D1417397

Second
Season

BOOKS BY JOSEPH MONNINGER

Second Season   1987
New Jersey   1986
The Summer Hunt   1983
The Family Man   1982

Second Season

JOSEPH MONNINGER

Atheneum   New York   1987

This is a work of fiction. Any references to
historical events; to real people, living or dead; or to
real locales are intended only to give the fiction a setting
in historical reality. Other names, characters, and incidents
either are the product of the author's imagination or are used fic-
titiously, and their resemblance, if any, to real-life counter-
parts is entirely coincidental.

Atheneum
Macmillan Publishing Comany
866 Third Avenue, New York, N.Y. 10022
Collier Macmillan Canada, Inc.

Library of Congress-in-Publication Data
Monninger, Joseph.
Second season.
I. Title.
PS3563.0526S4 1987   813'.54   87-12542
ISBN 0-689-11936-4

10 9 8 7 6 5 4 3 2 1

Printed in the United States of America

With love, Amy,
this book is again
for you.

For, Joe had actually laid his head down on the pillow at my side and put his arm round my neck, in his joy that I knew him.

"Which dear old Pip, old chap," said Joe, "you and me was ever friends. And when you're well enough to go out for a ride—what larks!"

—CHARLES DICKENS, *Great Expectations*

ONE

I

T WAS SNOWING when Brennan McCalmont carried the Christmas tree from his station wagon and propped it against the side of the house. The snow fell quietly in the yard, through the white birches and onto the green wreath that already leaned against a sagging basement window screen. Brennan took a step back and looked up at the house. Smoke rose from the brick chimney and cut the snowflakes wherever it passed. He watched the smoke for a few moments, the snow flicking on his eyelids, then pounded with his gloved hand on the side of the house and waited for someone to appear at the window. When no one did, he knocked again until he saw his wife, Linda, pull open the window.

"What do you need, honey?" she asked.

"Is Michael coming out with the stand or not, sweetheart? I told him to come out twenty minutes ago."

"I'll see what he's doing."

"Tell him to hurry. It's getting cold."

The window shut. Brennan let the tree swing down and lean against the house. It was getting colder, probably down to twenty degrees by now, and he blew into his gloves. He did ten jumping jacks and ran in place for a few seconds. The movement didn't warm him, and he thought about going inside and looking for the stand himself. Then Michael appeared on the back steps, his hair too long, his coat unbuttoned. It was plain to Brennan that Michael didn't plan on remaining outside.

"Here's the stand," Michael said, holding it out.

"Is it going to walk over here?"

Michael made a loud, exasperated sound, then came down the steps. He wore brown leather work boots, which he kept permanently untied. They made a dumb sound when he walked, like bread being patted. He carried the tree stand at his side.

"Anyone else coming out?" Brennan asked.

3

"Kate said she might come. But she was crying a few minutes ago, so I don't know. Louey's looking for his mittens."

"How about Mom?"

"I don't know. I don't think so."

"Well, this is a man's job, right? Just you and me, we can do it."

"Dad, I've got to call Franky."

"This is the tree-trimming ceremony, in case you didn't guess by now."

"I've got to call Franky."

"Tell Franky this is a tradition that goes way back, at least to 1971."

"Dad, I just have to talk to him."

"Okay, so talk to him. Just help me get this stand on right."

Brennan reached and grabbed Michael and began wrestling with him. Michael didn't move. Brennan felt himself swinging on Michael, spinning around, but Michael wouldn't play. It was always this way, and Brennan told himself that he would have to learn someday that Michael was not going to respond to roughhousing. Linda kept telling him to learn something about computers, to meet the boy halfway, but to wander into Michael's room was like visiting a hospital or a tracking station. Brennan avoided it when he could.

"All right, all right, I win," he said when it became clear Michael refused even to lock up with him. "Get me the small saw from the garage, please. Hurry up and we can get this thing done and get the tree up."

"All right."

He was getting cold. While Michael was in the garage, Brennan sprinted up the back stairs and stepped into the kitchen. He went to the broom closet and took down a bottle of brandy. He pulled the cork, drank off a swig, then jammed the cork back on top. He put the bottle up and waited, listening to the house around him. The old Christmas album was on, brought out like black china each year at this time, and he followed Bing Crosby through "Silent Night," his heart responding in such pure fondness, such familiarity with Bing, that it made him feel at once silly and divinely proud—proud of Bing, proud of the fact that Bing had sung to them all for forty years.

4

After a time he reached up, took another sip, then put the bottle back. He turned and had started for the door when he saw Louey there. Unaware of being watched, Louey worked his hand over the knob, slowly, careful as a safecracker, until he seemed satisfied the knob had turned. Then he leaned back and yanked, almost stumbling when the door gave way. He regained his balance and stood for a moment, his pale skin too white against his navy blue ski cap.

"Louey, you looking for me?" Brennan asked, and went over to his son.

"You want me outside?" Louey asked, his voice soft.

"Sure. How are you feeling?"

"All right. Maybe a little tired."

"You want to ride, I'll carry you down."

"No, I'm all right."

"Let me carry you."

"No, really, I'm okay."

Brennan gave Louey a kiss on the forehead. Louey pulled back, but only a little, which Brennan felt was fair enough for a ten-year-old. Brennan held the door steady while Louey passed through, then followed him out.

"Where did you go, Dad?" Michael asked, standing by the tree.

"I went to Jamaica," Brennan said, going down the stairs. "I smoked a lot of ganja there. Reefer, Daddy-o. You dig me? I heap big reggae man."

"Dad, you're ridiculous sometimes."

"You think so? Man, I a Rastafarian. I a party boy, man. I sing songs and live on welfare. I wear my hair in dreadlocks."

Louey laughed, but it was a weak, soft laugh. Beside him, Michael kicked at the saw and shook his head. Just then Kate stepped out on the steps and held the door open for McGregor, the family's Scottie. Kate wore a sweater and jeans and looked as if she had been crying. She stepped back on the doorsill and watched for a second before going back inside. Louey whistled and put his hand out.

"Aye, McGregor, you old Scot, are ya out for a walk on the glen then?" Brennan called. "Is it the high road or the low road we'll be taking today, laddie?"

5

"Dad, that makes the five millionth time you've said that," Michael said.

"Aye, but the Mad Scot and I know old Nessy may be about. Don't we there, Mr. McGregor, McBriar, McBaney?"

McGregor came cautiously down the steps, then took a run in the yard and barked a few times at the snow. Louey walked after him, his hand still out for the dog. Michael picked up the saw and twanged it a couple of times in his hands.

"Are we ready to put the stand on?" Michael said. "I'd like to call Franky before he turns thirty."

Brennan lifted the tree away from the wall and carried it to the stairs. He wedged the butt of the tree straight up in the air. He was warming now to the work and wondered if he shouldn't go back inside and have another snort.

"Michael, cut off any of the smaller branches, okay? I'll hold the tree steady. Louey, you chase the Mad Scot until we can't hear ourselves think. Everyone have his job?"

Brennan took a step to the side and grabbed the trunk of the tree, his arms sinking into the boughs. Michael hacked at a few of the branches, and the butt of the tree jigged back and forth. The white meat of the new pine smelled sharp and sweet in the cold air. Brennan glanced once at Louey and saw he had finally caught McGregor. McGregor was trapped against Louey's chest, his legs suspended, his furry eyebrows coated with snow.

When Michael had cut the smaller branches away, Brennan brought the stand over and fit it on the trunk. It fit easily, to his surprise, and he had only to pound it lightly with his palm to get it as secure as it needed to be.

"Easy, huh?" he said, stepping back and motioning for Michael to tighten the screws that clamped the tree in the stand. "This is the first time in my forty-two years that the tree stand went on the first time. Just like that . . . it's up."

"Dad, is this supposed to be a Kodak commercial or something?"

"No, it's supposed to be Christmas."

When the screws were tight, Brennan lifted the tree and turned it up on the stand. It leaned to the left, but it seemed solid enough.

Brennan tugged it a few times from different angles. The tree wobbled but never seriously.

"Louey, how do you like it?" Brennan called.

"Good."

"How good? Real good?"

"It looks pretty good."

"Okay, it's official. Michael, why don't you put the tools away, then come on back and help me lift it in? Louey, you want to open the door for us?"

"Okay."

Brennan stood in the cold and watched Louey climb the steps. Louey raised each foot slowly, planting it firmly before he could trust himself to lift his back leg free. It reminded Brennan of films he had seen of mountain climbers, their ice picks in front of them, their thick boots double the diameter of their legs.

Finally Louey stepped inside and held the door as wide as possible. McGregor slipped past Brennan's leg, sniffed once at the tree, then ran up the stairs and into the house.

"Ready?" Brennan said.

"Okay."

Brennan took the butt end of the tree and went in first. He paused for just a moment to get past Louey, careful not to press him against the door. He guided the tree through the dining room, then slowed to pass through the small hallway leading into the living room. He smelled the fire even before he saw it, and he turned quickly to see Linda feeding a few middle-sized branches into the flames. Her blond hair was tied back, and she looked very young. She was short, maybe five-four, but her figure was long and slender. With her hair up like that, she looked as if she were still in college, still in a dorm room somewhere, eating popcorn.

"Make way, make way," Brennan called. The wood was just really catching for the first time, and the smell filled the room. "The little fir tree is here. Make way."

"It's beautiful. Really, it may be the best tree ever," Linda said.

"You think so? Then why was everyone calling me a cheapskate when I bought it? I told you it was a beauty."

7

"It's lucky it's going to be in a corner," Michael said.

"Oh, yeah, wise guy?"

"Careful of the lamp," Linda said.

"Where's Kate?"

"Upstairs. She's in one of her desperate phases. No one has asked her to the Snowball."

"Oh, Jesus, just what we need right now."

"It's very important to her, so don't make fun," said Linda.

Brennan put the butt down and held it while Michael pushed the tree to its full height. Louey came in, slowly taking off his jacket. He sat on the couch, apparently exhausted from his trip outdoors.

"Turn it a little to the left now. You can see one of the bare spots there," Linda said, stepping back and looking at the tree. She crossed her arms. Brennan reached a hand in and lifted the tree, twisting it just slightly to the left. He watched her evaluate it, her head going back and forth, and he suddenly felt himself smiling. He smiled at her because she looked beautiful in the firelight and because she was mother to his children and because it was Christmas and the room smelled of pine and roast and cookies. He smiled because he knew she loved Christmas and went to great lengths to make everything right, and he was happy to stand in the corner of the living room with the tree scratching his arm, just to make it perfect. He also knew that he would make love to her that night, that they would be locked together, her legs up around his back, the blankets rich and deep around them. He would fall into her, ride into her, and she would meet him with her warmth, with the passion she gave him that was whole and fully apart from the children.

"How about now?" he asked her.

"Better. Put it down. There. That's right. That's perfect. It's fullest right there."

"How about it, Michael? You like it?"

"It looks good."

"Calm down, Michael. Don't get so excited."

"I said it looks good. You want me to write a poem about it?"

"I'd love for you to write a poem about it," Brennan said. "What do you think, Louey?"

8

"It's better-looking than I thought it would be. It looked really scrawny out in the yard."

"It's a pretty tree. We always get a pretty tree," Linda said.

"Now, where's Kate? I'm going to run up and get her. Michael, do you want to make your call now? Why don't you call Franky, then we'll all trim the tree together? How's that?"

Brennan went out of the living room and climbed the stairs to the second floor. Kate's room was the first on the right, the biggest room upstairs except for the master bedroom. A scratch pad hung from the door beside a plastic cutout of Snoopy. Brennan knocked softly and pushed open the door.

Kate stood in front of her floor-length mirror, her torso turned to catch a glance at her back and bottom. She wore a blue leotard with leg warmers. The room smelled close. It smelled of perspiration and powder and perfume. A workout tape was on her cassette player, a woman's voice calling, "One, two, and three . . . stretch it out . . . four, bend and, five, twist, nowww."

Brennan stepped in, doing a few dance steps as he entered, kicking his legs up spastically. He took a few steps backward and forward, kicked up like a chorus line dancer, and clapped his hands as he stepped back.

"One, cottage cheese, two, eat less fatttt, three, get a girdle."

"Dad, don't try to make everything wonderful because it isn't."

"You are. You're wonderful."

"I'm fat," Kate said, turning around. She put her arms flat at her sides and looked so intently at her image in the mirror that Brennan felt pain for her. "I'm at least five pounds overweight."

"Bull."

"I am."

"You've got a great figure. You do. I'm talking like a man now."

"Dad, I'm fat, and there's no use trying to talk me out of it."

"Okay, okay."

"I am fat."

"Okay."

He stood for a moment in the center of the room, the music still thumping, his daughter in front of him. Looking at her, he knew she

9

was not beautiful in the way she wanted to be—she was not the peppy, cute girl high school boys seemed always to want. Instead, she would be a beautiful woman, an amazingly beautiful woman, and it made him hurt to realize she could not see that in herself yet. He could see her beauty beginning in so many ways, in the push of her cheekbones, the grace around her neck, the swing of her hair, even the long lines of her legs, but he knew it was useless to tell her so.

She walked over and turned off the workout tape. The sound of Bing starting on "White Christmas" came up the stairs. Brennan listened, feeling somehow apologetic that Bing filled the silence. Kate stood curled next to the tape player, her eye now and then slipping to the mirror.

"Listen, we—" he started, but she cut him off.

"I'm not eating anything. I hate this whole season. Tell Mom if she bakes anything else, I'll run away. I'll become anorexic. I swear I will."

"You don't have to eat if you don't want to."

"Then tell her to stop baking."

"I can't do that. She can bake if she wants to. It's her Christmas, too."

"She puts the food out to tempt me."

"Oh, come on. That's a little much, isn't it? Your mother wants you to be popular."

"Don't ever say that word."

"You know what I mean."

She put her hands over her eyes and started crying. Brennan moved to her and hugged her. He held her against his shoulder and rocked her quietly. He thought of doing a few dance steps with her, to kid her out of it, but she kept crying and he simply held on to her. After he had rocked her for a time, he whispered slowly in her ear.

" 'You may talk o' gin an' beer,' " he said. "Come on, you know it."

She shook her head against his shoulder, but she didn't move away. He held her more tightly and started again.

" 'You may talk o' gin an' beer'—how does it go?"

"I don't know."

"You used to know. You used to know it all. How does it go from there?"

" 'Quartered safe' . . . you know."

"No, I don't. How does it go?"

From deep in his shoulder she whispered the beginning of the poem. He smelled her breath, warm and clean, and the sad odor of her tears.

" 'You may talk o' gin an' beer/When you're quartered safe out 'ere/An' you're sent to penny-fights an' Aldershot it;/But if it comes to slaughter/You will do your work on water,/An' you'll lick the bloomin' boots of 'im that's got it.' "

"It makes me happy you remember that," he said.

"I remember."

"Come down in a little, okay? Louey would like it. You don't have to eat anything. Just help us trim the tree, all right?"

"All right."

He let her go and went back downstairs. McGregor lay next to the fire. Linda had cleared the coffee table and was now setting out the ornaments. She pulled them out from a large brown box and removed their tissue wrapping; she held each one up for general admiration and to mark its place in posterity. Louey had not leaned forward to help. He stayed where he had first sat, his jacket still only half off his shoulders.

"How about a drink?" Brennan asked her. "You ready for a little eggnog?"

"I'd love some eggnog. Is Kate okay?"

"She's fine. Just don't push any food on her."

"I never do."

"I know, but she feels fat. Did you feel that way when you were sixteen?"

"Who can remember that far back? I'm forty-one. That was twenty-five years ago."

"No, I mean it. Was it like that for you?"

Linda stopped and looked at the ornaments. She picked up a small wooden horse and dangled it in front of her.

"I guess so," she said. "I guess it was just like that."

"I'll get some eggnog. You want anything, Louey?"

"No, thanks."

"And turn down the oven, okay? You can pull out that last sheet of cookies. Put the oven down to three hundred," Linda said.

He went to the kitchen and found Michael sprawled out in a chair. Michael talked into the phone like an executive, a wheeler-dealer, his head back, his voice surprisingly expansive, his legs hanging over the arm of the chair. But as soon as Brennan stepped fully into the room, he saw Michael pull up and cover the phone, his voice diminishing to a whisper. It reminded Brennan of a Styrofoam cup melting on a warm electric coil.

"Hello, Franky!" Brennan called, ducking once quickly toward the phone.

"Franky says hi, Dad."

Brennan went to the stove, turned the oven down, took out the cookie sheet, then went to the broom closet to get brandy for the eggnog. The eggnog was homemade and frothy—an old family recipe that one of them, Brennan couldn't remember which, had brought to the marriage. Now he put two glasses on the counter and poured the eggnog in a thick stream. He sprinkled in some nutmeg from the spice rack over the stove, slipped in a finger of brandy, and had begun to pick up the glasses when he saw Michael signaling him. Michael pointed at the glasses, at the brandy, then made a drinking motion and pointed at himself.

"You want one?" Brennan asked.

Michael nodded.

"You really want some brandy? Can you handle it?"

"Yes, of course I can," Michael whispered.

Brennan shrugged and fixed a third glass. Back in the living room, Brennan handed an eggnog to Linda and sat down on the couch next to Louey.

"Michael's having one, too," he told her.

"One what?"

"A drink. An eggnog."

"Do you think it's all right?"

"He's going to college next year. He'll be okay. To tell the truth, it's sort of nice to see him interested in something besides his computer."

Linda got to her knees and lifted her glass. Brennan touched his glass to hers, then leaned across the table and kissed her. Louey snorted and said, "Oh, jeez."

"Merry Christmas, honey."

"Merry Christmas."

He drank some of the eggnog and stayed close to the table, inspecting the ornaments with Louey, watching Linda unwrap the last few. Many of the ornaments he recognized at once from his own childhood up in Massachusetts. They seemed ancient to him, somehow outmoded, like suspenders or a wooden-handled shaving brush. The rest of the ornaments were from Linda's family. He could recall seeing them on the tree when he had first gone to her parents' home. Aggie, Linda's widowed mother, had made him stand beside the blue spruce and inspect the decorations that Linda had acquired as a teenager. As Aggie talked, Linda popped in and out of the room, carrying cookies and pine boughs and mistletoe. He had stood with a tepid glass of eggnog in his hand, listening to Aggie tell him about her daughter in such a way that he knew he was supposed to take her off the tree in some unexplained manner—sweep her away and marry her—and that the ornaments would be passed on with her. Both women had understood, and he had pretended not to understand so that he could feel them welcoming him into their family. He had only half listened as Aggie described Linda's penchant for the gaudiest bulbs she could find, just catching himself in time to see that the tree had been hung with ornaments that said things like "Miami Christmas" or "Happy Birthday, Baby Jesus." But then there had been a moment when Linda came in and Aggie was still, and all three of them had exchanged a look. It has been a look of love and acceptance and continuance. One family gives way to another, and it isn't birth or anything at all explosive. It was more like masonry, he decided, like rocks settling into mortar and cement.

He was still watching Linda unwrap the ornaments when Kate

came in, carrying a cup of eggnog. Brennan was tempted to ask her if she had spiked it with brandy but then decided against it. He raised his cup.

"Merry Christmas, darling," he said.

"Merry Christmas, Dad. Merry Christmas, Mom."

She toasted them both, then went down on her knees next to Linda.

"Oh, I remember all of these. All of them," she said.

She picked up two or three and tried them on as earrings. She modeled one after another and turned to where Louey sat, his body slowly uncurling to get him out of the chair.

"What do you think?" she asked Louey each time.

"You're a babe," he said.

Michael came in eating a cookie. His eggnog was half gone.

"Is it time for the star?" he asked.

"I guess we can put it up anytime," Linda said. "Are you ready, Brennan?"

"I guess so."

Brennan stood and took the star when Linda handed it to him. He held it for a second and waited for Louey. Louey tried to climb off the couch; but it was difficult for him, and Michael ended up holding out a hand to his brother. Kate put back the ornaments and stood next to her mother.

"Are we ready?" Brennan asked.

"I think so," Linda told him.

Brennan led them over to the tree, carrying the star in front of him. He felt the warmth of the fire on his legs as he stood judging the distance to the top of the tree. He could reach it. It wasn't more than six and a half or seven feet.

Louey came up then, and Brennan lifted him, a little shocked that Louey could be so light. He lifted Louey very carefully, afraid to bruise him, afraid of doing anything at all. He put the star in Louey's hand and whispered for Louey to wait until the others were ready. Brennan watched his wife, his oldest son, and his daughter move around the tree. Louey held the star out, and each of them reached up along the tree. Brennan helped guide the star, not at all burdened by Louey's weight. Then he felt the others guiding it as well, their arms reaching for one another over the tree. The star slipped over the topmost branch, the hollow plastic making a ticking sound as it slid over the pine needles.

Brennan moved the dining room chair away from the table legs and judged the angle. It was a sharp dogleg right into the kitchen, probably a par three, but he wanted to design the hole to his advantage. He was down two strokes to Louey. Louey was a master at bank shots, and whenever it was his turn to design the hole, he invariably forced Brennan to bank off a pair of wingtips or the sideboard in order to get into position for a lay-up shot. To get back at Louey, Brennan played doglegs and tried to get Louey on the linoleum in the kitchen as often as possible. The linoleum was old and worn, and it was possible, when a shot was hit too hard or off line, to have the ball roll for minutes on the sloping floor, the knick of its flesh rising in pitch each time it found a new angle.

"Dogleg right, par three. The hole is the Coke can we used for the par four," Brennan said now, walking back to the tee area in the den.

"Any out of bounds?"

"Only if you go into the living room, but you'd really have to rap it. You can play it off the chair legs if you want to. Whose honors?"

"My honors."

Brennan watched Louey bend over his putter. Louey's motor control was still good. He was relaxed over the ball, solid. Yet there remained a tentativeness about Louey's motions that made Brennan think of the leukemia inside his son's body. It was there, swinging as Louey swung, rocking back as Louey rocked. Brennan imagined the leukemia to be an animal living inside Louey's blood system. It was not a crab. That was cancer, and anyway a crab was too hard for what Brennan imagined the disease to be. No, watching as he did now, Brennan pictured a salamander instead. This sickness would have soft skin, a serpent's head, a tail that might be pulled off by birds and remain wiggling to confuse the bright eyes, the hungry beak. Light would cause it to find shelter under rocks or in the mucus of spring earth and decomposed branches. Despite what the doctors sometimes claimed, Brennan knew no light or ray would find it.

Brennan put his hands to his mouth and leaned his own putter against his thigh.

"The crowd is quiet. They are on the ninth tee. Louey McCalmont is ahead by two strokes, and he has honors. The no talking sign is up. . . . Louey swings, and it's a long drive down the center, well stroked, nicely played, but no, no, the ball is coming up directly behind a large tree. It will be a difficult shot for young McCalmont."

"Christ, it went right behind the chair leg," Louey said, stepping away.

"Into the woods."

"I can still bank it into the kitchen."

"But it will be extremely difficult to hold the green. Remember the linoleum."

"I can handle the linoleum."

Brennan set his own ball down and calculated his shot. He wanted to lay up almost against the dining room wall, giving himself a clear shot into the kitchen and a possible bank shot toward the Coke can. It did not enter his mind to miss the shot deliberately. Louey was too sharp. He would spot it, and that would end forever their matches of miniature golf around the house.

"I'm going to hit a two iron," said Brennan. "I want to control this shot just down the right side of the fairway."

"Chicken," Louey said.

"No, it's the percentage shot on these doglegs. You're in the woods, remember. You can lose two strokes on the linoleum."

"We'll see."

Brennan hit his shot and the ball went too long. It hit against the dining room wall and stopped only a few inches away from the molding. Brennan knew he would be forced to hit the next shot lefty.

"In the rough," Louey hooted.

"No way. It's a clear chip shot onto the green."

Kate came down then, wearing a bulky sweater and tight jeans. Earphones dangled on both sides of her head. Brennan could hear the music across the room. It was New Year's Eve, and she didn't have a date.

"Is it okay if I have Janey over?" Kate asked. Her voice was too loud.

"What?" Brennan yelled back.

"Janey."

"Turn it down," Brennan told her.

She pulled the earphones down to her neck, and they hung there like a stethoscope. Louey pushed her gently to one side and began trying out ways to hit the ball under the chair legs. Brennan noted that he didn't have a clear shot. Louey would have to take a short punch at the ball and hope for the best.

"Can I have Janey over?" Kate asked again. "She's by herself tonight, too."

"She can come over if she promises to keep her hands off Louey. He can't be expected to fight off your wanton friends all his life."

"Isn't that my Walkman?" Louey asked, looking at his sister for the first time.

"My batteries died."

"You could ask, you know."

"I could, but I didn't. Dad, can she come over or not? I'm supposed to call her right back."

"Sure she can. I don't care. You guys can't go out, though. Michael's already over at Franky's."

"We won't."

"And no one in. I don't want to come home to a party."

"Chill out, Dad."

Kate ran back upstairs.

"Who's away?" Louey asked.

"You are. Go ahead and hit."

Louey lined up his shot, checked his swing several times to make sure he wouldn't clang his club against the wooden struts, then chopped at the ball. He hit it too hard, and it shot off the wall beside the kitchen door and rolled almost back to where it started out.

"Trouble city," Louey said.

"This could be my break."

"You're going to have to hit lefty."

"I know, but it doesn't matter. I'll be on the green in two."

Brennan turned his putter around and stroked the ball softly. It barely had enough speed to reach the linoleum. McGregor, from his rug near the dishwasher, looked up and inspected the ball. It rolled slowly across the floor, stopping and starting as it found different grooves in the tiles.

Louey hit again, this time with a free backswing, and his ball shot into the kitchen. It banked off one of the kitchen table legs and began rolling up toward the Coke can stationed near the oven. Louey laughed and ran to follow the ball, but he smacked his hip on the doorway.

"Jesus," Brennan said. "You okay?"

Louey had stopped at once and stood completely still. He did not look at his hip. Instead, he seemed to hold his body rigid as if some other sense would tell him the extent of the injury. Watching him, Brennan almost believed Louey could hear the blood in his body rushing in to pad the area, or perhaps he could sense the extent of the inevitable bruise that would form deep in the hollow of his hip.

"I'm all right," Louey said.

"You sure? You hit it pretty good."

"I'm okay."

Louey went forward to find his ball. Brennan followed him. He had to fight the impulse to lift Louey's shirt and inspect the bruise. Yet without looking, he already knew what the bruise would be like. It would darken and fail to heal completely, leaving a dark pool, a shadow under the skin.

He went in and lined up his next shot. Louey's ball had rolled close to the Coke can. It was a short putt for a four. Even if Brennan made this shot, he lost the match by a stroke.

He hit the ball and watched it miss. It rolled past and sideways, working its way toward the dishwasher. Louey tapped his shot home.

"The world champion," Louey said, lifting his hands over his head.

"That's only nine holes. We play the rest tomorrow."

"Then putt out."

"Give me a six. I've got to get your mom going."

Brennan handed Louey his club, took a beer out of the kitchen, then went upstairs. Linda stood in front of the large bathroom mirror, putting on earrings and smoking a joint. She often smoked a joint when she had the bathroom steam to cover the odor. Now the window was open, and she ducked to it each time after she took a drag and shot a stream of smoke out into the cold air.

"It's the eternal hippie," Brennan said, coming in and glancing at himself in the mirror over her shoulder.

"I'm not a hippie. I'm going to be a workingwoman again in a month or two," she said, concentrating on the mirror.

"How was the real estate course last night?" asked Brennan. "Did you go to class zonked out, too?"

"No, I don't go zonked out. I'm at the head of my class."

"And you like it?"

"Yeah, I like it," she said, finding his eyes in the mirror. "I didn't know if I would at first. It's so different from teaching English lit to tenth graders, but I think business is going to be okay. It's all the same anyway; you just try to get along with people. Besides, it's going to bring in some money."

"We could use it. But you like it better than teaching?"

"You know what I'm realizing? I'm finding out that I've always been frightened of money. It was like everyone else in the world should be able to make it, but not me. I wasn't worthy of it or something. It's some sort of Protestant work ethic. We should work, but we shouldn't get paid. That's why teaching got to be so terrible, didn't it? You hated it, too. But I'm just learning the ropes with real estate," she said, and stopped to take a deep drag and then blow it out the window.

"You'll be great at it."

"I think maybe I will."

"You were a great teacher."

"I was a master of the overhead projector."

Brennan leaned close to the mirror and inspected his face. He was glad to see he didn't need to shave again before he went out.

"You know, I think the kids know you get tanked up in here," Brennan said.

"They do not."

19

"They don't think you're burning rope in here."

"Well, they have to prove it. Their suspicions wouldn't stand up in a court of law. How do I look?"

She wore a blue dress with a white collar. Brennan didn't particularly like the white collar, but he didn't say anything.

"Terrific. Wonderful."

She put out the joint with a sharp pinch of her fingers. He grabbed her and kissed her. He held her for a second in his arms, then kissed the side of her neck. She took his chin in her hand and held it steady, forcing him to look at them both in the mirror.

"We've got lines," she said. "I was just standing here and suddenly I realized I'm old. It's all there, isn't it? How long has it been happening?"

"You're not old."

"I am. I'm old. This dress looks too young for me."

"It does not. You're as beautiful as the day I met you."

"No, seriously, tell me something you mean. Are we just mature, or are we old?"

"Mature."

She pulled his chin closer to the mirror. He pressed his head against hers. Side by side, cheek by cheek, he looked first at her face, then at his. She was right, of course. He had noticed it recently. He smiled at their reflection, but this only made the lines gouge deeper around his eyes. Besides, she wouldn't smile back. She stared at them both.

"We've been together twenty years," he whispered. "We can't look just the same."

"I know," she said.

It was such a lonely thing to say, such a quiet understanding, that he turned and kissed her again. He kissed her softly on the cheek, then thought better of it and kissed her hard on the mouth until she had to lift her hand and brace herself against his chest. Afterward she put her head against his shoulder for just a moment.

"Kate's staying in with Louey. Janey's coming over," he said quietly against her hair.

"Good. I'll tell Kate to let Janey spend the night if she wants."

"See if you can get a look at Louey's hip. He banged it on the doorway."

"Which side?"

"His right side."

"All right."

She pushed away and went to speak with Kate. He took a large drink of beer and went to fish a tie out of his closet. Standing in front of the bedroom mirror, he flicked his collar up and looped the tie around his neck, his hands working automatically to start the knot. He felt good. So what if he was getting older? He looked in the mirror and examined himself. He was all right. He was dignified. He needed to do sit-ups, and he needed to start jogging; but he knew he had reached an easy place where he could forgive himself almost anything. Why begin it all when he knew he wouldn't keep going with it? He never did. If he actually kept up the exercise, he told himself, he wouldn't be thinking of starting it now.

He was still knotting his tie when Kate came in, the Walkman gone. She sat on the bed and watched him finish. He put a little cologne in his hands, slapped them together, then tapped his cheeks quickly.

"It smells like a forest fire in here," she said. She tossed a small throw pillow in the air and caught it, clapping her hands once, then twice, while the pillow was in the air.

"The chimney leaks, I think."

"That must be it," Katy said deadpan. "Can we order pizza?"

"When? Now?"

"No, when Janey comes over. Louey said he wanted some, too."

"Do you have money?"

"Dad, why do you think I'm here?"

"I don't know. Am I supposed to pay for pizza?"

"Well, you're not paying for a baby-sitter."

"Louey's hardly a baby."

"You know what I mean."

"You mean, since I'm stuffed with money, I should give you some. Is that it?"

"Yes, exactly."

"Did I just hear you say how handsome your father is? I didn't hear exactly what you said."

"My father is a handsome man."

"How handsome? Right now you've got a few anchovies."

"He's a hunk."

"That's better."

He took out a ten and gave it to her. She grabbed it, kissed him, then went off yelling for Louey. He turned back to the mirror and, in that instant, saw it was there: His resemblance to a middle-aged Sinatra still caught him sometimes. It came just fleetingly, too vaguely ever to ask anyone else about it, but he was sure it was there. He squared himself to the mirror, put his hands in his pants loops, and looked again. Sinatra, he thought. Sinatra primping for Saturday night.

Sitting in the car while it warmed up, listening to a talk show on home loans, Brennan admitted to himself he liked a good party. He liked being able to drink as much as he wanted, and he liked the chance to flirt. More than that, he liked the feeling of people's houses on the night of a party. It was good to walk in and see the carpet with vacuum swipes across the pile, good to be surprised by little dishes of nuts, by cheese puffs, by canapés and rich sauces. He liked to see other men throw their heads back as they snapped in a nut or two, their drinks swaddled in napkins, their ties brighter than they would ever be at the office. He enjoyed the upstairs haunts, carrying the coats up, going to the bathroom, watching the dull lights in the bedrooms, seeing little haloes from the bedside lamps illuminating circles on the walls. It excited him to pass a woman in the upstairs hallway, to smell her perfume, to see the beds beyond an open door. It was ridiculous, of course, but he couldn't help it. It was the potential of the evening that always pleased him. Things could happen, the unexpected, and the liquor made him open to chance and circumstance.

Tonight there would be a sauna, and this made Brennan nervous. It had made a number of people nervous, and he had listened as Linda

discussed the whole matter with Margaret, her best friend from college, as they went over possible scenarios, wondering aloud if they
all would be called on to throw off their clothes at midnight. The
party and sauna were at the Samuelses', old friends, who had put the
sauna in because Freddy Samuels suffered from psoriasis and needed
sun and heat for his skin. Freddy had read in a medical journal somewhere that psoriasis patients in Europe were often sent to Iceland to
bathe in the volcanic steam, and he had taken the idea and transplanted
it to New Jersey. Freddy had found only one American doctor to
recommend the benefits of a sauna, but that was all he had needed.
The sauna had gone in, dug into the backyard, complete with tanning
lights and a miniature solarium.

But the medical excuse hadn't carried much weight in the neigh-
borhood. No, there was something newly licentious about Freddy,
about his wife, Pam, and it was not difficult to picture them screwing
in the steam room, then romping out to the solarium. The sauna
seemed, somehow, to be a landmark for a new territory in their marriage. Perhaps it was forced, Brennan couldn't tell, but Fred and Pam
were undergoing a sexual renaissance. It made Brennan feel old and
tame. He asked himself and Linda over and over what was the harm
in it, but he could not shake the suspicion that there was something
faintly lurid about the whole thing.

He waited until the car was warm enough, then walked back up
to the house for Linda. She came out the door, locking it behind her,
as he came up the steps.

"His hip is all black-and-blue," she said. She looked worried, not
even concerned with the cold. She had a small house gift under her
arm. "Maybe we should take him to the doctor."

"And what would the doctor do?"

"I don't know. It's just so black-and-blue."

"Honey, he'll be okay. We've got to let him call the shots on a lot
of this. Any other kid and I'd say no, but Louey's not like that."

"He's trying to be too tough just because of all that sports stuff."

"I don't think so. Really not on this. Did you tell Kate to keep an
eye on him?"

"Yes. She promised to check him before he went to bed."

23

"There you go then. We're only going to be ten minutes away. It won't make the bruise any better if we stay home."

She nodded and checked the door once more. He put his arm around her as he walked her down to the car.

Ten minutes later they were pulling up in front of the Samuels house. Brennan heard music, some sort of jazz; then the door opened, and Freddy Samuels was there, grinning and holding up his drink. Freddy was dressed in a bright green jacket over an incredibly white shirt. His tie was gold and shiny. He appeared to have stepped off an island somewhere; he looked like the man who handed out trophies at golf tournaments.

"There they are, there they are," said Freddy. He kissed Linda on the cheek and shook Brennan's hand.

Brennan slapped Freddy on the shoulder, figuring all at once that it didn't matter if Freddy and Pam wanted to screw in jungle heat under their sun lamps. It was their business. He gave Freddy another swat and could not fight the impulse to let the swat carry more weight than necessary. He wanted to let Freddy know he was as vigorous as ever.

"Here you go, Linda, let me run your coat upstairs. Brennan, why don't you dig up drinks for you and your wife? Everyone helps themselves tonight, okay? If you can't find it, you can't have it."

One glance around the living room told Brennan they knew everyone at the party. It was the old push, people he had run with since he had come to New Jersey. Some of them had been friends of Linda's from college, the old Glassboro State connection. Some were from Westfield High School, where they both had taught, and like him, a lot of them had wandered into business. Actually he had met most of them through Linda—she was the one originally from New Jersey—but now they were a solid group, a crowd, and he could no longer remember precisely how each couple had joined up. Now and then they still surprised him by bringing up something Linda had done in the time before him. But it pleased him to know that most of them remembered how Linda and he had met while teaching in the high school, how they had arranged to take lunch together in Cafeteria B,

Fifth Block. He recalled meeting some of Linda's women friends and seeing that look in their eyes, that expecttion that he would marry Linda, that he was the one. You could fall in love with a group and a way of life along with a particular person, and he supposed he had. They all went back, that was the thing.

He spotted Phil and Margaret Dedich, Sara and Jim Atwater, Jill and Donny Bloomer, all of them loosely bunched around the Samuelses' Christmas tree. The noise level rose briefly as the others spotted them, and Brennan stepped into the room, feeling somehow that nothing of this had changed from his own days as a high school student. They all might have been in a teen-ager's living room, celebrating a victory over Kiwammie High School. Nothing had changed. Nearly every party he had ever gone to had held this exact flavor, and he knew it would only heighten as he took one or two drinks, as he saw the men getting louder in one corner while the women became more openly flirtatious. Even now, as Phil Dedich slid up to him and touched his elbow, a joke beginning before Brennan had really settled into the atmosphere of the room, he allowed the illusion to grow more and more complete. Kiwammie High, he thought quickly, three touchdown passes and a quarterback sneak.

Then Phil had him and was leading him to the doorway of the kitchen behind the other men. Brennan looked for Linda, but she was also drifting away, entering the small covey of women who had collected by the picture window.

"What are you drinking tonight?" Phil asked. He was a short, thin man who seemed more tightly wrapped than he needed to be. He always reminded Brennan of Ty Cobb—short, nervous, aggressive.

"What are you having?" Brennan asked.

"Scotch. Whatever you decide on, stick with it. You remember how sick you got last New Year's. You switched around to everything."

"I wasn't that sick."

"Was he sick last year or not?" Phil said loudly as they entered the kitchen. The men took up positions next to the refrigerator. "What the hell am I asking you for? None of you guys would remember."

"He wasn't sick. He was washing the driveway," Donny Bloomer said. Bloomer was a round-shouldered old jock who had worked himself into being an A-class squash player.

"He was sick as a dog," Phil told Donny. "Give him a beer."

Jim Atwater, the oldest member of their group, the only one whose hair was completely gray, pulled open the refrigerator and handed Brennan a beer. It was a Heineken. Before he thought, Brennan tried to unscrew the cap with his fingers and managed to gouge his palm.

"Jesus, he's so used to drinking his domestic crap he does it out of habit," Bloomer said.

"That's not a Pabst Blue Ribbon," Phil said.

"I wish it were," Brennan said, stung a little.

"What?" asked Atwater. "You mean to say you really like Pabst more than Heineken?"

"I do."

"He's just playing ignorant," Donny said. "He does it on purpose. Real men don't like anything imported. Real men like beer brewed in Newark."

"I think they closed that brewery," Donny said. "I remember going on a tour. It was right next to Route Twenty-two, just past the old airport. I took the kids there once. I think it was a Cub Scout troop. You should have heard the questions they asked. They had the guide just about crazy by the end of it."

"I don't like having to like Heineken," Brennan said, surprising himself. When everyone looked at him, he said, "It's fashionable to like imported beers, so what? Everybody wants Mercedes and BMWs. I know a guy who lives in Europe who says the big status symbol over there is an enormous Cadillac."

"But it isn't drinking Budweiser," Phil said. "They don't go chic and drink Rolling Rock, do they?"

Pam Samuels walked in, carrying a tray of hors d'oeuvres. She had straight black hair with just a hint of gray, and tonight she wore a tight red dress. The dress was absolutely perfect, and Brennan felt the men responding to it as he did. Bloomer stood up straight against the refrigerator, and even Jim Atwater watched her place the tray next to the sink.

26

"What are you men plotting?" she asked. "Aren't you ever going to come in and join the party? I might as well just clean the kitchen and let the rest of the house go to hell."

"We'll be in in a second. We're planning a theme," Phil said. "I think this party needs a theme."

"Like what?"

"Like a murder mystery."

"You mean a game," Pam said, then moved again, this time to the refrigerator. "You come up with one and I'll play it."

Bloomer coughed, and Phil pretended to hold his heart as if her words had triggered an attack; but Pam didn't take the double entendre farther. Brennan watched her lift ice out of the freezer, her dress riding up slightly, her stockings providing just enough friction to hold the hem an instant before releasing it, and wondered what it would be like to kiss her, to press her against the refrigerator and kiss the back of her neck. He imagined her turning a moment, lifting her shoulder to prevent him from going too deeply into her neck, then his lips tasting her skin, the dry, wonderful taste of her hair. He would smell her, inhale her, and his arms would lock just under her breasts until she leaned back into him and went slack.

She stayed a minute more, then returned to the living room, passing through the door at the same moment Freddy entered. He appeared amazingly vigorous and prosperous.

"Everybody get a drink?" he asked, coming in and rinsing his hands at the sink. "You all set?"

"All set," Bloomer said.

"We were just saying this party needs a theme," said Phil.

"You were saying it," Atwater corrected.

"Okay, I was."

"We could discuss man's inhumanity to man," Bloomer said.

"No, I mean a purpose to the party. A reason to drink. That's it."

Freddy straightened up and dried his hands on a paper towel from the roll hanging under the cabinet. He shook his head and nodded at Phil.

"This guy always want to play something. You ever seen anyone like him?"

"It's not a game; it's a theme."

Brennan helped himself to another beer, then excused himself and went into the living room. He checked to make sure Linda had a drink. She had a large glass of wine, a glass as large as a brandy snifter, which she swirled at him as he stood by her. He lifted his beer and toasted her back.

Sara Atwater was telling a story about the first time Jim had taken their youngest daughter, Melodie, to her swim class. Jim had thought he would simply hand Melodie over to the swim instructor, but the instructor had given them warm-up exercises. In tune to a piano, he and Melodie had walked in a small circle, following other children, all of them singing "Baa Baa Black Sheep." When the part came for them to bleat, "Yess, sir, yess, sir," they were told to put their hands to their ears and wiggle them like ram's ears.

Brennan listened to the end, laughed with the others, then put his hand on Linda's shoulder. He wanted the physical contact. He didn't know why, but he always found ways to touch her whenever they were in public. It was silly, he knew, yet he couldn't help himself. She put her arm loosely around his leg.

Brennan finished his beer while Pam put on a record. It was a medley of songs sung by Ella Fitzgerald. Linda tapped her fingers on his leg, and he rubbed her more gently.

After a time Brennan went to the kitchen for another beer, then climbed the back steps to the bathroom. He washed his hands at the sink, taking a long time to stare into his eyes. "Nineteen eighty-six," he said aloud. Nineteen eighty-six, his own forty-second year. It was spinning past him now, at this moment, but it did no good to say so. Already it was twenty years since college. Twenty years! Brennan could not accommodate the thought, could not make it real. He could remember the time only in seasons, in memories of sport, and so he could picture young Cassius Clay dancing in front of George Chuvalo, or Mays standing at the plate as if it were a stickball box, or Arnold Palmer swinging his flat wood and tossing a cigarette away as the crowd, Arnie's Army, shouted for him to charge. These were photographs to him, newsreels, but now and then, when Palmer appeared to push motor oil, or a story broke about the reconciliation between

28

Mays and the San Francisco Giants, Brennan felt cheated. These men should have stayed young. To watch them now, occasionally appearing in old-timers' games, or playing match golf with others on the senior tour, was almost more than Brennan could bear. He turned the channel on them or left the room whenever they came on, afraid that in their frailties they would steal his youth.

Brennan stood for a few more minutes in front of the mirror, then finally shook himself and took a good drink of beer. When he was done, he entered the master bedroom and sat on the bed. He was starting to feel just a little drunk, and that often made him sentimental. He told himself to slow down—he had all night. He was sure the party would go until two or three at the earliest. There was no hurry. The Samuelses' parties were notorious for going late. It was expected. Freddy Samuels would stoke them with alcohol until the mere hour became scandalous enough to prove them all reckless.

He took another drink, then lifted the phone and dialed his number. It was answered on the third ring by Louey, a surprise since Louey rarely made it to the phone in time to beat Michael or Kate.

"Hey, you," Brennan said.

"We on for the rest of the golf match tomorrow?"

"You bet. What are you doing?"

"Nothing. The pizza guy's supposed to be here soon."

"Did Janey get there?"

"Yes. They're upstairs."

"What are they doing?"

"I don't know. It sounded like they were dancing a little while ago."

"How are you feeling?"

"Okay."

"How's that hip?"

"It's fine. You don't have to worry about it. Kate told me she had to look at it before I go to bed."

Brennan put his hand on his forehead. He felt very tired suddenly but then realized perhaps it was only the beer getting to him.

"Louey, you think I push you too much on all this sports stuff?"

"No, why?"

"Your mom says I do sometimes. I don't mean to. If I do, I'm sorry."

"You don't push me."

"You sure?"

"I'm sure."

The phone was silent for a moment, Brennan shook his head, sorry he had gone into it. It was the way they talked, that was all, and it meant nothing more than that. He had been wrong to listen to Linda.

Then Louey said, "I know what you mean. Don't worry about it."

"All right. I'll take your word for it. I was just calling to check in. What game you watching?"

"Georgetown and Houston."

"Who's ahead?"

"Georgetown by three. They're in the fourth quarter."

"I'll take Georgetown for three dollars."

"Give me the three points."

"No way. Even bet."

"All right, you're on."

"Okay, over and out."

"Over and out."

Brennan took a gulp of beer as he hung up the phone. He took another drink of beer, almost draining the bottle, then jumped up and snapped into a quarterback's stance. He turned the bottle sideways and pretended to take it from the center. The steps came back to him, though he didn't have enough room to perform them all. Right foot, left foot, ball cocked at the ear, eyes downfield. Scan the defense, scan the linebacker's drop, check for zone, check keys, count the timing out in cadence with the receiver's pattern. Zing, it was there, and he imagined the sharp nose of the ball snapping against the receiver's pads, complete for fifteen yards.

Still up, he hustled downstairs, the beer working in him now. He knew he was going to get drunk, very drunk, and he did a silly little shuffle step halfway across the living rom floor when he caught Linda's eyes. The step was a hop-skip, a Three Stooges routine, and he did another one even though Linda shook her head.

"Men's sauna," he said when he walked into the kitchen. "What do you say, Freddy? Let's get this party rolling."

"We were just talking about that," Donny said. "You up for one? I'm up for one if you are."

"Everything's set up. We kept the heat on. We've got towels for everyone. We didn't know if people would want to or not," Freddy said, putting down his drink, his look grateful.

Brennan felt the idea catch. He grabbed two more beers out of the refrigerator, opened them both, and toasted himself by clanging one bottle against the other. Then he toasted with Jim Atwater, who was drinking straight scotch. Phil Dedich stuck his head into the living room and called, "Men's sauna. You women can enter at your own risk."

"Aww, you guys aren't really, are you?" one woman said, but Brennan couldn't identify the voice.

Freddy led them down a back hallway, past the garage. Brennan smelled heat before they were even close. Next to him Dedich carried a bottle of Chablis and a long-stemmed wineglass. They all were a little drunk, Brennan realized, so it did not surprise him to see Bloomer knock his shoulder on the doorway as they stepped into the sauna area.

The sauna was located off a low-ceilinged rec room. On the far side, near the door, Brennan saw the entrance to the solarium. Directly across from it was the door to the sauna. A small weight machine stood in the middle. The machine had five or six functions: a sit-up board; a bench press; a lat pulley. Brennan suddenly felt jealous of Freddy. He imagined Freddy's body growing harder, his strength returning.

"This is some place. I saw it when you were putting it in, but I had no idea it would turn out like this," Atwater said, leaning on the sit-up board. "Really nice, Freddy."

"You like it?" asked Freddy. He seemed very excited by this move into his sauna. "We didn't know if it was going to be worth it. I mean, how many times have you bought things and then just didn't use them? We still have a stationary bicycle that no one uses, and a couple of months ago, don't tell anyone, but Pam bought a goddamn mini-trampoline and almost killed herself bouncing up and down. You think she uses it anymore? Christ, no."

"We got a rowing machine," Bloomer said, looking around for Atwater, who had a bottle of scotch with him, then holding out his glass for a refill, "and for the first fucking month I rowed across the Atlantic and back. Honestly, I figured out the mileage, and I made it to Greenland on a straight line. Then I gave it up. I don't even know why, but I did."

"You feel better?" Brennan asked Freddy.

"Oh, much. Not only do I feel better, I sleep better. I take a sauna some nights before I go to bed, and I sleep the best I've slept in years."

Dedich began taking off his clothes. He hung his shirt and pants on a row of hooks by the solarium. Brennan moved over to the weight machine. He lay down under the twin arms of the bench press and lifted. The weight came up easily, and he rolled his head back to see how many of the black disks he had lifted.

"What's it set on?" he asked.

Freddy came over and looked down.

"A hundred. I do three sets of fifteen reps."

"Jesus," Brennan said, pumping the weight two or three times, trying to see if he could do the same workout. "That's pretty good, isn't it? I'm trying to remember what I used to do."

"But you were a jock," Freddy said. "I never was."

"Yes, but you're in better shape now."

"Oh, I don't know."

"I'm way out of shape."

When Brennan sat up, he felt the blood high in his head. He couldn't kid himself it was only the beer. He felt flushed and dizzy and angry for being so soft. He wasn't positive, but he thought he remembered doing ten repetitions of two hundred pounds in the old YMCA.

The rest of the men were almost naked. Freddy got up and handed them towels. Brennan took a drink of beer and listened to his heart flapping inside his chest. In the distance he heard the women coming down the hallway, their voices high and excited. He hoped the redness would go away before they entered.

"We're naked," Donny called to the women. "We're as naked as Romans."

Before the women came in, Atwater and Bloomer jumped into the sauna. Freddy started undressing, and it struck Brennan as sort of slimy that Freddy was going to do a striptease just as the women arrived. Brennan thought again of Pam and Freddy rocking away in the sauna. Freddy was a pimp. He was a good guy, but he was a pimp.

Phil Dedich let out a little yelp as the women came in. He was tugging at his pants leg, which had somehow caught on his ankle.

"There's my husband," Margaret Dedich said. "Doesn't he send shivers up your spine?"

"This damn pants leg," Phil said, finally getting it loose. He stood in his boxer shorts, facing the women. They filled the room with their perfume.

"Now, are we all really going to undress and go in there?" Linda asked. "I don't know if I'd ever be able to look any of you in the face again."

"We've really come to this, haven't we? We're all going to ogle each other, then go home and rerun the whole thing in living color. I can't stand it," Margaret said, laughing.

"Ozzie and Harriet never did this," Sara Atwater said.

Phil turned his back to the women, pulled down his underwear, then ducked into the sauna.

"Oh, my God," Jill Bloomer said. She was a thick woman who looked most comfortable in a golf skirt with a white paper towel hanging out of the back belt. "Phil's got a cute little bum, doesn't he?"

"He looked like a little cottontail hopping in there," Margaret said, and laughed.

By this time Freddy was down to his underwear. He wore some sort of European brand that made his penis and scrotum look like the snout of a dog. His pubic hair sprang up out of the top.

33

"Freddy, those are quite revealing," Jill said, hanging on the lat pulley. "You look like an Olympic swimmer."

"Aren't you getting undressed, Brennan?" Linda asked, smiling.

"In front of you four? I wouldn't dream of it."

Freddy shucked off his underwear, not bothering to turn all the way around. He was a showman. He walked casually into the sauna, grabbing a towel off the rack as he went. He had the body of a bantamweight.

"Well, ladies, we have to decide on our course of action," Pam said. "Is it an orgy or not?"

"Not for me. I was thinner in my last life," Jill said, and took a long drink.

"Me too," Sara said. "If I had to do over again, I wouldn't even have been born in front of men."

"Let's go back then and let Brennan undress in peace," Pam said. "I never knew he was so shy."

The women went out, and Brennan undressed. He patted his stomach a couple of times, disgusted at the way it fluttered. Like sailcoth catching a ruffle. Like wind moving over grass.

Brennan was at breakfast when he heard Roger Maris was dead. Sitting at the kitchen table, a bowl of Cheerios in front of him, he raised his hand for quiet, though no one paid any attention. He jumped up, passing Linda as she crossed to the table with juice for the kids, and reached the tiny television as the newscaster's voice broke off for clips of Maris in 1961.

"Quiet," Brennan said.

"What is it?" asked Linda, turning to look. Her left ear was almost deaf, a leftover from a virus when she was a kid, and she sometimes missed things.

"Quiet. Maris died."

"Maris who?" Kate asked.

"Roger Maris," Louey told her.

"Who's that?" Kate asked again.

34

"He invented the automatic pinsetter," Michael said. "He's a great name in professional bowling."

"Could you please be quiet!" Brennan said, too loud, he knew, but he wanted to listen. Ironically there was nothing to hear. The "Today Show" news ran a black-and-white film of Roger Maris in 1961, the splendid season when he had hit sixty-one homers. Brennan leaned closer, blocking the television on purpose. This was not their time, not their season, and he didn't want Michael or any of the others to make a joke out of Maris's passing. He stared at the television, trying to understand that Roger Maris, the great Maris, was dead.

The film ran in silence. Brennan saw Maris take that beautiful swing of his, that lefty Yankee Stadium swing, and he watched Maris start to run, then trot as it became obvious the ball was gone. Who was the announcer? Brennan tried to remember. Was it Mel Allen or Red Barber? The Scooter? Who had called that final home run, the sixty-first, to put him past Ruth? He watched Maris round first, his uniform baggy by modern standards, but his body beneath the thick wool as tight as any ball player's needed to be. Maris lifted his hat, and there was his crew cut, his dark eyebrows, his muscled arms. The clip faded out into a commercial for Manhattan Renault.

"Christ, Dad, he was just a baseball player," Michael said.

"He was a great baseball player," Brennan said without turning around.

"Just for one season though, wasn't it, Dad?" Louey asked.

"You don't have to be great for more than one season. The point is that he was great at all."

Brennan turned the TV off and returned to the table. He was running late now. It still hadn't sunk in that Roger Maris was dead. He took a sip of coffee and looked at Michael.

"Haircut today, right Michael?" he said.

"And, Michael, afterward you're meeting me downtown at John Frank's to look at suits. I'm going to be at class, then I'm going straight to John Frank's," Linda said, in between drinks of juice. "You're going up there next week.'

35

"I don't know why I have to wear a suit," Michael said. "Professors at colleges don't wear suits."

"You're being interviewed. You want to make the right impression," Linda said.

"What does a suit have to do with whether or not I can do the work at college?"

"Oh, Michael, grow up," Kate said. Brennan noticed she ate only dry toast and a glass of juice. "How can you be so smart and still be so dumb?"

"Here, here," said Louey.

"I hate all these phony games. You should have seen how stupid the applications were. 'Tell us your greatest achievement,' " Michael said in a falsetto, pretending to read off a napkin. " 'Tell us what you believe to be the greatest invention in the history of mankind.' Jesus, it's so ridiculous."

"But you still need a haircut and a decent suit of clothes," Linda said. "Ridiculous or not, the rules are the rules."

Brennan took a last sip of coffee and stood. He glanced at the clock over the stove and saw it was seven twenty-three. At seven thirty he could catch the news and hear all about Maris.

"I've got to go," he said. "See you all tonight."

"Dad, I need money for the haircut," Michael said.

"Your mom will give it to you."

"I don't have any," Linda said, standing up to see him out the door. "Do you have something to give him?"

Brennan flipped out his wallet and handed Michael a five. Michael held it to the light and inspected it.

"This is a five. You don't see many of these anymore. I keep forgetting that Dad thinks we're living in 1959," Michael said. "He still thinks Ike is president."

"How much does it cost then?" Brennan asked, taking the car keys off the hook by the door. "I pay twelve bucks in Newark."

"Yes, but look what you get," Kate said.

"What's wrong with my hair?"

"Dad, that's resodding the whole yard. Michael just wants to prune the hedges."

"It does cost a little more," Linda said.

Brennan grabbed the five back and handed him a twenty. Michael smiled and tucked it in his shirt pocket.

"I want change," said Brennan. "And don't let him do anything fancy to you."

"No, Dad, I'll ask him to dull the scissors too."

Linda stopped him before he got to the door. She nodded at him to indicate that she wanted a word with him in private. He glanced at his watch once more. It was late. "Two seconds," he said, then followed her into the living room, where they stood in front of the large wall mirror. They often had their talks there, and Brennan always felt that seeing themselves reflected kept their discussions level. It was like being on camera, and whenever he spoke, he could not keep his eye from catching a glimpse of his profile.

"I'm not going," Linda said.

"Going where?"

"To the reunion. I just don't want to. High school reunions are ridiculous."

"Okay."

"Do you think I should?" she asked.

"I think you should do what you want. It's really up to you."

She looked at herself in the mirror. He looked at her too. He liked the way she was that morning. She looked a little rumpled, as if she had come out of bed too quickly. He knew she had been debating whether or not she should attend the reunion ever since she had received the invitation. He also knew that this was not necessarily the final word but only the step on the way to a decision. She had a private world of self-assessment, worries that she never talked about but that he could sometimes see on her face. It always surprised him when one of these private thoughts bubbled up to the surface. He loved listening to her then; it was like pulling up an earthy plug, a core sample from which he could guess at her feelings.

When she spoke again, it was to her own reflection as much as to him.

"I'm between jobs right now, and that's the first thing everybody would ask. 'What are you doing?' I can't stand all that."

37

"Okay."

"Do you think I'm being silly?"

"No."

"I mean, it's really just a way for everybody to check their progress, isn't it? It isn't good-spirited at all."

"I'm with you."

"Okay, so that's settled."

Linda walked him back to the kitchen and kissed him at the door, then he was out, running to the car. It was seven-thirty-four. He wondered if Maris had been the lead story. Of course, it wasn't as important as Qaddafi, or terrorists, or the price of gold, but sometimes the news people understood what a story meant.

He had the car moving down Lawrence Avenue toward Route 22 before the news came on. The normal stories slipped by but he couldn't find any mention of Maris's death. He flicked around the stations, finally ending up with a young announcer whose voice sounded puny and stupid. The announcer wouldn't have the slightest idea what Maris could have meant to the sports world. That was the problem with the news. Nothing had any weight, nothing shocked anyone. Everything was tailored to fit between two commercials and a pop song, then it was gone. Brennan had some hope for the late-evening news. By then the stations would be out talking to the old ballplayers, and the players might cut through the crap enough to say what it meant to see Maris gone. Perhaps Mantle would say something. Maybe Berra, or Tom Tresh, or Hector Lopez, if he was still alive himself.

Brennan made it to his office by eight fifty-five. It was not really an office, just a cubicle, but it was all his. He dropped his briefcase on his desk, then glanced through the mail stacked on his blotter. There was nothing important, only a few letters stuffed with invoices, and he left them where they were, unopened. Some new boxes had been moved in over the weekend, and he saw from the printing on the sides that they were filled with football helmets. He snapped open one box and pulled out a helmet with a linebacker's face mask attached. The helmet was a new production number that the design team had developed after a year's work. It was supposed to reduce injuries by spreading out the shock of contact, by not passing it onto the neck and spine, but it looked the same to Brennan. He slapped it a couple times against his open palm, then carried it with him when he left to look for coffee.

He ran into Glenn Shuhan in the hallway. Shuhan was thin and tall, an old forward on one of the Big Five teams out of Philadelphia. Shuhan was the district sales supervisor, Brennan's boss. It had been Shuhan who'd hired Brennan when he left teaching and coaching five years ago and made the jump to sales. Brennan liked the man but never quite felt comfortable around him.

"Hey," Shuhan said now, pointing at the helmet, "what do you think?"

"I just got it. It looks okay."

"Let me see," Shuhan said, walking more slowly now.

He was carrying a coffee cup and handed it to Brennan so he could use both hands. He hit the helmet against his palm, then looked at it straight on, turning it ever so slightly to see its shape. Then he twirled it by the earholes and looked inside. The foam rubber was thick and completely filled the hard exterior shell.

"It doesn't look any different from our other models," Shuhan said. "What's the selling point?"

"It's supposed to disperse the shock of contact better. The design people said they would send over some sort of diagram to back it up."

"It's a wonder anyone will even make these things. Do you know how many times we were sued last year over head and neck injuries?" asked Shuhan, taking his cup back and giving the helmet to Brennan. "Seven times that I know of. A helmet actually cracked down in Texas, and the boy is still getting migraines. They teach the kids to use the helmets as weapons, then they wonder why they break. We're having a hell of a time getting coverage."

"Did they pay off on all seven?"

"I don't know. On some of them they did. It's cheaper in the long run than to go into litigation."

Brennan walked beside Shuhan to the coffee station. Two secretaries were there, both of them temporaries Brennan recognized from the previous week. New women constantly appeared to type and file, most of them looking similar enough so that Brennan was never quite sure whether or not he was saying hello to a temp he had worked with before or to someone entirely new. He smiled at them, helped himself to Coffeemate, and waited for his turn at the coffee urn.

"Did you hear about Maris?" he asked Shuhan.

"What about him?"

"He must have died last night. There was a clip on the TV this morning, but I couldn't find anything on the way in."

"I think he died last year," Shuhan said. "I think it was in December. I thought you were going to say they found out he was a fairy or something."

"I just saw a clip," Brennan said. "I didn't hear the announcer because my kids were talking."

"Maybe it was a nostalgia piece. Maybe it was one of those films they're always showing about the guys who died the year before—that kind of stuff."

Shuhan pushed down the lever on the coffee urn and filled both their cups. Brennan wondered how he had missed Maris's death. It didn't seem possible. Maybe Shuhan was wrong. Either way, he couldn't quite figure what he wanted to say. All he knew was that his mind had been filled with Maris the entire ride this morning.

Shuhan was called away by Franklin in the next office, and Brennan was left alone to go back to his desk. He decided to make phone calls until noon, have lunch, then stop in Roselle Park for a three o'clock appointment. He had been courting the Roselle Park School District for three months, and he thought it was about to bite.

Brennan had another call to make, but he put this one off until the middle of the morning. He gave himself a half hour delay, then another half hour, and would have kept doing it if he hadn't begun to worry that Dr. Breisky might leave for lunch. Doctors were hard enough to contact, and Brennan finally realized he couldn't put it off any longer. He stood, closed the door, then went back and put the phone in the center of his desk.

"Dr. Breisky," he asked when he reached Overlook Hospital.

"Who's calling, please?"

"Brennan McCalmont. I'm calling about my son."

40

"One moment, please."

The receptionist put him on hold. He closed his eyes and rubbed his forehead. He imagined his call climbing the floors. It would stop finally at Floor 7, Oncology, only to hang at the nurses' station until Dr. Breisky could be located. Despite the efficiency and the bustle, the attempts at order everywhere in the hospital, Brennan knew Breisky would be difficult to find. Breisky was a quiet man, more of a technician than a doctor, who floated somewhere behind the anonymity of the white beams and toxic chemical compounds with which he treated his patients. He did not spend a great deal of time on the floor. He limited his contact with patients, especially the children, because, it seemed to Brennan, they got to him. It was not their pain—although Breisky was not entirely insensitive to that, Brennan was sure—but his inability to cure them that kept him away.

It was ten minutes, perhaps longer, before Breisky finally picked up. He sounded a little out of breath. Brennan heard him fumbling with a chart, no doubt recalling names and facts. Then he began speaking very rapidly, assessing the results of the first chemotherapy. It had been effective, he said, but it was only the beginning of a series of treatments. It was too early to make any predictions.

"When would my son have to come in again?" asked Brennan.

"Soon. Next week."

"I'm going up to New England next week. Is there any other time?"

"No, it really should be next week. It's the right timing, the right interval between treatments. We've already put it off because of Christmas and the holidays. We really shouldn't postpone it any longer. I'm sure you understand."

"Are you positive?"

"Positive. It's really the right time for this, Mr. McCalmont. Trust me."

"I just wanted to be with him."

"Of course. Perhaps there's a way to reschedule your trip?"

"No, I'm afraid not. It's just that Louey had such a hard time with that first treatment."

41

"That's not unusual. He's a boy on the edge of puberty, and then to find people around him injecting him, hooking him up to an IV, well, it's normal. We have many reactions like his."

Louey's not like that, Brennan wanted to say, but thanked the doctor instead and hung up. Brennan suddenly found himself breathing hard. His heart beat in his chest, and he wondered, almost curious to feel it happening, if this wasn't the beginning of a heart attack. People died at his age. People went like candles. He put his head down on the desk and tried to relax. He thought once of Maris, then pictured Louey screaming in the hospital room, yanking the IV from his arm, punching and slapping the nurse who happened to be passing by when he began yelling. Louey McCalmont, the sweetest boy Brennan had ever known, had stood on the bed, screaming at them all, using words Brennan had never believed Louey knew, defying any of them to come close. "I'm going home!" he had screamed. "I'm going home!" he yelled over and over, the veins on his neck tight, his face red, a streak of blood dripping down the inside of his arm. And even as he yelled it, Brennan had seen the exhaustion cut into his violence, had seen Louey's eyes suddenly glaze with the knowledge that this was futile. He seemed dazed with the shock of his own rebellion and staggered on the bed, his feet sinking into the mattress as if in a bedroom farce, his spit flicking in the light as he shouted, "You're all crazy! You're all fucking crazy!" He had stood them off for a few more minutes, his nose running, his chest shuddering, until Brennan had stepped forward and held out his arms.

Brennan pulled his car into the service lane off the parkway. He flicked his brights at the white signs directing buses one way, cars another, and followed the car signs until he spotted the pay phone set below a sharp corner of the McDonald's roof.

He parked against the curb, a violation, but he didn't expect to be long. He grabbed a bunch of change he kept handy for tolls and went into the booth. He dialed the number quickly, concentrating to make sure he didn't forget, then waited as the exchange clicked several times. Finally it was picked up by a young man who said too loudly, " 'Sports Talk.' Where you calling from?"

"I'm out on the Garden State."

"What's your name and question?"

"Brennan. I want to ask him about Roger Maris."

"Okay, listen to the show on the phone. Turn down your radio."

"I don't have a radio here. I was listening in the car."

"Okay, when you hear Art ask for you, jump in. Make sure you're paying attention because he won't wait long."

Brennan held the phone in the crook of his neck and wrapped his coat closer. It was cold in the phone booth. He looked up and saw the sky was gray. It could snow. He wished for a huge snowstorm, a giant blizzard that would slow everything down and make them all stop. He wanted snow up to the windows, snow over the doors, so they all could just stay in and sleep and eat good meals. He imagined building a fire, a good fire with logs of ash or hickory, which he would keep going all night long. Perhaps the whole family would pull out sleeping bags, as they did when the kids were smaller, and sleep near the fire, camping out in their own home, each of them taking turns telling ghost stories.

He was still looking at the sky when Art Rust, Jr., the host of "Sports Talk," came on the line.

"Hello, you're next on 'Sports Talk,' " Art Rust, Jr., said. "Who's this?"

"Brennan. I'm calling you from the Garden State."

"Don't brag about it," said Art in a voice Brennan knew was joking. Still, the abruptness of the comment, the aggressiveness of it, made him falter. Brennan coughed and cleared his throat, then tried to clarify himself.

"I mean, from the parkway," he said.

"What's your question there, friend?"

"It's not really a question. I just wanted to ask you about Maris."

"What about him? Great ballplayer. He had one of the truly great seasons in the history of the sport. Truly great. People forget he could play right field as well as anyone around. He had a great arm. No, he wasn't just a fluke."

"I remember that season," Brennan said, conscious he was stumbling badly now, trying to remember what he had called about. "Maybe this sounds stupid, but did he just die? I saw a clip on TV this morning."

"He died late last year, partner. It was a great loss."

"Roger Maris is dead?" Brennan asked, trying to gather it in.

"I'm afraid so. A great right fielder in his day. It was one hell of a year he had."

Brennan didn't listen closely to this last bit. Roger Maris, the great Maris, was dead. He suddenly felt very close to crying. How did he miss it? Maybe Maris had died when Louey was in the hospital or something, he didn't remember. He knew he wanted to talk about his swing, about the pure beauty of it, and how it had struck him to see it again on the morning news, but he wasn't sure Rust would understand.

"I guess I just wanted to say I'll miss Roger Maris," Brennan finished lamely.

"We all will, baby, thanks for calling."

The line clicked, and Brennan heard the beginning of a commercial jingle. He was back on the outside, listening in to the show. He hung up the phone and pulled his coat tighter. It was cold suddenly, and he couldn't shake it.

Standing with Linda and Kate, Brennan watched Michael walk up and down the upstairs hallway. The new suit Michael modeled was slightly too big. The pants nicked the tops of his black wing tips, occasionally snagging in the new, stiff shoelaces. The seat of his pants bagged the tiniest bit behind, not enough to have altered, but enough to make it obvious Michael was not accustomed to wearing a suit. Still, Michael looked good, as good as Brennan had ever seen him look, and he called Michael closer to help him straighten his tie.

"Is this a Windsor knot or a regular?" he asked Michael.

"Regular."

"You might want to see if you can get this knot a little thicker. It would look better."

"Use Dad's tie bar," said Kate, stepping forward to remove a piece of lint from Michael's pants leg. "They look sexy anyway."

"I'll look like an ad salesman," Michael said, his neck stretched to give Brennan room to work.

"You will not. Everyone's wearing them," Kate said, again taking lint off Michael's pants. "You were right, Mom, this is a nice color on him."

"I thought gray with his coloring," Linda said. "He's dark enough."

"He's a winter," Kate said.

Brennan finished with the knot. It was better, straighter, although Michael's neck still did not fill out the collar. Michael stepped back and looked in the mirror attached to the door of the linen closet.

"Women will flunk their exams if they see me," Michael said. "They'll never be able to concentrate again."

"You have to promise me," Linda said, leaning against the door of their bedroom, "that you will hang that up as soon as you get finished for the day. Promise?"

"I promise."

"Really promise. That suit cost good money."

"I thought they accepted only bad money at John Frank's, Mom."

"You know what I'm saying."

"All right, that's it," Brennan said, smoothing the cloth once more over Michael's shoulders. "We all should get to bed. Michael, hang that suit up now. Put it back in the clothes bag, okay?"

"Okay."

Brennan waited for Linda to step into the bedroom, then closed the door behind them. The bedroom was cold. Brennan crossed to the bed and turned on the electric blanket. The switch was almost buried under Linda's real estate books. Linda went into the bathroom.

"I'm going to say good night to Kate," Brennan said. "I won't see her in the morning."

"Okay. Make sure Michael's hanging up that suit, will you?"

"I'll check him."

Brennan went out into the hallway once more. He heard Kate's stereo playing softly in the closest room. Michael's room was at the far end of the hallway, past Louey's. Brennan knocked before he

45

entered and caught Michael standing in his boxers, his skinny chest and arms raised in gooseflesh. Brennan saw computer parts on every surface.

"You hanging up the suit?"

"Jesus, this thing gets more attention than I do."

"Did you hang it up or not?"

"Yes."

"Okay, we're up at four tomorrow morning. You have your alarm set?"

"All set."

"All right then, see you in the morning. The suit looked great. It really did."

"Thanks, Dad."

Brennan closed the door and went to Kate's room. She had changed into a flannel nightgown and was sitting on her bed, brushing her hair. A Western civ book was open on the bed beside her. Brennan saw something about Julius Caesar, another page about aqueducts.

"We'll be up early, so we won't see you tomorrow, sweetheart," said Brennan. "Everything okay with you?"

"Yes, why?"

"No reason. What's this on the stereo?"

"Bruce Springsteen."

"You like him?"

"He's okay. You'd like him. He sings all about baseball and stuff."

"Give me his tape someday and I'll listen to it on the way in to work."

"You didn't listen to Adam Ant."

"I couldn't, Kate. What is he anyway? All these rock stars are like comic book heroes. They all have these costumes and identities they put on when they step onstage."

Her hair crackled. She put the brush down to keep the book from closing.

"Listen," Brennan said, "this next week isn't going to be too easy around here. Your mom's going to be up at the hospital from Tuesday on, just about, and when she comes home, she's not going to be good for much. You think you could cook some meals? You know, just make it a little easier on her?"

"I'll be up to see Louey, too."

"I know, but just sometimes if you could? Just be on the lookout for her, okay? She'll probably be a little anxious. Just see where you can pitch in, all right?"

"Okay, Dad."

Brennan kissed Kate good night, then went back to his bedroom. Linda was already reading in bed, something about mortgage rates. Brennan went into the bathroom and showered. He stayed in the shower longer than necessary, allowing the water to hit his shoulders and neck. Finally he stepped out and dried himself. He was warm enough now to wear just a towel into the bedroom. He lay on top of the covers, his weight pulling the blanket tight over Linda's thighs and stomach. He propped himself on his elbows beside her.

"Did he hang it up?" asked Linda, setting the book to one side. The book had a cover that showed a young couple going into their first dream house.

"I didn't check him. He's pretty excited."

"You still going to leave at four?"

"I don't want to get caught in that traffic going out to Connecticut. The Tappan Zee Bridge is terrible in the morning."

"It's so early, though."

"We'll be okay."

He inched forward on his elbows and kissed her shoulder. He waited for his penis to stir, wondering how it would respond but feeling nothing. He kissed her again, this time kissing up toward her throat. His lips touched the round flute of her collarbone.

"You think Louey understands why I have to go?" he asked, letting his head rest on her shoulder for a moment.

"Sure he does."

"Sometimes I still think I should cancel."

"Michael would be heartbroken. Besides, it's late enough already. Most of the kids went up in the fall, when they applied to colleges. Remember what the social worker said. She said you have to be sure not to slight your other children just because one of them is sick. She said that can cause a lot of bitterness."

"What the hell did she know? She kept calling me Benny, for God's sake. She couldn't even remember my name."

"She got the names mixed up. But the point was still a good one."

Brennan kissed her shoulder some more. It was a good point, he knew, and despite how ridiculous he had found the social worker, how ridiculous she had been, he believed what she had said. Be careful of your other children. He closed his eyes, his lips just touching the side of her neck, climbing into her hair and behind her ear, imagining his children like eggs, or glasses slipping from a box suddenly torn at the bottom.

But these thoughts faded as Linda's lips touched his cheek, his ear. Her hand wedged in between him and the covers to pull down the sheet. "Come under," she said, and he did, shedding the towel like skin, crawling under and into the heat. Her body was warm, and he realized suddenly he was cold. She retracted from him for an instant; then she pushed into him, the knob of her pubis jabbing his hip, her arms like bands or heated towels crisscrossed over his back.

He went down her body, kissing her breasts, her arms, kissing rib by rib until he felt her thighs spread an inch, rolling more than spreading, then another inch. He smelled her then and put his mouth on her vagina, his legs ludicrously sticking out from under the heat, his legs cold, but her body there above him, gloriously opening. Abracadabra, he thought. He licked quietly, his pulse and tongue and penis all connected somehow, until her arm came down and pulled him up, a survivor's hand extended to a fading swimmer, and he climbed her body, shinnying, until his penis was deep inside her and she was moving.

"Brennan," she said.

He moved on top of her, beginning to sweat a little, the lines of the electric blanket like a harness on top of him. He raised himself up until just his penis and her vagina were in contact. "Just that," he said, "just that." And she lifted to him, a baby ape hanging onto its mother's belly, a glider rocking on a porch underneath a white frame, her weight pendulous and wonderful.

"Come now," she said, "come in me."

He knew from this that she was tired, prepared to have it over, although he also knew it did not mean she was not enjoying herself. He moved a little side to side, inviting her to be playful, but she tightened her arms on him and whispered again into his ear. "Now," she said, "come in me." But he was not quite there, not yet, and he went faster, closing his eyes tighter, feeling the heat build around him. Deep, deep, a socket, he thought, his hands moving to cup her buttocks, her legs rising until they created a single hinge to connect them at the hips. She reached down and touched his balls, and it was so kind, such a thoughtful thing to do that he felt the sperm lifting in him.

"Oh, you're good," he said, and meant it every way, any way she cared to take it. A good lover, a good cunt, a good mother and friend. At the same time he came in her, his body shivering, his penis still perched on the pedestal of her palm.

Still in her, he rolled to one side and held her. Her right leg hung over his hip, but the notch of her vagina was tighter now. He squeezed her and rocked her, holding her head against his shoulder. Already he felt sleep moving up from their groins, the blood sifting back to their brains and hearts and limbs.

"You're a wonderful woman," he whispered.

She didn't answer. She was away, gone to dreams, gone to wherever she went each night. Her body twitched once, twice; then her head bucked up and knocked lightly against his jaw. He lay beside her, feeling his penis slowly pull away from her, but he fell asleep before he had left her entirely.

When he awoke at the alarm, she was curled in a tight ball on the far side of the bed. He looked at the window and saw it was dark. He knew it was cold simply from looking at the windowpanes and hearing the wind. Far away he heard a car spinning on ice. When he threw back the covers, the car caught asphalt and moved away.

He met Michael down in the kitchen. Two cereal bowls were already out, the cereal set beside them. Michael grabbed the milk from the refrigerator while Brennan poured them each a bowl of Cheerios.

"Did you think of anything we've forgotten?" asked Brennan.

"You have all the directions? I don't have any maps or anything."

"Yes."

"Then that's everything."

"You have the names of the people you're supposed to see at each college?"

"Yes. I've got all the letters with me."

They ate in silence. It was too early to talk. Brennan turned on the radio and heard an all-night talk show slowly wrapping up. It made him sad. It was always a little sad to see the sun rise when you had been up all night, and he heard this in the callers' voices when they spoke to the talk master. A few minutes later Brennan heard the weather report. Dry and sunny but cold, highs in the low twenties. He reminded himself to bring his sunglasses.

He let Michael run the bowls under water while he checked his briefcase once more. He had a number of papers he wanted to be sure to bring along. He had the deed for the house in Massachusetts to remember, as well as two maps of New England. He had also brought along three contracts he had promised Shuhan to look over, along with the blueprints the design team had finally sent to him. He had to stay up on the job. With Louey, he had already taken off more time than he should.

"I'm ready, Dad," Michael said.

"I'm all set."

Brennan let Michael out and locked the door after them. Then he jogged to the car, careful on the frost that had collected on the driveway. The night was very cold. Brennan saw the stars clearly and heard the trees knocking against each other.

He drove slowly to Route 22, letting his station wagon warm up, then pressed the accelerator when they gained the parkway north. Michael leaned against the door and slept. That was all right. Brennan liked seeing the night lights, the cars moving so smoothly on the highways. Distance. They covered distance, tricking nature somehow by using the night and waking up in some new place. Go to sleep a kid, wake up a college applicant, a Yale or Harvard man. It could happen. It was happening to Michael. That was another thing the social worker had said: Things will pale beside your son's illness. Things will seem insignificant. Brennan supposed Michael must have felt that at times. How do you compete with a sibling who is dying? How do you draw attention to yourself? Besides, it all had seemed so easy to Michael: 780 verbal, 800 math, IQ in the high 140s. Michael had been a straight A student since his first day in school, since he had begun piecing together puzzles more rapidly than other children, talking sooner and more intelligently, learning the alphabet one day and appearing at the dinner table the next to show his mother a sentence he had thought up—not just a word, but a sentence, a concept it took most children years to understand. It all had been natural, and Brennan could only liken it to the performance of a great athlete, an athlete so talented his pure abilty made an explanation of his talent absurd. Questioned, he would only shrug, just as Michael sometimes did when Brennan asked him how he knew something. It came, it stuck.

Yale Man, Harvard Man. Brennan liked the sound of it, even though he suspected he was, at that moment, delivering his son to a life he himself would never understand. It would be subtle—books, painters, music, even the right type of shoe, the proper break in a trouser leg. He was paying for ideas, and the ideas would take his son away. What would he do, Brennan asked himself, the first time his son was condescending toward him? It would be different from the stupid arguments they had together now. No, this condescension would be real and perhaps merited. Brennan felt a sudden dread of the conversation he knew was inevitable. It would come, he was sure, and it was futile to try to predict what would trigger it. Perhaps it would be only a mispronunciation, fouling up the name of a foreign city or butchering one of the Arab names that dominated the news these days. Maybe they would serve the wrong wine at a meal. Maybe they would not serve wine at all, only beer, and Michael would use that to clout them with his knowledge, his wider world. However it came, Brennan knew the seed of it was now in their lives, undiscovered, waiting for Michael's sharper eye. It did not seem fair, but Brennan accepted it for something they all would have to go through.

Watching Michael grow, he had always known the time would come for him to boost his son over the fence just to find himself left behind, scrambling against the cement, comically frantic.

Brennan rolled his shoulders and rubbed his stomach. To his right he began to see just the faintest promise of sunlight. To the west the stars were already becoming pale. Brennan promised himself a cup of coffee as soon as they made it over the Tappan Zee Bridge. He would have one cup in the restaurant, another in the car afterward.

Brennan finished the last of his onion soup and wiped his mouth with a napkin. The soup had been a good choice. He thought about ordering another bowl, then decided against it. He wondered for a second how many calories were contained in a bowl of onion soup. He never liked to consider his body a machine, but that was the truth of it. The body burned only so much, and all the rest was extra. He thought of his potbelly as wood stacked under the eaves of a New England house. It would be used, sooner or later. No one died fat, he thought, not if he lived long enough.

He checked his watch once more, then stood and asked the waiter for the phone. The phone was back by the men's room, wedged between the wall and a cigarette machine. The wall was cut with deep pen gouges, numbers to call for blow jobs, hand jobs, fucking, and term papers. A poem above the phone started, "Call me Willy,/Call me silly," but then the writer apparently ran out of inspiration. Different words were scratched in to suggest the next line—Dilly? Pilly? Frilly?—but the poem had run out of room.

Kate answered and accepted the charges.

"Dad, where are you?" she asked.

"At Brown. In Providence."

"We thought so, but you took the schedule with you."

"Is something wrong?"

"No, nothing really. Mom just wanted to keep track of where you were. Is Michael with you?"

"No, he's talking to the computer guy up here. He went off with him somewhere to see the system."

"What fun."

"It is to Michael," Brennan said. "I'm meeting him over in the gym in a few minutes. The admissions guy gave us a pass and said we could work out."

"Does he like Brown?"

"I think so. He liked Yale. I like Brown better, I think. I like Providence better than New Haven."

"What?" Kate asked, and Brennan knew she was speaking to Linda. Kate's voice drifted away, then came back.

"Mom wants to talk to you. Say hello to Michael for me. Love you, Dad."

"Love you, too."

Brennan listened to the phone being passed and pictured Linda swinging her head slightly to move the hair off her ear. She always had to switch the phone to her left ear since her right was so poor. He heard the stove rattle, and Kate said something else. Then water ran, and finally Linda said hello.

"Hi, sweetheart," she said, "how's the trip going?"

"Fine. Michael's already going Ivy League."

"Is he?"

"But did you know Ivy League isn't ivy at all? I mean, it isn't a plant. Ivy is actually IV, the Roman numerals. It means four, the first four colleges."

"I didn't know that. Which four?"

"I don't know. Harvard's one of them."

"So Michael's enjoying himself?"

"He's talking computers with everyone. I told Kate, he's over looking at the computer system right now."

"I'm so glad he'll have people who can talk computers with him."

"I think we're going to be able to swing it financially," Brennan said softly, turning to the corner. "I've talked to some of the financial aid people, and they said if he's accepted we'll probably get some help."

"That's wonderful."

"They've been helpful. I didn't have to bring it up or anything. They knew most of my questions before I asked them."

"That's fine," Linda said, but he knew, hearing her take a breath, that it was coming now: The news about Louey was bad and she was thinking of how to say it. Her ring hit the phone, and he pictured her switching hands, glancing at Kate, perhaps making turning motions with her wrist to ask Kate to turn off the water.

"Go ahead," he said.

"Well, listen," she said, "Louey's real sick, honey. He's been vomiting almost continuously. Dr. Breisky says it's to be expected, and I called Margaret, and she said her uncle had the same thing, the same treatment, and that's what happens."

"What do you mean, 'that's what happens'?"

"I mean, the vomiting. That's what the chemotherapy does. That's how it works. He was sick the last time, too."

"Is he conscious? The doctor didn't say he'd be that sick."

"Yes, he did."

"Not that sick, he didn't."

"He implied it, darling. I suppose he didn't want to be too graphic. We did know, honey. It was in that information he gave us. Even the caseworker said so."

"He did not, damn it. No one said he'd be sick all the time. Not the whole goddamn time. I thought that place was a hospital! They're supposed to make him well. What the hell is that medicine anyway, dripping radioactive crap through a kid's veins?"

"Brennan, I know, honey."

"What is it, a fucking change of oil?"

"I know."

Brennan closed his eyes and felt his breath coming hard. When he looked again, he saw his waiter peek around the corner to check what was going on. Brennan covered the mouthpiece and held the phone away from his ear.

"Stock market," he said to the waiter.

"You okay, mister?"

"Yes, I'm okay."

"You want your bill?"

"No, I want to wreck this fucking hole and then you can bill me, all right? Is that what you want to hear?"

54

"Jesus, relax, would you? The manager sent me over here."

Under his hand Brennan heard Linda calling for him. He waited until the waiter moved away, then put the phone back to his ear.

"Listen," Brennan interrupted, "has Breisky been in to see him?"

"Yes, right after he went on the IV."

"Fucking IV League, huh? Louey beat Michael to that, didn't he? What did Breisky say?"

"Nothing, honey. It's just a procedure to him. It's not his fault, really. He has a lot of patients."

"Sure he does, the bastard. If you can get hold of the prick, tell him to visit at least twice a day. Tell him we're paying him good money for his services."

"I'll tell him what I can, Brennan."

That was it then. Brennan waited for Linda to say something else, but it was over.

"I'll tell you what," Brennan said, watching the waiter pass with a tray of beer, "I'm going to get off now. I'm no good right now, okay? Let me just hang up, and maybe I'll call you tonight when things calm down."

"All right, honey."

"It's not you."

"I know."

Brennan hung up and waited a second for his breathing to slow. He stared at the graffiti. MARTHA BURPS THE WORM ALL TERM. He read the line ten or twelve times, all the while wondering if he should call Linda back and start all over. What annoyed him most was that he had not taken down all the particulars of Louey's condition. Again he pictured the leukemia moving through the bloodstream, a lizard, a creature able to escape anything. Sleeping, he knew, salamanders sprang from frozen logs. Flame did not kill them, and neither did light. Flame released them; flame woke them.

He stood quietly for a few moments longer, catching his breath, then paid and headed for the gym. As he walked toward campus, the wind struck him in the face. He pulled his collar tighter. He had to ask a student for directions, but finally he saw the field house. He crossed the parking lot and went in, showing his pass to the security guard seated inside a small booth. As soon as he was past the guard, he saw Michael leaning against a waist-level wall, looking down at the track and basketball courts. He had their gym bag, but he hadn't changed yet.

"How was it?" Brennan asked, putting his arm on his son's shoulder. "Did you break into the Pentagon's system?"

"We launched some missiles at Canada."

"Is it a good system?"

"The system's okay. There are a lot of terminals around campus, so you can get on almost anytime you want. They've got mailing, the whole thing. Computer majors get extra time on the terminals."

"So is this the best one so far?"

"I guess so. I like Mr. Compson," Michael said, turning to look at a pickup game of basketball going on beneath them. "What did you do?"

"I had a bowl of soup. Did you get anything to eat?"

"We had a sandwich."

"You want to run a little then?"

"If you do. You sure you're up to it?"

"Once in shape, always in shape."

"How was Louey?" asked Michael. He picked up the gym bag and balanced it on the wall. "Did you get hold of Mom?"

"Not great," Brennan said. "He's pretty sick."

"The chemotherapy?"

"Yes."

"He didn't turn into Mr. Hyde again, did he?"

"No, he's just real sick."

"Dad, you think this chemotherapy is worth it? I read that information Mom had. It sounds like the treatment is worse than the disease."

"What else can we do?"

"I don't know. I just hate to see him have to go through all that."

"Listen," Brennan said, "let's run a little bit. I could use a run."

Brennan followed Michael down into the visitors' locker room. It was small and hot, but nearly empty. Brennan changed quickly into his gym shorts and sneakers. It gave him a good feeling to be ready for a workout, to be standing in a locker room again. That much didn't change. He bobbed back and forth, waiting for Michael, trying to loosen his muscles. He felt stiff and tired. His lower back throbbed near his spine, and his hamstrings stretched and yawned. Touching his toes, his legs vibrating, he pictured wire cables pegged into soft spring dirt beside a circus tent.

"Dad, why did you give up running?" Michael asked, sitting on the bench to pull on his sneakers. "You were pretty consistent about it for a while, weren't you?"

"Twenty-five miles a week."

"What happened?"

"I got bored with it."

"You miss it?"

"I don't know. It's good not to have to do it, I have more time, but I felt better when I was doing it. I could go upstairs better. You know, that sort of thing."

"You should start again."

"Freddy's running. He's lifting weights, too. He's got a whole sauna in his basement."

"You should," Michael said, finally finished.

"Maybe I will," Brennan agreed, feeling his face turning crimson. He bobbed down two or three times, attentive to the strained muscles in his back and legs.

Out on the track, running slowly, Brennan felt himself comfortable for the first time in days. His legs felt thick and slow, but there was a peacefulness in finding them solid after so much neglect. Michael jogged with him for a lap or so, then gradually pulled away, his long legs supple and fluid, his stride taking him into a rhythm with two or three other runners. Brennan took up the pace of a heavy coed, her large butt flexing under gray sweat pants, her ponytail swishing side to side. Watching her run, her toes slightly splayed, her gait wide, he doubted she would ever lose the weight she wanted to shed. Yet there was something heroic about her perseverance, and after following her for three laps, he jogged past, huffing a little and raising his eyebrows at her, trying in some way to signal that it all was a struggle. She smiled back, slightly self-conscious, and Brennan stuck his thumbs up, a motion so ridiculous he saw her smile fade.

But it was all right. He was running now, moving along at a decent clip. Once an all-American, always an all-American. His body responded slowly, sluggishly, but with something of the grace of an old actor struggling to his feet to rumble a line in a voice too broad and resonant for a modern stage. It was still there. He stutter-stepped twice, faking a little, then let his stride lengthen. Muscles flexed high up in his hips, and he felt his back loosen. His breathing was good, his blood pumping normally. He felt himself approaching that good state when the mind jumps at its own thoughts, tracking them in whatever direction it chose, while he could sit back, someplace deep near his spine, and simply watch.

"How you feeling?" Michael asked, coming up beside him, lapping him, Brennan knew, but didn't care. "You look good."

"How many laps to a mile?" asked Brennan.

"About fourteen, I think."

"How many have you done?"

"Eight."

"Okay, I'll do a mile, then quit. Am I really red?"

"No, not too bad. You look sunburned, that's all."

"The peak of health."

Michael stayed beside him for another two laps, then went off again. Brennan saw a boy with a long fiberglass pole run at a vaulting pit, plant the pole, then bounce up five or six feet, finally sinking back down. A coach yelled, "Good, good," and clapped his hands, resin or chalk rising in small clouds across his chest.

Running now, sweating freely, his legs finally limber, Brennan felt all right, felt okay. For a moment he thought of football, of green grass with white stripes, the bleachers jammed, the cheerleaders kicking. He stutter-stepped twice, faking to his left, then jiggled his upper body. Two hundred and five pounds, a good fifteen overweight, but what could you do? He was Brennan the Bull, Brennan the Beautiful, with a gun at his shoulder and coolness in action. Flanker right hook, tight end sideline flare, fullback stay, halfback dip on the linebacker.

58

On one, ready. He clapped his hands and finished the mile, his pass to the hooking flanker going zing, snap.

Brennan saw the Deerfield River to his left as he followed the Mohawk Trail. From the swell of the river he knew the dam must be down. Great arrows of white churning water broke over rocks and chafed the banks. Brennan slowed to look more closely at the river, remembering a pool somewhere along the far edge, marked by a beech, where he had caught the same trout three times in one summer. It had been a big trout, a German brown, and he had examined it closely to see the three separate nicks he had left on its upper lip. Twice he had taken it with a Coachman just under the surface, but the last time he had settled a perfect Pale Evening Dun on its rise, knowing before the fly had actually touched the surface that the fish would take it. And just before it had rushed up, Brennan had a chance to feel the warm evening, the wild insect hum, the beautiful crush of water on his knees. Now, he had thought, and as simply as that the fish was on, wriggling downstream and back up, while Brennan let the line go where it would, content to know he had hooked it.

Now, however, he could not locate the pool. He slowed the car and strained to see out the window; but it was winter, and the trees did not look the same. A car behind him honked and Michael turned to look.

"There's a car behind you, Dad," he said.

"I know. Let him go around."

"What are you looking for?"

"A pool I used to fish."

"The guy's about to come through the windshield. You better let him past, Dad."

Brennan edged his station wagon over and let the car, a Mitsubishi, fly past. The driver flipped the finger at him. Brennan nodded and pulled back into the lane.

"They hate out-of-towners up here," Brennan said, watching the green and white Massachuetts plate disappear. "They get a million tourists a year up and down this road."

"Looking for wampum?"

"Looking for wampum."

"I can't believe you lived up here," Michael said. "Weren't you bored stiff?"

"No, it was all right. We didn't do the things you do now. It was pretty innocent. We fished and hung around. It was okay."

"You really didn't have electricity? I mean, were you serious when you told us all that stuff?"

"We got it when I was twelve or so. My dad never wanted it. It was my mom who finally talked him into it. Afterwards, though, he liked it more than any of us. He watched TV and listened to the radio. And around the community people started getting electric milkers. That was a big thing."

They were coming into Charlemont. The town was really only two rows of buildings, the right side more tightly packed, the left side somehow eroding into the parking lot of a Mobil station. Carter Hardware was still there, Brennan noted, as were Plenty's Dry Goods and Plug's Fishing Tackle. Another store had opened on the river side, but it was impossible to tell from the sign outside the door what it sold. The sign said GRUMPHY's and nothing else.

Brennan saw the statue of the Mohawk Indian and pulled his car into the municipal parking lot just outside the courthouse doors. He looked to find Harvey's truck in its usual spot, but it wasn't there. Brennan turned off the engine and reached into the glove compartment for the envelope he had brought containing the deed, the lease he had signed with the Adamses, and the last two bounced checks. A cold wind from the river hit the car in violent bursts.

Michael asked, "Should we go in? Did Uncle Harvey get a new truck?"

"In a second. Let me just make sure everything's here."

"Is Uncle Harvey expecting us?"

"Sometime today."

"I could run in and see if he's there."

"No, I'll just be a second."

Brennan checked everything one last time, then hit Michael's knee and climbed out. It was very cold, yet the air was good and clean.

60

Brennan smelled the river and woodsmoke. He took a few deep breaths. On the other side of the car Michael jogged in place.

"Harvey will be back in a second, even if he's out," Brennan said.

"If you say so."

"You hungry?"

"No."

"Harvey will want to eat an early dinner. Maybe he'll want to go by the house, but if he's ready for dinner, just go along with him, okay?"

"Sure."

Brennan held the envelope close to his chest as he went up the stairs of the courthouse. As soon as they were inside, Brennan felt good, dry heat and heard a radiator hissing. The floors were wood and slightly bowed. Three doors opened off the hallway, each one with a small sign indicating the function of the communicating office. One sign, larger than the rest, said FISHING LICENSES. That was Harvey's office.

Brennan thought perhaps there were people he should recognize, people he should say hello to, but he hoped Harvey would be back before he had to stumble through old names. Michael grabbed a seat and immediately picked up something to read. It was a brochure on the Mohawk State Forest, the lettering formed from tomahawks. Brennan slapped his envelope against his own leg and began reading the bulletin board, which was nailed up next to the Office of Motor Vehicles. Sewing machine for sale, $75. Ethan Allen maple table, with leaves, $45 or best offer. Quartz heater, $35. Brennan read the names on the slips, the tiny strips of paper under each one like braided buckskin. Up near the top a special section was devoted exclusively to fishing gear. Brennan saw a sign for a graphite rod for $125, a fly-tying vise included.

"It says here," Michael said from the bench, a short hiss of steam rising up to cover his voice momentarily, "that the Mohawks traveled the whole area and settled only seasonally next to the Deerfield. They stayed for the fishing."

"It was a trail west, wasn't it?"

"That's what it says."

"I never did get it all straight," said Brennan, his eyes still on the bulletin board. "It was always just Indians. No one said much about who they were or what they did. I could never remember the difference between the Mohicans and the Mohawks. Which one is the haircut?"

"I think they both are," Michael said, not really listening any longer.

Pretty soon the door opened, and it was Harvey. He wore a light golfing jacket over a thick ski sweater. He also wore a red hunting hat which did not fit at all with the golf jacket. The flaps were down on the hat, and for a moment it made Harvey looked compressed, gave him the appearance of an old man, until he flipped it off and clapped his hands.

"I saw those ugly New Jersey plates out there," he shouted. "Christ, what are they now? Sky blue? What's that supposed to be, pool water blue? You can't see the sky there, that's for sure."

"Hi, Uncle Harvey," Michael said, standing.

"Christ, Michael, is that you?" Harvey asked, stepping forward and hugging him. "Up here on the college swing, are you? Look at you! You seventeen or eighteen?"

"Eighteen."

"Jesus, and look at this old goat. Brennan McCalmont, the Deerfield all-American. How are you, Brennan? Gee, it's good to see you."

Brennan hugged Harvey and felt himself hugged back. He slapped Harvey twice on the back, happy for the first time in days, in months. Harvey's jacket whistled as he pulled away. He snapped his hunting hat against Brennan's leg, and Brennan reached up one last time to punch Harvey lightly on the shoulder.

"You know," Harvey said, taking a spot between Brennan and Michael, "I was just seeing about this Adams business. You rented your goddamn house to a hooker! Did you know that?"

"No, come on."

"You did. That Gretchen, the one you liked so much, she was doing a little business in your house. Nothing big, you see, it was just different guys on the weekends. You wouldn't have guessed it, would you?"

62

"No, she looked awfully good to me."

"Pretty girl, wasn't she? She was always baking bread whenever I went by. The house was plenty dirty, but she always had some sort of loaf in there. It was never cinnamon bread or just plain white either—she always had something like wolfsbane or yellow tansy smashed in with it. She'd take all the leftovers and pump them into a huge loaf of bread. She said it was nutritious."

"Dad's a good judge of character," Michael said.

"Isn't he? Not only that, the girl's turning tricks, but not enough to pay the rent. How's that? Your father has a way with finances."

Harvey slapped Michael with his hunting hat and grinned.

"Now, what do you say?" Harvey continued. "Why don't I run you over to your house and get you set up? Then we go over to mine. Ginny has a little something planned for dinner, and then we can just sit around and talk. How would that be?"

"Great," Brennan said. "Michael, why don't you ride with Harvey and tell him about colleges? I'll follow."

"Okay," Michael said.

"Good," Harvey said, "I want to hear about that."

Harvey yelled to someone in another office; a female voice responded; then he slipped on his hat once more. He pulled open the door and led them across the parking lot, his jacket flapping, his hatbrim fighting to fly straight up.

"What's the river like these days?" Brennan asked over the wind. "The fishing still good?"

"When the dam's down. They ruined it for natural hatches. Still, it's pretty good if you know where to go. I don't do it much myself anymore."

"How's the power plant working out?"

"Cheap electricity and jobs. People around here won't knock it. There isn't much industry."

Harvey and Michael jumped into Harvey's old Ford pickup. It started on the first turn. Brennan climbed into his station wagon and followed them out of the parking lot, turning right onto the Mohawk Trail. He drove slowly, looking now at the river, now at the old clapboard houses on either side of the road. The houses looked pretty much the same. Old Man Billing's house still had a WORMS FOR SALE sign pegged into the front yard, but back behind the house Brennan saw the old man's garage had burned down. A mile farther along he saw where one house had been entirely abandoned. The roof had caved in, and the front porch had snapped outward, buckling and rolling toward the road. Brennan tried to remember who had lived there but could summon only a few vague faces.

He saw his own house when the road separated from the bed of the Deerfield River. It was built of white clapboard and had a high, steep roof. The porch that ringed the house was wide and sturdy. In the summer it was a wonderful place to sit, and Brennan, turning up the short driveway, remembered evenings coming back from the river, his father and mother two dark forms in the last light, their rockers mewing, their voices calling out to him as he crossed the meadow up to the house, "They biting?" And if he had caught fish, the cats, Lewis and Clark, would track him, padding softly through the tall grass, their bodies thrust forward to sniff at his creel, while he took the last few steps up to the porch, the smell of mosquito dope suddenly heavy and dense all about him. "Three," he would say, or seven or nine, then go to clean the fish at the side of the house, the cats wild until they received the intestines. He would arrange the long, sleek bodies of the fish on a white china plate in the kitchen, their eyes stunned and glassy, their forms so perfect as to be almost rude beside the rusted sink.

Now he pulled to a halt beside Harvey's truck and shut down the engine. Michael was out at once. Harvey grabbed his keys off the seat as Brennan came over to stand next to him. The back step to the door had been replaced with old fieldstones.

"It's run-down a little," Harvey said. "I was telling Michael on the ride over that Gretchen left and no one even knew it. She just wasn't around for a while, and when no check came to the office, I figured I'd look into it. She wasn't here, and there wasn't any sort of note. She just took off."

"What about the guy?" asked Brennan, watching Harvey try a key in the back door. "What was his name? Bobby or something? No word from him?"

"None."

"Did he go to some other job?"

"I don't know," Harvey said, still sorting through keys. "These people are old hippies. We've got them all around here. They don't really want to work, and they don't really want to farm; but they like living out in the country. They aren't even genuine hippies. These people are the leftovers. I feel sorry for them, really. They're all over this area because people like you have moved away. A small place like this can't really be farmed, and there isn't any industry around, so what the hell are people going to do with old houses like this? All you can hope for is they don't burn the place down."

Harvey pushed open the door. They stepped into the kitchen, and Brennan smelled the cold and mildew deep in the wood. Michael flapped his arms while Harvey stepped through into the small living room.

"I can see my breath in here," Michael said.

"I didn't want to start the stove until you were here," Harvey said from inside. He banged on something in the stove. "It isn't a good idea to have it going with no one around."

"No, of course not," Brennan said, for some reason moving to the sink to see if the water still worked. "Is the stove in good condition?" He turned the faucet and a stream of water shot out.

"I had it cleaned out. A lot of creosote built up on it because she was heating with whatever she could—cheap wood, old boxes. I think she burned most of her garbage in it."

"This place needs to be aired out," Michael said, going in to join Harvey.

"Needs to be lived in," Harvey said.

Brennan turned off the water and stepped into the living room. The room was tight; the ceiling, too low. Harvey already had the fire going. Brennan saw that Ginny must have been in to clean after the Adams girl had left. The dining room table was covered with a clean tablecloth, and a few dried flowers were arranged as a centerpiece.

"That's already throwing some heat," Michael said.

"Oh, these things work pretty well once they're going. Almost everyone in the area has a wood stove. It's no big deal anymore."

65

"You and Ginny have been awfully nice to take care of the house like this," Brennan said.

"Well, it's a good old place. I have a lot of memories attached to this house."

"So do I."

"Of course you do," Harvey said, opening the small Pyrex door and throwing in another stick of wood. "You sure you want to sell it?"

"I'm sure."

"The market isn't great, you know. What I said about all the hippies and things is true. New people aren't moving in here."

"We just can't make it up here enough to keep it. It isn't worthwhile."

"Dad, couldn't we just keep it in the family?" Michael said. "It wouldn't cost anything."

"It costs something. Ask Harvey. It needs a new roof, doesn't it, Harvey?"

"And the plumbing needs work. There's no doubt it needs some money put into it. Still, it's a nice house in the summer."

For a moment no one said anything. Brennan stepped closer to the stove. He felt the heat building now. Forty-five thousand dollars. That had been Harvey's best guess, but he wondered now if the house would bring even that. It was a depressed area. Yes, the river was beautiful and filled with trout, but you couldn't live on them. And the truth was, it was not really a summer house. There was no summer community, nothing even mildly suggestive of a resort. It was a house near a good river, and that was all. Brennan hoped it would bring $45,000. He didn't think he'd pay that much for it himself.

Michael went out for the bags. Brennan looked into the living room but then came back near the stove. Harvey had the fire going now, and the wood cracked and pinged against the metal. He heard the chimney expand once, its yawn at the heat pressing against the hole cut in the roof.

"Louey's in the hospital?" Harvey said when Michael went out for a second load. "Michael said he's in for more tests."

"For more chemotherapy."

66

"Jesus, that's tough. I'm sorry. Louey is a wonderful boy."

"I need the money, Harv. I wouldn't sell it if I didn't."

"I know. I just hate to see it go."

"I wish it were summer. I'd like to try the river once more."

"They do some ice fishing up on Pillar Lake. We could rig you up for that."

"No, thanks. I never went for ice fishing."

"Neither did I."

The wood popped again. Brennan stepped closer, the heat finally penetrating.

"I really appreciate your taking care of the house," Brennan said once more.

"You'd do it for me."

"I guess I would."

"Then we're even," Harvey said, his red hat tight around his face.

Brennan pushed back from the table, absolutely filled. He had had two helpings of pot roast, one and a half of boiled potatoes, and a full serving of carrots, creamed onions, and home-baked bread. He knew there was pie for dessert. He had seen it when they came in through the kitchen—a wide deep-dish apple pie, beautifully brown and flaky. Perhaps there would be ice cream, Brennan couldn't tell. At the moment he wanted nothing but a cup of coffee and a glass of water.

"You know," Harvey said from the head of the table, "I have a surprise for you, Brennan. Michael, you're going to have to see this, too."

"What's that?" Ginny, Harvey's wife, called from the kitchen. "Are you going downstairs? Do you want to take your coffee with you?"

"Can we? I want to show him my projects."

"It's all ready. Just give me a second."

Ginny came in a moment later, carrying a tray of coffee and cream. Brennan had known her from high school. She and Harvey had dated through their senior year, then married as soon as Harvey had returned from Springfield College. Now, looking at her as she served the coffee,

Brennan found he had a fondness for her that was separate and apart from his fondness for Harvey. Ginny Russel. He still thought of her as Ginny Russel even though she had taken Harvey's name twenty-two years ago.

"This is decaffeinated," Harvey said, standing and passing around the cups. "I can't sleep if I drink coffee this late."

"Do you drink coffee, Michael?" asked Ginny. "Our Pat did the last time he was home from school, and I don't know why, but it surprised me. I didn't think twice when he went for a beer, but the coffee really got to me."

"Sometimes I have it," Michael said. "Maybe with a little extra milk."

"Here you go."

"Come on now," Harvey said, lifting his cup and motioning toward the kitchen. "You've got to see some of the projects I've been working on."

"He disappears every night this way," Ginny said as Brennan rose and prepared to follow. "He goes down there and turns the radio up and he can't hear you if you stand on the top step and scream."

"They've got a good talk show out of Boston I can catch," Harvey said. " 'Sports Huddle.' "

Brennan followed Michael and Harvey into the kitchen, then down the basement stairs. Harvey stopped once and flicked on a light, and Brennan heard a fluorescent tube coming alive below.

"Have you seen this room before?" Harvey asked. "Was it fixed up last time you were up here?"

"Almost," Brennan said.

"Holy mackerel!" said Michael, the spoon in his coffee cup swinging and scraping against the china.

As soon as he was down low enough, Brennan saw that the basement had been converted into a rec room and Harvey had moved his stuffed animal collection into the far right corner, partially under the stairs. The collection had flowed over the workbench, ringing it and taking up most of the wall. Now there were animals over half the room, scattered across the floor or propped on tables. A few of them were nearly waist-high. Brennan saw a huge barn owl and a hawk of

68

some sort perched on a T-shaped stand. There were other animals—squirrels, a chipmunk, a huge salmon, and a beaver—but some he could not see except for their eyes.

"Uncle Harvey, how many animals do you have now?" asked Michael.

"About fifty, I guess," Harvey said, moving forward and flicking on lights as he went. "I'm getting pretty good. I'm putting some things out on consignment with a guy down in Springfield. It's a sideline."

"Where do you get the animals?" Michael asked.

"Hunting season mostly. Sometimes people bring in things to stuff . . . you know, they shoot a good-sized buck and want the head mounted. Like I said, it's a sideline."

Brennan moved closer. Harvey flicked on a small light over the workbench to illuminate a row of small birds, delicately posed, their wings outstretched, their talons reaching for an imaginary branch. They were well done. Harvey had captured something about each bird to keep it alive.

"We get some things off the highway, too, of course. I got a red-tailed hawk that way. It was a beautiful specimen and wasn't even damaged by the car that hit it. Probably just twanged by the antenna. Wonderful bird."

"How do you know how to pose them?" Brennan asked.

"I look in books. Lately I've been taking slides of different animals, mostly birds, but they help. See, it's more than just stuffing dead animals. I want to make them look alive somehow."

"Sure, of course."

"But this isn't why I brought you down here," Harvey said. "You want a little brandy in that?"

"Do you have some down here?"

"In my bench," Harvey said, and opened the center cabinet under the work surface. He pulled out a bottle of Rémy. "How about you, Michael? You want a touch?"

"Sure. Can I, Dad?"

"Why not?"

Harvey poured a finger of brandy into each of their coffee cups, then put the bottle back. Brennan was beginning to feel comfortable with the animals. He examined the owl more closely. It was a beautiful bird, larger and more massive than he would have imagined. The bird's breast was wide and powerfully muscled. He tried to see where Harvey had made his incisions, but the work was too well done.

"That's a horned owl," Harvey said. "Isn't it magnificent?"

"You're good, Harv."

"I'm getting there. Now, listen, Michael, you're in for a treat. I'm going to take you back in time. You, too, Brennan. Come on over here. You can look at the animals later if you want."

Harvey turned off two or three lights and moved over to a small sitting area that had obviously been used by the family as a TV room. Brennan sat on an old, dusty couch and waited. Michael sat in a rocker. Harvey went to the TV and fiddled with the VCR. When he was done, he crossed to the bottom of the steps and yelled up to Ginny.

"You coming down, honey?"

"In a minute. Go ahead and get started."

"Sure?"

"Go ahead. You need more coffee?"

"No, thanks."

Harvey came back and stood in front of them. He reached behind the TV screen and turned off the overhead light.

"Ready?" he asked.

"What's this all about, Uncle Harvey?"

"You'll see."

The television came on. At first it was only a gray picture with some white static running through it. Then an image jumped across the screen and disappeared. Brennan felt Harvey sit down on the couch beside him.

"Recognize it?" asked Harvey.

"No idea."

"You will."

And as Harvey said this, Brennan saw the screen turn white, a banner made from a sheet danced across the field of vision. CHARLE-MONT IS THE CHAMP, the banner said, and Brennan felt something weak and frightened move in his stomach. He leaned forward, his

70

coffee almost sloshing over the rim, and saw the camera finally focus on a beautiful field of green grass. A line of boys ran through the goal posts and leaped at the white banner, and Brennan saw himself, aged seventeen, leading them onto the field.

"Oh, my God," he said.

"Charlemont versus Plainstown, 1961," Harvey said, and touched Brennan's knee.

"Dad, is that really you? Is that you right there?" Michael asked, his voice excited. "God, it doesn't even look like you."

"That's him," Harvey said, "team captain."

"Where are you, Uncle Harvey?"

"Back on the left. You'll see me. Number eight-five."

"What number are you, Dad? I couldn't see it?"

"Fourteen."

"Old number fourteen," Harvey said. "Did they retire it, Brennan?"

"I stole it."

"You still hold the records."

"Where did you get this?"

"It's the new thing. Everyone's converting the old Super-eights to video. I had a guy in Springfield do it. Coach Hoch gave me the films."

"I can't believe he kept them," Brennan said.

"He did. He has them all. He coached for what? Seventeen years? He's got every year, every game. He was worried the whole time I had them."

"How is Hoch?"

"Fine. You should stop and see him if you get a chance. He's getting old."

Brennan wanted to ask more questions, but the two teams were ready to play. The tape went blurry during the kickoff, and Brennan couldn't follow the ball; but he saw Kenny McCay, their fastest player, suddenly running forward. McCay cut across the field, dodged one Plainstown man, then picked up a wall of blockers. Brennan was surprised to find his memory calling back every detail of the run, and he watched as McCay slipped one more tackle, then fell out of bounds as he was hit by a Plainstown player. First and ten, Charlemont ball.

"Here you come, Dad," Michael said, his finger out almost touching the screen. "Look at how you run! You still drag your foot out like that!"

"I do not," Brennan said.

"You do. Ask Mom."

"Here we go," Harvey said as Charlemont broke its huddle and came toward the line.

Brennan took a sip of brandy. Nineteen sixty-one. He was amazed at how old-fashioned his uniform looked. Two players on the near side, he couldn't remember their names, wore old bell-shaped helmets, their earholes swelled out. All the linemen wore high tops. He tried to find Harvey, but he was lined up away from the camera.

"Off tackle right," said Harvey. "Didn't we always start with that?"

"With Grey running."

"Here it goes."

Brennan watched himself take the snap from Floyd and spin to hand off to Grey. Grey took the hand-off and angled forward, cutting toward the right sideline, where he was supposed to run between a double team and a trap block. Something went wrong, and Grey was hit almost before he regained the line of scrimmage. The Plainstown player jumped up and waved his fist at the crowd.

Brennan knew what was next. Second and eleven. He took a little more brandy and was shocked to find himself suddenly close to tears. It wasn't fair, somehow, to be exposed like this. It wasn't fair to look back. He leaned forward and examined the boy, himself at seventeen, as he broke from the huddle and spit on his hands, arrogant, cocky. He had weighed 175, not more, and his stomach had been completely flat. His walk was looser, more confident. And for a fleeting moment Brennan recalled the feeling of cleats on grass, the solid feeling of traction and strength and mobility—of power and faith in himself. He remembered the feeling in his stomach as he walked toward the line, the pass play already called, his hands reaching forward to touch his center's butt. Hutt, hutt, huttttt. There had been an instant where he had smelled grass and mud, and he had known, he had known absolutely, that he would take his drop and drill a pass to Harvey, to Grey circling out of the backfield, to Merrill, the tight end. All-county, all-state, he was the king for one season, in his prime, crisp and sweet in muscle, and he *knew it* even as he felt the ball hit his palm and took his first step back. Huh, huh, uh, he breathed, brought the ball up, read the linebackers' drops, then spotted Merrill crossing behind them, looping in a circle pattern. Fluid and smooth, he thought, and then the ball was off, without his full knowledge of throwing it, and he took two steps to cover in case of interception; but he knew it was there, saw it zing, snap into Merrill's hands, complete for fourteen and a first. Yes, yes, yes.

"I was open long," Harvey said.

"We needed a first."

"Dad, that was you? I can't even see it, you know what I mean? I know it's you, but I can't really see you."

"That's the Silver Bullet." Harvey laughed. "That's him in the flesh."

"I remember this too well," said Brennan. "I remember everything about it."

"So do I. I remember the whole season. I remember most of the plays."

"You have all the games?"

"Just three or four. I have the game against Montville, when you threw that duck to me and I caught it in the end zone. You remember?"

"Yes."

"Hoch said you were the best he'd ever seen on the high school level."

"Only on the high school level, though. The competition gets pretty steep after that."

"You had a good college career."

"But nothing like this. It was a wonderful time in life."

Ginny came down, carrying the apple pie, and Harvey turned off the machine until she had a chance to cut out pieces. Harvey got up and came back with more brandy. He gave them all a little more.

"Can you believe these films?" Ginny asked. "Wait until you see some of the crowd shots. We saw your mother and dad in one."

"And you," Harvey said. "We've got a wonderful shot of Ginny shouting something. She was wearing a—what was it?"

"It was awful. It was my 'American Bandstand' look. I had a ponytail and the whole thing. You should see it."

"The Montville game, too," Harvey said.

Ginny sat on the arm of the couch, a coffee cup on her lap, while Harvey turned the video back on. It was first and ten again, but Brennan gave up trying to keep track of the situation. Instead, he watched himself, watched how he took the snap from center and moved, light-footed, quick, in command. Once the camera panned the hometown stands, and Harvey leaned forward to point out different people; but Brennan could see only the trees behind the grandstand, the mottled colors of the leaves. Fall. The cheerleaders did a quick cancan, their skirts long by modern standards. He saw Melissa Powers, his high school sweetheart, raise her hands to her mouth and cheer, two mittened hands forming a funnel, her face so sincere it made his stomach tighten just to see it. "Gooooo, Chargers." And then the film was back on the players, and he saw himself dropping once more, his style remarkably poised, his feet good, the pocket forming around him. His internal clock counted with the boy on the film, one, two, three, throw it, throw it, and he saw a Plainstown player hit him from behind, blindsided, and remembered the shock of falling, the ball almost hopping from his hand.

"God, you were hit," Michael said.

"Maddox was that guy's name. He went on to play at Notre Dame. I was supposed to block him on some of these plays," Harvey said. "He was too damn strong. He was like a man already at that point."

"It seems so long ago, doesn't it?" asked Ginny. "I can remember what I wore to those games, almost every one, but it's so long ago."

"Louey would love to see these," Michael said.

"Take them with you," Harvey said, taking another piece of pie. "You can send them back or copy them. Whatever you want to do."

"Mom would love to see them. So would Kate."

"We'll see," Brennan said.

"Here it goes, here it goes," Harvey said suddenly.

Brennan saw Harvey break into the open, and he saw the ball

74

lofted in his direction. It was a good spiral, thrown over the right shoulder. The ball and Harvey intersected perfectly, and he watched Harvey's gentle hands take it in, two steps from the end zone.

"The Silver Bullet," Harvey said.

Easter was two days away. Brennan had taken the morning train to New York and had stayed in the city all afternoon, talking to customers. All the stores on Madison were stocked with candy, with chocolate rabbits and pink marshmallow chickens. Brennan stopped at half a dozen windows and examined the stock. He didn't understand the connection between Christ's rising and chocolate. He hoped to God Linda wouldn't buy those chocolate eggs with raw cream inside—it looked like a yolk, and he had to leave the room whenever anyone ate one. Some of them even had a little yellow food dye, or custard, or whatever the hell it was, to make the whole thing look authentic. Linda bought them just to get to him, and the kids ended up chasing him around the house, threatening to bite into them.

He wanted a tree for Linda, and riding out on the three-thirty Central Jersey, Raritan Line, he decided to stop by Vargas's to pick one up. He had no idea what kind of tree to get her, but she had been hinting around about needing a tree to throw some shade on her garden. Maybe a maple, he thought. Maybe a sycamore, with pinto bark and that strange shedding it did. He ruled out any sort of evergreen. Evergreens were acidic, he knew that much, and they would probably throw off the soil balance in Linda's garden.

At Newark he switched trains, showed the conductor his pass, then settled back. It was almost hot in the car. The railroad had passed a rule to ban all smoking at the beginning of the year, but he saw a few people still smoking cigarettes down low. He found a copy of the *Post* on the seat in front of him. He turned around to the sports page and saw a big article on the Mets down in spring training. Gooden was as hot as he was last year. Another article said something about Mattingly of the Yankees, but he couldn't concentrate on it. He rested the paper on his lap and stared out the window.

He got off in Westfield and walked down Quimby, up toward

Broad. The clock on the Central Jersey Trust said 4:23, 51 DEGREES. It was still light and sunny. He pulled at his tie. He smelled the ground when he passed the Presbyterian church. It was a muddy, rich smell, and he stopped next to Mindowaskin to breathe it. A pair of ducks swam toward him, expecting bread, but he held out his hands and showed his open palms.

It took him ten more minutes to get to Vargas's Nursery. It was about an acre of land, set back off East Broad. The office was connected to a greenhouse. Brennan wandered through a small forest of trees, all of them waist-high, until a pretty young girl came out and put her hand up to shade her eyes. She was twenty-one or -two, perhaps a little more, her skin absolutely beautiful. She had blond hair, just touched by brown, which hung loosely to her shoulders.

"Can I help you?" she asked.

"I want to get a tree for my wife. It's an Easter present."

"Do you know what kind?" she asked, coming forward. She smiled or squinted, Brennan couldn't tell which. He felt a ridiculous urge to make her smile again, to say something witty, but instead, he simply smiled back.

"Something that will be shady."

"Normal soil?"

"I guess so. It will be close to a garden."

"Well," she said, and took a few steps around a small clump of trees, "you can get something traditional. We have plenty of maples and beech. You could have a chestnut . . . they grow quickly."

"Which would you recommend?"

"How about a copper beech? They're beautiful."

"Do they have low branches? I mean, too low for shade?"

"You can prune them, but you're probably right. What else? Why not a larch?"

It was perhaps the heat of the sun or the lean of the girl as she put her hand up again, but he came very close to saying something stupid. He looked closely at her hips, at her thighs as they tucked in against her blue jeans. He wanted to put his hand against the side of her breast, lightly, firmly, then gradually pull her closer and closer. He would kiss her neck. He would kiss the side of her neck until she

76

lifted her hair, faint and weak against him, their groins gradually shifting until he was certain she would pin herself against him.

But she moved away from the sun, bending to check the label on a large sapling, twisting the burlap sack that contained its roots. Business.

"This is a larch right here. They grow in almost anything."

"They're pine?"

"Cone-bearing, but the needles are deciduous. It's a pretty tree."

"I think maybe I should go with something easier. Do you have oaks?"

"Sure. You can't miss with an oak. They're really the best tree around here for overall growth. We sell a lot of them."

He spent a few more minutes examining the various kinds of oaks, picked a plain white oak, then went into the greenhouse with her and left his address. She promised to deliver it on Easter Sunday, early in the morning. If it didn't take to the soil, she said, the nursery would guarantee a new one.

He thanked her and left, warm enough now to slip off his raincoat. Spring fever. Walking the half mile to his house, he still saw her, saw the way she moved in jeans, the small gaps in her shirt. He decided she would wear white bras and beautiful, soft underwear. He imagined the flesh between the belt line of her jeans and the top of her panties, the skin as white and soft as an earlobe. Younger women, young girls. He wondered why men were blamed for chasing young women. Even now, thinking of her, he felt his blood lift in his stomach in a way he could not even faintly control.

He went in the front door of the house, feeling better now than he had in days. Tomorrow was Good Friday, a day off; then he had the entire weekend. Hanging up his jacket, he decided to call Freddy for a run. Freddy was turning into some sort of marathoner with stringy legs and about a thousand different T-shirts. Brennan himself was up to fifteen miles a week, sometimes eighteen. His legs felt better. His wind was good, better now that he had dropped a few pounds.

"Who's home?" he called up the stairs.

He heard a record going, the music loud. He jogged up the stairs. The music came from Kate's room, and when he knocked, it lowered.

77

"Who's there?" she called.

"Prince and the Revolution."

"Dad?"

"It's Bob Geldof and the Boon Town Rats."

Kate opened the door. She wore jeans and a football jersey. The jersey had been a present from Jason Melk, her new boyfriend. Brennan didn't know if it meant they were going steady or what. She was more popular now. One winter in the soil and she had come up a new plant.

"Where is everyone?" he asked.

"Out back, gardening. Isn't everyone always gardening in this family?"

"Are they? What are you doing?"

"I was trying to do homework."

"On Thursday night? With the whole weekend ahead of you?"

"I want to get it out of the way."

"Who you listening to?"

"A-ha."

"That's a group?"

"They're from Sweden or somewhere."

"And their name is A-ha? That's really their name?"

"Yes."

"Who's number seventy-three for the Westfield Blue Devils?"

"Dad . . ."

"Are you playing this year?"

"Dad, stop it."

"I'm all for women's lib, but do you think you ought to try out for tackle? Why not something a little more delicate, like a flanker or split end?"

"Dad, can I get back to my homework, or do you want to be mean to me some more?"

"You're squaresville. The cool cats are changing and heading out to the backyard. You with me, Daddy-o?"

"Oh, God."

Kate closed the door. Brennan went into his room, changed to running shorts and a heavy sweat shirt, and called Freddy. Freddy said to give him a half hour and he would be by. Brennan hung up and went downstairs.

The back door was open. McGregor lay on the steps, taking in the sun and the warmth of the concrete stoop. Brennan spotted Linda in the center of the garden, turning the earth with a pitchfork. Louey was in a lawn chair set out in the sun. He wore a baseball cap to shade his eyes and cover his bald spots.

"The king of the castle is home," he said, stepping out. "Greetings, peasants."

"Hi, Dad."

"Just in time to help me turn this soil," Linda said.

"I? I, the king of all I see? This is menial work, my dear."

"He's in a weird mood," Kate called from an upstairs window.

"Are you running, Dad?"

"In about a half hour I will once again show my athletic prowess, yes, son. Does that answer your question?"

"I watched the Franklin game after school. You didn't have much athletic prowess there."

"It wasn't one of my better games, was it?"

"You stunk up the place."

"I know, I know. I wish Harvey wouldn't keep sending those tapes."

Brennan jumped off the top step and McGregor barked. The shock of landing registered all the way up in his groin.

"Jarts?" he asked Louey. "You up for them?"

"Sure."

"Grab them from the garage. I want to kiss your mother."

Kate whistled. Louey got up slowly, his body stiff and awkward, his legs too thin. He walked to the garage.

"You want me to help?" he asked Linda.

"No, that's okay. I like to do it."

Brennan stepped over the chunky soil. It smelled like spring. A few birds called from up in the trees. McGregor yawned, his chain hitting on the concrete.

Brennan kissed Linda. She felt good in his arms. She was warm from the sun, warm from work. He was still kissing her when he

79

suddenly felt her leg go behind his in a neat judo trip, and he fell backward, landing in the fresh dirt. Linda jumped on top of him.

"You two are so queer!" Kate yelled from the window.

But Linda kissed him, laughing and pushing him into the dirt, bringing his hand up with a cake of mud and pressing it into his palm. He kissed her hard and tasted dirt on her lips.

"This weather," she whispered in his ear.

"I know."

Kate whistled again from upstairs.

"Louey, don't go around the corner," Kate said. "They're in the middle of a spring mating ritual."

"We're supposed to play Jarts."

"First Dad has to whinny and canter around the yard. Mom, if I did that, you'd have a cow."

"You're not married," Linda called from on top of him.

"Besides, I'm giving her my football jersey next week," Brennan said.

"You two belong in some sort of manual."

Linda climbed off him. Brennan remained on the dirt for a moment longer. Where the dirt had been turned, it was warm and soft. He put both hands in it and squeezed.

"Come on, up and out of there. I want to get this turned," said Linda.

"What are you planting first?"

"A little of everything. I'm late according to the almanac."

"I want to have a pumpkin. One pumpkin."

"They get all over everything."

"That's all right. Will you plant one for me?"

"Sure."

Brennan stood and helped Louey set up the Jarts. This was a game the doctor had recommended. No horseshoes to bang against his leg, nothing metal or hard. It required a minimum of strength, only a wrist snap, and it would give him a little exercise as he walked back and forth to the scoring rings.

Louey went first and looped his Jart to within a few inches of the ring. Brennan lobbed his high and saw it land a good two feet off. Louey put his next one in the ring. Brennan overshot the whole thing.

"Three for the ring, one for closest," Louey said.

"Four-nothing."

"I beat Michael yesterday."

"Where is Michael?"

"Over at Franky's."

Freddy came up the driveway while Louey was throwing to end the game. He had already jogged a mile. He ran in place next to Linda while Brennan did some quick stretching. Louey collected the Jarts.

"This husband of yours is getting in shape," Freddy said to Linda. "I can barely keep up with him. How many you want to run today, Silver Bullet?"

"Maybe three or four."

"Why don't we go down to Gumpert and do the track there for a while, then jog back this way?"

"All right."

"Weather like this makes you want to run."

Brennan bounced a couple of times, then nodded at Freddy. Freddy waved to Linda and said good-bye to Louey. Brennan took up Freddy's stride, which was long and good. Freddy was more of a runner than Brennan.

"Louey looks pretty good, everything considered," Freddy said when they were out on Woodland, running toward East Broad.

"He's doing okay."

"It must be tough on all of you."

"It is. It's tough on Linda."

"I can imagine."

Brennan didn't want to talk. He ran next to Freddy, feeling his blood move in the old way. Back in shape. It was coming, and he felt it. Tight legs, tight ass, tight chest—that was the way to be. It was a big craze now, everyone running around in leotards, but Brennan felt his running going all the way back to boyhood, to springs thirty years ago. That was the difference. People just coming into fitness didn't know. They danced around studios and did exercises with Hula-Hoops and Frisbees, the old geezers checking their pulses, the women looking in mirrors, but they couldn't get back to anything because they'd never been there. That was the thing they missed. Getting in shape was just a way of going back.

TWO

BRENNAN loved conferences, loved hotels, loved breakfasts in small coffee shops that served mint-flavored toothpicks with the bill. Conferences were something he hadn't known about in his coaching days. There had been a few clinics, even a few wild ones, but they were nothing like business conferences. Coaching conferences were low-budget; business conferences spread it out, laid it on. That was what business was about, showing off, and Brennan felt just right, and strangely important, as he walked through the lobby, his shoes slick on the carpeting, the ting of elevator and cash register bells somehow making all the movement musical.

He paused in the middle of the lobby to wait for Guy Layton, who had stopped in the bathroom after breakfast. Brennan looked around. Don Meredith was supposed to be coming today. Meredith was the keynote speaker for the conference. There had been some talk about Namath's coming; but that had fallen through, or at least the rumor had fallen through, and Meredith was chosen. That was okay. Brennan would have preferred Namath, but he was satisfied with Meredith. The guy he really wanted was Cosell, but he was told that Cosell rarely did banquets anymore. Even Meredith did these things only as a friend of a friend. He didn't need the money. It was just to keep his hand in.

Brennan was still in the middle of the lobby when Guy Layton came up.

"Ready?" Layton asked, lighting a cigar. It was perfect that Layton had wooden matches he could strike with a quick flick. He stood still and puffed at the edge of the flame.

"All set."

"Christ, look at that sun. I heard over the radio this morning it's only forty degrees in New York City."

"Any snow?"

"No, just black crud that sticks around until late April. Spring won't come."

"It was warm around Easter."

"It's always warm around Easter; then it always gets cold again. That's spring in New York. That's why they schedule the conference down here. You know what the weather's going to be like in Florida. You can count on it. Mark my word, the whole damn country's going to end up living down here. You'll see."

Layton had his cigar going. Brennan liked the way Layton looked with a cigar, with his Lacoste shirt, his mild tan, his new haircut. Brennan always felt as if he were going places when he hung around Layton. It wasn't that Brennan was fawning or thought Layton a better man. It was just that Layton believed so much in his own success that it became addictive. Layton was big on tipping, big on ordering the most extravagant meals. It wasn't gourmet eating. He went for things like surf 'n' turf, or Ponderosa steaks, or giant Alaskan king crab. He liked to cover a tray when he ordered, liked to see the waitress appear with her arm weighed down, a small murmur following in her wake. And sitting behind the enormous platter, a lobster bib tied around his neck, or an AIN'T A RIB TO SPARE apron over his white shirt and tie, Layton was a type, an example of the American businessman that even Brennan appreciated. Babbitt, yes, a little bit, Brennan admitted, but a man who was enjoying himself. His expense account was wide, and he waded in it. Layton would have been confused by a guy like Harvey, by Harvey's economy and parsimonious wood chopping, not because he didn't understand the necessity of it but because he wouldn't comprehend how Harvey could ignore all the money floating around. Surf 'n' turf or stuffed owl. Layton knew where he stood.

Brennan waited a moment longer, until Layton's cigar was smoking just right, then walked beside him out into the warm Florida sunshine. The light was brilliant, but welcome, and he was content to stand and wait for the valet to bring around the rented Nova, while Layton jingled his change and smoked.

"You much of a golfer?" asked Layton.

"Not really. I used to play when I was a kid. Caddies could play on Mondays."

"I used to play a fair game, in the eighties somewhere, but it's all been shot. Who has time to keep it up?"

"I know what you mean."

"Some guys," Layton said, spinning the cigar ash slowly until it flaked away, "they spend all their time out on the course. I had a buddy like that in Cincinnati. He got his handicap down to three or something, and he was hacking away at it until he found out his wife was working on her own handicap up in this other guy's bedroom. You can't do everything at once."

"Did he give it up?"

"No, he divorced her." Layton laughed.

A young kid brought the car up and jumped out, too servile, but Layton slipped him something anyway. Brennan climbed in the passenger side, feeling relaxed and strong. The pancakes he had eaten for breakfast were warm and solid in his stomach. He could have rolled his head back against the warm upholstery and slept for hours. Everything considered, this was okay. People said teachers had a racket, what with their summer vacations, but they couldn't hold a candle to businessmen. Golf on Thursday, one day of presentations, then home for the weekend. He knew as well as everyone else that nothing was really expected of them here. He was supposed to listen, get some details on the new equipment lines, and be inspired by Meredith. Perks. He drooped his arm out of the side window and let the sun bake it.

The course was fifteen minutes out of town, but Layton knew where he was going and drove with confidence. They passed orange groves and signs for Disney World. Brennan saw the green of the golf course before they came to the entrance. A sign above the gate said WELCOME REISEL. Brennan noticed that only the WELCOME portion of the sign was permanent.

"This is a beautiful golf course," Layton said, driving the Nova around slowly, looking for a parking slot. "They used to have signs posted on different roughs telling you to forget your ball because of the alligators and things. You see snakes out here sunning sometimes."

"You're kidding."

"No, I'm dead serious. I still don't go in the damn rough if I hit one there. I figure I'll take the stroke and keep my leg."

Layton parked the Nova and they locked up. The heat was building. Brennan heard a cicada start to call as they crossed the parking lot.

"Hot, huh?" asked Layton. "Gets hot enough in Florida, the old people start dying all over the place. Shuffleboard coronaries, strokes, you name it. It's something."

"You think it's ninety?"

"Probably eight something. It will get to ninety by noon or so. The back nine is a son of a bitch."

A table of coffee and sweet rolls was spread out at the entrance to the clubhouse. The clubhouse was air-conditioned and cool. Brennan wanted a doughnut but kept himself from taking one. He had lost twelve pounds since January. He took a cup of black coffee and looked for an air-conditioning vent or a fan, anything to cool him off. His desire to play was suddenly gone, and he wondered if there was a polite way to back out. Then he thought about what there was to do back at the hotel, and he decided it wasn't worth the trouble to get out of the foursome.

They were teamed up with Latts and Miller, two sales reps from Denver. Brennan shook both men's hands. Together they went over to a bulletin board and looked at some of the bonuses offered for low score, low team score, low foursome score, closest to the pin on a par three, eagles. A new Ford Pinto was offered to anyone from Reisel who shot a hole in one. Brennan liked that. The chances were astronomical that anyone would hit one in, but it was a good move to wave the new car above the crowd. Reisel was willing. That was the message.

"Wonder if you can get the cash for the car," said Layton, now halfway down his cigar. "We just bought a new one."

"What kind did you get?" Miller asked, or perhaps it was Latts, Brennan had already forgotten who was who.

"A Jeep Wagoneer. It's a big damn thing and eats gas like crazy, but it will get you anywhere you want to go."

"Where do you want to go?" the other one asked. Brennan decided this was Latts.

"Go? Oh, I see what you mean." Layton laughed. "No, I mean, it's good for snow and everything else. You never get snowed in."

"You could drive it around the course," Brennan offered, not expecting it to be funny, but the newness of the group, everyone's uneasiness, made them laugh.

The sun was hotter when Brennan went out to warm up on the practice green. He dropped three balls on the Bermuda grass and putted them toward the hole. He had no feeling for the club. Two of the balls rolled past a good three yards. The third one hung way short. Touch, he reminded himself, but it was no use. He hit the balls at a second hole, but they came no closer.

He gave it up after a few more attempts, then went to stand with the other men watching the first tee. A few guys yelled at the foursome going off, laughing and pointing at the distant flag. "That way," someone yelled, and a heavyset man zipping off in a golf cart called back, "I thought we were playing ten." His ball had only gone fifteen yards to the right. The crowd watched him hit a dribbler onto the fairway.

"We're up," Layton said, coming slowly through the crowd in a cart. His cigar was down to a nub.

"Right now?"

"They bumped us up. One of the foursomes didn't show."

Layton tossed his cigar away. Brennan grabbed his clubs and put them on the electric cart. Layton's bag was already there, large and red, with a tightly rolled umbrella strapped to the side. His club covers had little tassels on them that Layton always called pasties.

Brennan walked to the tee with his driver. His arms and back felt stiff. He put the club behind him and stretched his arms backward. Something popped in his shoulder, then popped again. He bent forward and did a few light toe touches. Next to him, Layton swung his club back and forth, making the air whistle.

"Christ, I'm so damn stiff. You get older and you tighten up," he said.

"I've been doing a little stretching when I run. It feels good."

"I'll bet it does. I should do something, some sort of exercise, but I'm too lazy."

"I'm easing into it," Brennan said.

"You're an old jock, though. It's different for you."

"It's still a pain in the neck."

But it wasn't a pain in the neck. Brennan felt his body responding, loosening on command. That was what made it worthwhile. That's why he ran. He stretched a little more, then took a couple of practice swings. He felt strong. The club was light but centered. It felt as though he could hit the ball for miles, yet keep his swing smooth and easy.

"You two want to lead off?" Latts asked, coming up through the crowd. "Miller's still getting our cart squared away. We just heard we were bumped up."

"Sure, you guys loosen up," Layton said. "You want to show us how, Brennan?"

"You can."

"No, go ahead. Give us the direction."

Brennan shrugged, then dug in his pocket for a ball. He liked its whiteness against the green tee area. No red or orange or yellow balls for him. White was good enough, he thought as he teed the ball high. He put his club next to the ball and saw it was so high he risked popping it up. He tamped it down a little and checked again.

"They're far enough off," said Layton. "Go ahead when you're ready."

Brennan nodded and felt himself become calm. He was an athlete. He rolled his shoulders once more and sensed it was there, that it had never left, that he still knew his muscles and could call on them. He wagged the club softly behind the ball once or twice, waiting for an inner tick. Then, when it came, he brought the head slowly back. Next it was a whirl, a twist of color as the grass flicked by, the trees, the shirts of the men behind him, and he felt the club hit the ball perfectly, the heavy meat of the club sending a powerful shock and *understanding* all the way up his arms, and he knew if he did not hit another shot all day, he had at least hit this one. He looked up in time to see the ball entering its second level, a beautiful rise as it took on its final speed and distance, the line of the shot entirely straight and bisecting the fairway.

"Jesus Christ, you hit the hell out of it," Layton said.

"We've got a ringer playing with us," Latts said to Miller, who was finally coming through the crowd.

Brennan didn't look back. He waited until the ball landed and came to a stop, high and white, dead center.

Brennan sat on his bed in the semidark, his sheets rumpled from an afternoon nap. Remission. That was Brennan's one thought as he hung up the phone, his connection with New Jersey cut off. Remission. Linda had been very cautious, and she had repeated the warning several times—don't get your hopes up, this may be only temporary, don't go overboard—but Dr. Briesky had said it looked like remission. Breisky was cautious, that was his way, so if he was saying it was a remission, then it had to be. Louey the Lionhearted. He wished now that he had been more clearheaded when he had talked to Linda, but she had awakened him out of his nap. He had been exhausted after the golf, sunburned and tired from chopping his way around the course, and he had fallen asleep as soon as they came back. He closed his eyes and tried to reconstruct what Linda had said. Remission, no telltale signs of increased cell deterioration, good blood counts, good platelets. The salamander was gone, or at least holed up somewhere, hibernating, and that was all that mattered.

Slowly he let the joy in. He was aware this was a process like anything else, and he pictured himself working a valve. Easy, he said to himself. His mind filled gradually with images of Louey moving around the house, running, jumping—no, maybe not running and jumping, maybe that wouldn't return, but at least not bruising at the slightest touch. That was possible. Linda had said even his hair looked better.

Brennan grabbed the phone and called room service. He ordered up six beers in frosted mugs. Then he went into the bathroom and shaved, showered, and rubbed himself with skin cream. His arms and neck were red. People called a tan like this a truck driver's tan, but Brennan always thought of it as a caddie's tan. Go a loop, eighteen holes, ten dollars.

He opened the door when room service knocked and took the tray from a young Cuban boy.

"Put it on our bill," he told the boy, "and here, this is for you."

He gave the boy two bucks and closed the door. He lifted one beer and held it against his forehead. Suddenly he felt he wanted to thank someone, maybe God, but he had lost that way. But thinking this brought him close to tears, and he held the beer against his forehead, muttering, "Thank you, thank you," imagining some huge force in the universe taking his gratitude and humming louder with it. Finally he took a long drink, knocking back half the beer, wonderful and rich and cold enough to make his head ache softly.

He was on his second beer when Layton came in, a towel around his neck, his chest and legs badly burned.

"I fell asleep in the goddamned lounge chair," Layton said, obviously in pain. He turned and lifted his arms and legs, checking the redness. "What time's dinner?"

"About fifteen minutes."

"Do I look as red as I feel?"

"You look bad. Have a beer."

"Six beers? What's the occasion?"

"My boy's in remission."

"Why, that's wonderful," Layton said, and hit Brennan on the shoulder. "That's really something. When did you find out?"

"My wife called a little while ago."

"Well, congratulations," Layton said, and took a beer. He lifted it. "To good health for your son. That's the best news I've heard in a while."

"Just keep your fingers crossed," Brennan said, taking another long drink.

Fifteen minutes later Layton was ready. Brennan had finished three beers and carried his fourth down in the elevator. He felt primed. The exercise had made his legs and back weary, but he felt slim and on top of things. He took another sip as the door opened and suddenly there, standing in front of him, was Don Meredith. At first, in his drunkenness, Brennan judged Meredith to be a cardboard cutout, one of those life-sized placards he sometimes saw in movie theaters or at used-car lots. But then Meredith smiled. It was a good smile. Another man was next to Meredith, half whispering to him. Gradually Brennan realized that Layton had stepped out and was holding the door, the rubber gasket butting against his hand, and that they all were waiting for him to make way.

"Mr. Meredith," Brennan said, unable to move.

"Hi, there," Meredith said.

"Could I get your autograph for my son?"

"Brennan . . ." Layton said.

"On anything. Just your name. It would mean a great deal to him and to me."

"Sure," Meredith said, "who's got a pen?"

So there was a moment when everyone slapped his pockets and Brennan switched hands to hold his beer. Finally the man standing next to Meredith dug out a pen, and Layton gave Meredith the day's scorecard.

"You boys sure got your money's worth today," Meredith said, then quickly signed the front of the card.

"If it's not too much to ask, could you just put 'To Louey' above it? That would make it just—"

"Louey—e-y?" Meredith asked, writing.

"E-y."

"There you go."

Brennan stepped out of the elevator. He took the scorecard from Meredith.

"I really appreciate this," Brennan said. "He's been sick."

"Well, I hope he feels better."

"He is. He's feeling better right now."

The elevator closed. Brennan felt Layton slip a hand on his shoulder. Brennan patted the scorecard in his suit coat pocket and decided he didn't care if he'd had to act a little ridiculous to get the autograph. Dandy Don, he thought.

He followed Layton into the banquet room, two rooms, actually, connected by a folding door. The door had been rippled back, and now there were at least fifty yards of tables, all of them set with white linen and brown bread bowls in the center. A straight table was arranged on the dais, a podium dead center. The podium had the Reisel seal tacked onto the front. The air conditioning was on high, the hum almost obscuring a track of the Ray Conniff Singers swinging into "Raindrops Keep Falling on My Head." A large seating chart was posted next to the bar. Brennan checked for his seat and found he was sitting way in the back, almost in the men's room. He ordered another beer and toasted himself in a silica wall that threw out his reflection from behind the bar. Small fry and autograph hound, he nodded at himself.

"This fucking burn is killing me," Layton said, coming from the bar with a beer. "I mean, is it cold in here? It feels like it's freezing."

"No, it's nice. You've got that good lobster look."

"I can't even cross my legs."

"Drink some beer. That always helps."

"I haven't had a sunburn like this since I don't know when."

"That Meredith was a nice guy, wasn't he? The way he did that on the fly like that? I thought that was pretty kind of him," Brennan said.

"He wanted to get you out of the elevator. Besides, I hear he isn't going to speak for more than five minutes. They've got some guy who's climbed Everest instead."

"Who?"

"I don't know. Some guy. Hope he took his fucking sunscreen with him," Layton said, rolling his shoulders.

"You okay?"

"I don't know. I might have sun poisoning."

"You're pretty red."

"You know that was Brickett with Meredith? Brickett's on the board."

"I don't care."

"He might, though. Brickett's supposed to be a son of a bitch."

"He gave Meredith the pen. You should have given him your back to write on."

94

After dinner the Everest guy spoke first. He was introduced by Spearman, the company president. Spearman had to glance down at his notes to get the name straight, but the mountaineer didn't seem to mind. As soon as the mountaineer made it to the mike, he said, "O-ke-ke," which was, Brennan realized, his name properly pronounced. It was a tiny slap at Spearman.

The man began to speak. People were still drinking, but gradually the room became quiet. The mountaineer was an excellent speaker, a superb speaker. He talked about how the expedition was formed, who funded it, why the climbers chose their specific route. He mentioned equipment, which was, of course, the tenuous tie-in for the audience, but that really wasn't the point. Slowly be began to take them up the mountain. He had no slides to show, no ice picks or crampons to hold up. His words called up images until Brennan chose not to drink anything else while he spoke, for fear of ruining the illusion. Listening to him speak, Brennan was half with the expedition, half with Louey. He pictured Louey climbing, scrambling over rocks and going higher and higher, the salamander curled and sleeping in the heel of his boot.

Brennan stood watering the oak in the early-spring light, his feet bare, his ankles tickled by the border grass around Linda's garden. The oak was doing all right. It had had a moment of failure right at the start, transplant shock, Linda said, but now it was thriving.

Brennan put his thumb on the nozzle of the hose and sent a rain shower over the garden. The water caught some of the last light and pulled a rainbow out of the air. He watered the patch slowly, trying to judge the proper amount for each section. Linda didn't normally allow him to do the watering, but she was upstairs, helping Kate into her prom dress.

He watered the beans first, then moved along to peas and tomatoes. He gave each section a light dusting. People overwater, Linda always told him, and he was careful to restrain himself. He tried to imitate spring rainfall.

It was prom night. He had difficulty convincing himself that Kate was actually going to a prom. Michael had said no, of course, telling everyone who would listen that proms are stupid, but even he seemed a little disappointed now that he wasn't involved. Later he was going to Franky's house for a losers' party, probably to play poker and smoke cigars with five or six other computer heads; then they were going to go hang out in the high school parking lot and make fools of themselves. Socially retarded, Brennan thought. Computer heads.

The kitchen door opened behind him, and Brennan heard Louey and McGregor come out. Louey came down the stairs easily, almost as easily as he ever had. He was putting on weight, too, and looked much more sturdy. If his hair weren't still spotty, it would have been difficult to tell he had ever been sick.

"You should see them upstairs," Louey said. "Mom's trying to fix Kate's hair, and Kate's about ready to kill her."

"What's wrong with her hair?"

"Beats me. It looks the way it always does."

"How's the dress?"

"Pretty nice. It's pink. But I don't like the way it's cut around the shoulders. It looks stupid."

"Don't tell her that."

"And you know what?" Louey asked, holding his foot out to McGregor and wrestling with the dog for a moment. "I found out the theme of the prom is 'A Night in the Forest.' Can you believe it? They tried to turn the gym into a forest."

"Maybe the ropes will be vines."

"They made one set of bleachers into a garden path . . . you can go up it row by row until you've climbed the mountain. Then they have a lookout, like a scenic lookout, where you're supposed to stand and enjoy the panorama. Michael found out from Franky."

"Well, it sounds better than sitting around with a bunch of computer heads."

"Maybe. They've got a new game now, and it's pretty neat. You have to take a frog across a street filled with trucks and cars. If it gets hit, it makes a decent splatting noise. It's pretty cool."

Brennan moved around the garden. The soil smelled wet now. He watched McGregor sniff around the little wire fence Linda had put up to keep him out. Peas, tomatoes, squash, cukes, lettuce, peppers, five ears of corn for looks, sunflowers, and a pumpkin. Brennan watered the pumpkin last.

"You doing weights tonight?" Brennan asked Louey.

"Yep."

"Go easy, huh. You're still not a hundred percent."

"I will."

"How are you feeling, anyway?"

"Good."

"You don't feel weak at all?"

"No, not really. Sometimes I feel a little fluttery or something. Mostly I'm okay."

Brennan heard a car enter the driveway. Jason Melk. He had a name like a detective or a guy who eats radioactive bread and turns into a rhinoceros-man.

"Go tell him we're around back," he said to Louey.

"Don't you dare," Linda called from the upstairs bathroom window. "Let him come to the front door like a human being."

"How long have you been listening?" Brennan asked.

"Long enough."

"Go get the door then, Louey. I'll be right there."

Brennan turned off the hose while Louey ran inside. He took his time, figuring he would let Jason sweat. He looped the hose under the spigot in even coils.

"Dad?" Louey called.

"Coming."

He jogged up the stairs, aware of his bare feet, his baggy Bermudas. He thought maybe he should have changed, but it was too late now. Opening the screen door, he saw Louey standing in the dining room next to Jason Melk. Jason was a good foot taller and much broader. Even in his shiny tuxedo and red cummerbund, Jason was a tackle, a born tackle, with a wide mouth and a thick neck. A herbivore, Brennan thought, a ruminant.

Brennan stepped into the dining room and held out his hand.

"You must be Jason Melk," he said, too loud, he knew, but he didn't care. "Kate's told us a lot about you."

97

"Good, I hope, sir."

"Oh, all very good. You play for Westfield?"

"Football? Yes. I started last year."

"Tackle, right?" Louey said.

"Right tackle, yes."

"You guys were pretty good," Louey said.

"We had a good season."

"Who did you lose to? Scotch Plains?" asked Brennan.

"No, Union and Summit. They were better than us, so it really wasn't all that disgraceful. They were a lot better. We played pretty well against them."

"When does practice begin in the fall?"

"Well, we start getting together for Health Club in August. It's just training without equipment. Agility drills and that sort of thing. Coach Floson can't be on the field, but he can watch. He notices who's around."

Brennan liked this kid. He was clean-cut, polite, as solid as ham steak. Brennan was glad Kate had stuck to the herbivores, not the wolfish backs and wide receivers. She could depend on Jason Melk. He didn't know whether she had picked Melk or won him by some forfeit, but either way it was okay. At least she was happy now, not moping around as she did last summer.

"So are you ready for a night in the forest?" asked Louey, his smile crooked. "We heard they've turned the gym into a forest."

"They always try something. One time it was a Scottish glen. They played bagpipe music whenever they had to make an announcement."

"They still have a king and queen at these things?" asked Brennan.

"I don't know. Someone said they did."

Brennan was about to offer Melk a seat when he heard Kate coming downstairs. He heard her dress and her hand squeaking on the banister. Melk heard it, too, because he took a step to the side and looked up the staircase. He smiled broadly, and Brennan liked him even more for that wide smile, his lack of pretense.

"You look great," Melk said as Kate took the last step.

98

"So do you," Kate said.

Linda came down behind Kate, carrying a camera. She posed them against the mantel, then out on the front steps. She had to tell Jason to put his arm around Kate. Brennan stood behind Linda, watching them tentatively lean into each other. He wondered for a moment how old they were. Sixteen, he decided, then realized Jason was driving, so he had to be seventeen at least. In the flash of Linda's camera Brennan remembered himself standing on Melissa Powers's front porch, her father aiming the camera, the Chevy Biscayne waiting in the driveway, his tuxedo shirt tight around his neck. Melissa had worn a blue dress, cut low, so that all night he had seen the edge of her breasts, her nipples hidden from him by a pouch of soft white. She had worn powder, and he had breathed it as he stood on the porch; breathed lipstick and perfume and something that was only Melissa's, a woman smell, yes, but the scent he had on his clothes after a night of kissing her, taken from the pearl of her teeth. It was the smell of youth, or love, or the smell of light on the soft golden arm hairs that he saw when she fixed her hair. With it was mixed the smell of spring, dandelions and the crust of an egg, old nests, summer beginning.

Brennan turned the portable radio up loud. It echoed off the garage walls, but he didn't care. It was the Temptations playing "The Way You Do the Things You Do." He stood in front of the old dresser mirror and did a few turns, putting in the hand motions just as the Temps used to do, bending now and then to grab the mike. "You got a smile sooo brighttttt, you know you coulda been a ca-an-dle," he sang. He didn't know the next verse, so he spun again and came in on the chorus.

"Dad, do we have to listen to the oldies station?" Louey asked. He was wearing nothing but a pair of gym shorts and sneakers. He was doing slow curls with the dumbbells and watching himself in the mirror. He still had a small boy's muscles.

"The Temptations are the greatest."

"The Who."

"The Who might be permitted to carry the Temps' suitcases. They might be allowed to perform a warm-up act."

"You've never even heard anything The Who's sung."

" 'Talking About My Generation.' Stutterland. The thing is, these guys like Townshend actually believe they're serious artists. They don't even realize they're just playing pop music. They whack their guitars and some jerky kids think it's great."

"They don't do that anymore. They don't even tour. How about 'Pinball Wizard'? That's pretty good."

"How about 'My Girl'? You've got no soul, Louey. You were brought up on too much white bread."

"So were you."

"Yes, but I've lived, you see. I go way back. I've got roots. I'm as old as Bo Diddley."

Louey finished his set and put the dumbbell down. He flexed his arm a couple of times. Brennan picked up the dumbbell and did some quick curls. Keep the biceps tight. When his arms were tired, he did some presses, snapping the weights up and making them ring. He stared straight ahead, concentrating. A few moths flickered in the light overhead.

"Will you spot me on bench presses?" Louey asked when Brennan was finished. "I want to do three sets of fifteen reps."

"Call it a night then?"

"I've got to do my lats."

"You've done enough for tonight. You don't need to knock yourself out."

"Just a couple of sets on the lats."

"No way. I'll spot you on the bench presses; then we're done for tonight. Maybe I'll take you and Mom out for a root beer anyway. How would that be?"

"If you want."

"If I want?"

Louey laughed and lay back. He lifted the weight and began doing presses. "Hey, 98.6" came on the radio. Brennan watched himself in the mirror and sang, "Loving is the medicine that saved meeee, oh I love my babyyyy." Louey shook his head and muscled up another rep.

As soon as Louey was done with his third set. Brennan jogged to the house and found Linda. She was watching a "Bonanza" rerun. Brennan kissed her, giving her a quick sniff. He smelled marijuana.

"Come on, you pothead," he said. "Stewart's root beer."

"You're kidding."

"No, come on."

She loved Stewart's, loved all the junk in American culture. He could always get her to go to McDonald's or White Castle. She liked the Three Stooges and "Divorce Court." She would pass up any program on TV in order to watch the old monster movies—*Godzilla*, *Mighty Joe Young*, *King Kong*.

"Ben was just giving the boys a lecture," she said as she stood and turned off the TV. "I love it when he does that."

"Was Hop Sing around?"

"No, but Adam was there. This was before he decided to become a lawyer and move to San Francisco. Adam was gay, I think."

"He bought a condo on the bay."

Brennan hustled her out to the car. Louey was locking up the garage. Brennan whistled at him, and he climbed in back.

Then they were rolling, the windows down, music up high. Steppenwolf came on with "Get Your Motor Running." Brennan pumped the gas a little and revved it up in neutral at the stoplights. Louey ducked down behind the seat whenever they pulled up next to another car.

"My son Louey's right back here," Brennan announced, "but he's afraid to be seen with his parents."

"Dad . . ."

"Hear him, O people of the world?"

"Dad . . ."

"He thinks his parents are out of date. He thinks his parents are squaresville."

"You are," Linda said, laughing.

"I am? You really think I'm out of date?"

"Of course you are."

"How?"

"The music you like. The things you remember. The way you think of things . . . your reference points. You're hovering somehwere near 1965."

"I am not."

"Sure you are. So am I. There's nothing wrong with it."

"But I'm a hipcat. Come on, Louey, admit it. I know the new music."

"Some of it."

"Okay, some of it, but at least I know some. I like break dancing. How the hell are you supposed to stay up on things? Am I supposed to go out to discos? I stopped going to discos when the limbo came in."

"I could never limbo, could you?" Linda asked. "I hated the limbo and Twister. I never understood the point of Twister."

"It was to rub up against each other," Brennan said. "It was to cop a feel."

"Dad," Louey said.

"Who's Mr. Squaresville now, huh? I speak the truth, right, Hop Sing?"

"Right, Pa," Linda said.

Brennan pulled into the small Stewart's parking lot. The lot was rutted, and the car rocked up and down as he nosed into a spot. Another car was parked directly under the yellow neon light that lit up the Stewart's sign. The driver was about sixty.

"See?" Louey said. "You hit all the young spots."

"Quiet, he'll hear you." Linda said.

"I want French fries."

"Why did Stewart's die?" Brennan asked, slipping off his seat belt. "They're so much tackier than McDonald's ever dreamed of being."

"Tackier than Burger King even. Although Burger King's the only place on earth that announces everything you're going to eat to the entire restaurant. It's a selling point," Linda said.

"You want a whole meal?" Brennan asked Louey as he climbed out. "You want hamburgers and stuff?"

"Sure. I'm starved."

"You're always starved."

That was okay, Brennan thought. Better to be hungry than sick. Brennan ordered a giant hamburger, three French fries, and three king-sized root beers through the small sliding screen at the left end of the counter. A girl in an orange uniform filled up a tray with the drinks and called to someone else about the hamburger. She went to the service counter and dug out three helpings of fries.

"I'll bring the hamburger when it's ready, sir," the girl said. "That will be seven thirty-eight."

Brennan paid and carried the tray back to the car. He hung it on Linda's door so that he could still get in and out on his side. As he climbed back in, Linda handed him his root beer.

"The first sip of summer," Linda said.

"You think we should stop by the prom for a quick dance?" Brennan asked.

"I think so. What about you, Louey?"

"I'd lock myself in the trunk."

"Kate would like it," Linda said. "She'd probably tell Jason to cut in."

"Maybe we could get the band to play 'Moon River,'" Brennan said. "Maybe we could get the whole joint to do the alley cat."

The girl came out with the hamburger, and Linda passed it back to Louey. Brennan ate his fries slowly and sipped at his root beer. He leaned on his door, his arm draped out the window. Three weeks and school would be out. A month and they'd be at the Jersey shore, on vacation for a week, the house in Lavallette open to the sun and air. He wanted to get a Monopoly game for the week off. Maybe Clue, although he remembered that as being boring after a game or two. He would get Parcheesi and Labyrinth and maybe a bob-a-loop, one of those things Zorro's sidekick always played with. He would dig out the old set of horseshoes and play on the beach after everyone had gone home for the day. He could play with Louey or Michael, maybe Linda if he could talk her into it, or maybe he wouldn't play at all. Maybe he would just leave them out, letting someone else throw them, content to hear the ring of metal on metal, the sound of summer from years ago.

Forty-three thousand dollars. Brennan sat at his desk and examined the check. Four-three-zero-zero-zero. It was the biggest check he had ever handled in his life. It was the most money he had ever had at one time. It worked out to almost a thousand dollars for every year he had been on the earth. No, it worked out exactly, since he would be forty-three himself in December. A grand a year. He turned the check over, back and forth, reading and rereading the name, the numbers. Pay to the order of: Brennan McCalmont, Charlemont Savings, June 23, 1986.

Just looking at the check made him feel rich. He searched his emotions for a moment and was surprised to find that he didn't really have any regrets about selling the house. Harvey had attached a note that said a nice couple had bought it. The man liked to fish and was close to retirement. The woman was a gardener, like Linda, and she had talked about digging up a section of the field behind the house for a big vegetable patch. Good for them, Brennan thought. Good for the house. He hoped they would make it into a showplace and stuff in enough firewood and heat to take the dampness out of the walls forever.

He wondered now what to do with the $43,000. He possessed no illusions about his financial acumen. Other men talked about Ginnie Maes, and zero-coupon bonds, and mutual funds, but he understood only enough to follow the scent of financial conversations. High yield, high security, that's what he thought was best for this money, but of course, everyone wanted that. You couldn't get high yield without some risk. Still, he reminded himself, this was his nest egg. He knew very well that he would never be this far ahead again—at least not until Louey was well and Michael and Kate were finished with school. Maybe then, he thought, he would start to lay it away, bulking up for retirement. Until then he knew it was flat out and silently suspected that even the $43,000 would fade away faster than he could imagine.

He rolled his chair back. A man of means. What he would like to do, he thought, was to buy one thing and see if it would go up. He thought he would like to plunk down forty-three grand on a painting, or a statue, then send it out to auctions and see who nibbled. That would be something, to sit in an audience and watch your profit grow by people touching their noses, holding up a finger, winking, each change in the auctioneer's voice signifying another grand. Or maybe better still would be simply to lop off ten thousand and play with it, see what it could do, buy ten thousand of penny stocks and see what happened. People had built empires on less. That was the thing about capital: It gave you a future.

Around noon he went down the hall and stuck his head into Layton's office. Layton was on the phone and held up his finger to say he would be a minute. Brennan took a seat across the desk from him and looked at the different decorations Layton had hanging around. It was a mismatched collection of things—a few ears of Indian corn, a Mexican sombrero, a humidor for cigars. Somehow the decorations made it seem as if Layton were constantly ready to fly off to the islands or maybe take the afternoon off at the track. Work seemed to be his hobby, something he just dropped in to do now and then.

"So, what's up?" Layton asked when he finished with his call. "You eating lunch today?"

"I'm treating you."

"What's the occasion?"

"I sold the house up in Massachusetts."

"Did you really? Good deal. Where do you want to eat?"

"I don't care. Let's get a sandwich. I'm going to run over to the bank afterward. I want to get this deposited."

"Start earning interest, right? Let your money work for you."

"I've got to get an IRA started. I've never even had to worry about it before."

"An IRA," Layton said, pronouncing it like a man's name. "Tax-deferred. You'd better check out the new tax laws."

"Right."

"The government doesn't give you a break every day."

"No, I guess it doesn't."

Brennan waited for Layton while he slipped on his jacket and straightened his desk. Maybe it was a mistake to invite Layton to lunch, he thought. Layton would lay into him about how to invest the money, and he would probably be right, the guy was pretty good with money, but Brennan wasn't in the mood to hear it right now. Forty-three thousand dollars. It had a good sound, a magical sound, which he feared would be lost if Layton started hacking off five to go in this fund, twelve to go in another. Already Brennan had made one quick subtraction to see what Michael's first year at Brown would cost, but he had jammed the figure back into the lump, smoothing it until he left no scar.

Finally Layton was ready, and Brennan walked with him out into the sunshine. It was June and hot already. Newark was already in the middle of summer. The exhaust on MacKensie Street hung close to the ground. A few buses passed as they walked uptown, heading toward the sandwich place on Montgomery.

"Jesus, it's going to be a hot summer," Layton said. "I read in the *Farmer's Almanac* that it's supposed to be a blisterer."

"You read the *Farmer's Almanac*?"

"In the morning, slurping up cereal. It's pretty interesting."

"What else did it say?" asked Brennan, stopping for a second before crossing Wilmont. A black kid came by with a ghetto blaster blaring rap music. Brennan heard only one phrase: "You're not the guy you think I am." It didn't make sense.

"Rain is going to be lousy. They'll probably have to put the water limits on again. You know, Ed Koch will be running around turning off fountains and telling people not to water anything. That sort of stuff."

"Everything gets brown by August, no matter what they do."

"Do you know, though," Layton said, stopping for a second to swing his jacket off, "that there's as much water on the earth as there ever was? That's what the *Farmer's Almanac* says."

"So why the shortage? It's relocated?"

"And polluted. But the atmosphere is like a big bubble. Things don't get out. I don't know why, but it made me feel good to read that. All we have to do is keep the water clean and there will always be enough. You dump a bucket of water out in New Jersey, and it will end up somewhere, maybe the Delaware, maybe the Hudson River; but it will still be around. I like that."

"So do I."

Brennan stopped to listen to an old man playing a saw. The man sat against the Broadax building on a small campstool. He bent the saw forward and back, his bow finding strange sounds, his mouth changing slightly at each pitch. Brennan tossed a quarter onto a blanket spread out in front of the man.

"That guy's a long way from Tennessee," Layton said.

"Why does some guy decide to play the saw? That's what I always think about. Why not the clarinet, or the violin? Why's he pick the saw?"

"Because it's cheaper," Layton said.

It was crowded in Fellow's. Brennan had to ask twice for a table, but they finally got one as two other men stood to go. They sat down quickly, afraid to lose it, while the waitress bussed away the plates, a small tub of mayonnaise, and a few empty sugar packets.

"Two Heinekens," Brennan ordered.

"Be right with you," she said, pulling back.

Layton took out a pack of cigarettes. He lit one and leaned back in his chair.

"So you're rich, huh?" he said to Brennan.

"Hardly."

"You should think of investing it the right way. Go see someone. I've got a friend over at Merrill Lynch who's a financial adviser. He can set up your whole picture."

"Maybe I will."

"You've got to think long-term, too. You've got to figure out where you'll be at sixty-five. Sixty-five is boxcars in this business."

"That's twenty years from now."

"What are you, forty-two? That's twenty-three years from now."

"You really think about retirement?"

"I don't think about it. It's a fact. I don't think about it any more than the sun coming up. I just don't want to be an old peckerhead depending on my kids or living in some crappy old-age home. Money's the only thing that will get you respect when you're a geezer. You've got to hang the fucking will over their heads."

"You're nuts."

"Talk to me in twenty years."

The waitress returned with their beers. They were served in tall Pilsner glasses. Brennan held his up to the light.

"Cheers," he said to Layton.

"Cheers."

Brennan took a drink. The beer tasted perfect. Even though he pretended to prefer the crappy domestics, he liked European beers. He had never been to Europe, but he pictured them drinking big steins of beer in beautiful gardens. Austria or Germany, that's where he would go. Wines were too complicated, and he didn't think he'd trust himself in France or Italy, places where you had to order wines with everything. Beer and a Wienerschnitzel. You couldn't go wrong.

He patted the check in his pocket, wondering if he should tell Layton how much it was made out for. He thought maybe it wasn't polite not to, but then figured it wasn't Layton's business. Layton would have a ball-park figure anyway. Houses in northwest Masschusetts didn't sell for a hundred thousand. Forty-three thousand dollars was a good figure, more than he had expected to get. He touched the check again, once more thinking he would like to turn it into something solid, something he could point to and say, "That's worth forty-three thousand dollars." Maybe a painting was the answer. Maybe he should buy diamonds or silver.

The waitress came back, and they ordered. Layton had roast beef, the most expensive sandwich in the place, but that was just Layton. Brennan ordered some sort of bologna melt that he really didn't even want. He drank more beer.

"You going down to the shore for vacation?" asked Layton. "You taking the whole tribe?"

"Down to Lavallette. It's probably the last vacation we'll all have together."

"Michael's deserting the nest. Times flies, huh? How's Louey doing these days?"

"Okay. I think he's all right. He's lifting weights, and he's got a good appetite. The doctor's pleased with his progress."

"Good for him. Can he do everything he used to do? Play sports, the whole deal?"

"No, no contact sports anyway. It's still a remission. We have to keep reminding ourselves of that."

"How long does a remission last?"

"It depends. No one knows, really. It can be five, six years. It can be for a lifetime. It can be for a couple of weeks."

"What a crapshoot."

"I know."

After lunch Brennan left Layton and headed for the bank. It was hotter now, real summer weather. He passed three kids break-dancing on a piece of cardboard. He passed a man handing out flyers for a strip show. Each time Brennan tapped the check. Forty-three thousand dollars, bait for robbers, crooks, pimps. What would they do, he wondered, if they knew he had so much money? They ought to make a game show of it, give people money and see if they could make it from one end of Newark to the other.

The Chemical Bank lobby was wide and cool. A few potted plants stood next to the central pillar, their heavy leaves lifting in the air-conditioned currents. Brennan took his spot in the teller line. Standing there, watching the quiet order of the bank, he wondered if he could convert the check into cash. It would have to clear, of course, but maybe when it did, he could convince the manager to let him come in and hold the forty-three thousand back in one of the vaults. He wouldn't leave the bank. He just wanted to see what forty-three thousand in one-dollar bills would look like. What would it weigh? At some point, he figured, you have to cash in.

When it was his turn, Brennan approached the young man who stood behind the teller window. Manager trainee, learning the ropes, Brennan thought. His suit looked new.

"Good afternoon," the teller said. "May I help you?"

"I want to deposit this in savings."

"Did you fill out a slip?"

"Not yet. I was going to do that now."

Brennan pulled out one of his deposit tickets and filled in the information. One check, $43,000. He took his time writing the number, going leisurely over the zeros. He watched the teller's face when he passed over the deposit ticket. The kid frowned.

"You have to endorse it," he said.

"Of course."

Brennan signed it. The teller punched in the amount on the computer, then took Brennan's bankbook. There was a quick noise, and the book came back at Brennan. He took it and read the figure: $47,347—except for his house, his total worth.

"Could I ever get this whole amount in cash?" he asked the teller.

"When? Now?"

"No, some other time. When the check clears. I'd just like to see what it looks like."

"I don't know. I wouldn't advise your taking it in cash."

"I wouldn't take it. I'd just want to look at it here in the bank. Could that be arranged?"

"I suppose so. I don't know. Would you like to see Mr. Meese? He's my supervisor."

"Has anyone ever done it before?"

"I don't know. I could get Mr. Meese if you like."

"No, that's okay. I just thought it would be interesting to see what it looks like."

"I'm sure it would."

Brennan put his bankbook in his pocket. He walked across the lobby, thinking about what the money would look like. It occurred to him that it would look exactly like his old house.

He left the bank and went to Murphy's, a large sporting goods shop on Clarkson Boulevard. He had been in before to buy equipment for Louey, but now he went straight to the fishing gear. A young man in a tight-fitting red sports shirt came around from behind the gun counter and asked if he could help.

"I'm looking for a fly rod," Brennan said.

"Certainly," the young man said, "right over here."

It had been years since Brennan had priced a fly rod. The prices had gone up, that was sure, but the sight of the rods still excited him.

Most of them were made from new materials, things Brennan had read about but never used. Graphite, fiberglass. Brennan had always used cane.

"How's the graphite fish?" Brennan asked, whipping the tip back and forth, checking the balance of the rod by placing his finger next to the top of the hand grip.

"It's a good rod. I use one."

After looking at some other rods, Brennan decided to take the graphite number. It cost 230 bucks, an Eagle Claw, top of the line, but it was worth it. It came in a beautiful case inside a silver packing tube. Brennan gave Harvey's address to the kid and asked him to send it. The kid gave Brennan a receipt.

"Can I put a card in it?" Brennan asked.

"We don't have cards, but you can write a note."

Brennan took a pen and a piece of paper from the clerk. He went to one side of the counter and leaned down to write. Underneath the paper there were beautifully tied flies—Adams, Muddler Minnows, Hendericksons, Wulfs. Brennan stared at them for a moment, his mind unfocused, his mind drifting back to the Deerfield and the trout beside the copper beech.

"Dear Harv," Brennan wrote. "Thanks for selling the house. The money will come in handy.

"Here's something to say thanks. Maybe I'll be up this summer to watch you test it out. Your friend, Brennan McCalmont."

It was ten in the morning, and they had already been into five patches of bluefish. The fish had been ravenous, biting at anything, and Brennan had cranked in five before the captain called for lines in. No one bothered with the rubber sand eels Brennan had brought along. They fished straight spoons and reeled them as fast as they could, stirring the blues out of their deep feeding patterns. It was dumb fishing, Brennan thought, but exciting in its way. He liked the tug of the fish and the frenzied crack of them as he brought them into the boat. It was always something to be tied into a fish, to be tied into water. Besides, Brennan didn't care what the fishing was like. The sky was a perfect blue, and the water green. It smelled of miles and miles of open water, of pure, beautiful ocean. Behind him he could see Sea Girt and Belmar, but ahead was the whole Atlantic. Three thousand miles to England. Two months to the Orient.

He leaned on the railing and sipped a beer, feeling for the first time entirely on vacation. Michael stood on one side, Louey on the other. Between them they had caught seventeen fish, more than anyone back at the shore house would eat, but Brennan knew it was no use stopping. Blues would keep feeding, and they would keep catching them. It was a pattern of some sort, and even though Brennan wasn't sure what it stood for, he trusted it just the same. You couldn't release a blue anyway. It would bite the hell out of your hand. Blues were like solid logs, thick as a man's calf.

"Last go," the boat mate said, stepping behind them. He carried a white plastic bucket and wore black rubber boots folded down to below his knees. He was a square, heavyset kid who smoked cigarettes whenever he had a dry hand. His name was Carl.

"We turning around?" Louey asked.

"After this last patch."

"What time is it?" Michael asked.

"Ten, ten-fifteen. We'll put back in around one by the time everything's done. This is supposed to be a big patch. They're running like crazy. Full moon, you know?"

The engines slowed, cut. Brennan became aware of the waves hitting the bow. A sea gull fluttered next to a whitecap, lifted once, then settled. Far below, Brennan caught the slightest glimpse of the school. He saw only silver flashes glinting, but they went on for a hundred yards at least. They moved incredibly fast, too fast to comprehend completely. He let his jig drop and heard Louey shout beside him.

"On," Louey said.

"Big?" Michael asked.

"I think so. Pretty big."

"How many does that give you?"

"Seven."

"If you land it, it gives you seven. On," Michael said.

Brennan reeled in, hoping no fish would strike. He wanted to clear the way for Michael and Louey, but a fish hit his spoon, missed it; then another took it. He felt the heavy tug in his shoulders and felt the first frantic rush of the fish. It wasn't big, maybe three or four pounds, but it ran like a bigger fish, stringing out to the bow of the boat before turning back.

"There's a million fish down there," Louey said. "I can see them from here."

"It's a big run," Carl said behind them, his bucket down, a gaff now in his hands.

"Who you going to take first?" Brennan asked him.

"I'll take Louey's. Then Michael's; then you. Steer him over, Louey."

Louey strained at the reel. He jacked his pole higher. The fish swung around, finally breaking the surface just next to the boat. Carl gaffed him in one quick move, the shepherd's hook stabbing into the fish and jerking him clear of the water. In the next instant the fish was flapping on the deck behind them, its heavy body banging against the passenger cabins.

"Now you, Mike," Carl said.

Carl gaffed Michael's fish, then Brennan's. Eighteen, nineteen fish, Brennan thought. That made nearly forty fillets, which was too much, way too much fish. Kate didn't even eat the things, and Linda wasn't wild about them.

"Carl," Brennan asked, "you know anyone that would want some fish? We've got more than we can handle."

"Sometimes there are some guys at the dock that will take them. I don't want them. I'm starting to hate fish. Times like this, the fish are all over. I always think of it as a big bowl of soup spinning, you know, like after you're done stirring. The whole thing's just moving around slowly, coming close enough sometimes so you can scoop out the noodles right from the shore."

"Is surf casting worth it?"

"Anything's worth it this time of year."

"On," Louey said again.

His line went out, slowly ticking against the heavy drag. It was a big fish. Louey leaned the pole against the railing and weighted the butt with his chest. Brennan watched him, wondering how big a blue could get. He figured twenty-some pounds, maybe bigger, he didn't know. A blue that size would be a heavy, wild thing.

"That's a good one," Carl said. "That could take the pot."

"How much is in the pot?" Michael asked, still reeling fast for his own fish.

"Fifty bucks or so. Play him, Louey. Don't try to horse in a fish that size. You've got to let him run around a little."

"I don't know if I can hold him," Louey said.

"You want me to take him?" asked Brennan. "You say something if he gets to be too much."

"No, I've got him."

"Could be a bonito. Sometimes they run with the blues," Carl said.

"Up here?" Michael asked. "I thought they were down South."

"No, they come up this way. They're in the tuna family, just real streamlined. They're dense, too. You catch one the same size as a blue and it will probably be heavier."

"You really think it could be the biggest fish today?" Louey asked, his arms straining now. He didn't turn to look at Carl. He concentrated on the fish.

"Could be. A guy down the other side caught a pretty good one on the second patch."

Brennan swung his line in and hooked the spoon to the lowest guide on the rod. He was done for the day. He rubbed his arms with his can of beer. It was hot now, probably up around ninety. He felt sunburned and a little tired. He drank more beer and watched Louey pulling against the fish. No one had seen it yet. It was still far too down below the surface.

"He's running again," Louey said.

"Let him take it a little," Carl told him. "He'll come back this way."

"He's really heavy."

"You feel all right?" Michael asked him.

"I'm fine. I wish he would come up so I could see him."

"What's a bonito taste like?" Brennan asked Carl.

"Like bluefish. Maybe it's better, lighter. It tastes like tuna, really."

"Chicken of the Sea," Michael said. "Hey, Charlie Tuna, come on up here."

"The rest of the patch is pretty much gone," Carl said.

"It must be a bonito," Brennan said.

It was three or four more minutes before the fish finally came up. It thrashed around, its sharp dorsal fin cutting the surface. It was a bonito. The captain, smoking a cigar on the upper deck, came over to their side of the boat.

"You got a shark trailing it," he called down. "It's circling right now."

"Where?" Carl asked.

"Out beyond, maybe fifteen feet."

"We can't see it from here."

"Looks like a blue shark. They're up here this time of year. Could even be a white."

"How big?" Brennan asked.

"Big enough. Three feet, maybe four or five."

"What should I do? Will he take the fish?" Louey yelled up.

"Damn straight he'll take the fish," the captain said. "I don't know why he's hanging off."

"Reel, Louey," Carl told him. "You've got to get him in here. Get him close enough and I'll gaff him."

"Leave the shark alone if he takes it. Cut free," the captain said. "I don't want the bastard on board."

"He couldn't bring him in on that anyway. Not if he's more than a foot or two," Carl said.

Louey tried to reel, but it was slow going. He had to keep the butt of his pole in his stomach, just under his ribs, while his right hand fought to turn the crank. Brennan put a hand up to shade his own eyes and tried to see the shark. The bonito flapped against the water, hitting it hard with its tail, and from there Brennan surveyed an arc about fifteen feet farther out. He didn't see anything. He took a step back and stood on one of the small benches against the passenger cabin, but he still couldn't spot the shark. He stepped back to the railing.

"Here he comes," the captain said.

"Now?" Carl asked.

"Nowwwooaaw," the captain yelled, excited. "He missed it. He just nosed it."

"Something hit it. He hit it," Louey shouted.

"Is he still on there?" asked Carl.

"I think so. Yes, he's still on."

"Maybe you've got Jaws on there with it," Michael said.

But then Brennan saw the shark. It was very large and pale. Its dorsal fin stood a foot out of the water. No, not a foot. That was an exaggeration, but it was there, frightening for him to look at even standing in a solid boat on a beautiful day. It swam past the boat, and a yell went up from people all the way down the railing. Two guys at the end threw their spoons out at it. "Cut that out," the captain shouted. Yet even as the captain yelled, the shark was moving. It seemed to arch like a cat, its fin momentarily rising even farther out of the water; then it charged Louey's fish. "Shit," Carl said, but it was too late. The shark hit the bonito dead on, its open mouth causing the water to churn, the pole in Louey's hands giving a tremendous nod. There was a quick splash; then the shark was gone, the line limp.

"Took it," the captain said. "Didn't miss it twice."

"That was amazing," Michael said.

"Jesus, Louey, I thought you were going to hook the shark, too," Carl said.

"Looked like a damn white," the captain said. "I couldn't say for sure, but it looked like one."

The captain blew the whistle for up lines, and the engines bubbled. Louey reeled in the slack. Brennan saw right away that the spoon had been bitten in half. It was a clean bite, almost perfectly straight across. Louey showed it to Michael. A few other fishermen came over to look at it. Brennan took a seat against the passenger cabin and broke out another beer from the cooler under the bench.

He lay in the coolness of the master bedroom, the evening air blowing across his chest, the sheet light and soft against him. He felt Linda's lips gliding over his penis, her tongue just touching, prodding him. He felt he could come, but he turned his face to the open window and let her glide, enjoying the sensation, hoping he tasted of salt as she had tasted to him. He touched her hair and softly cupped the base of her skull. His mind drifted to the women of his past, to slips and skirts hiked unconsciously, to a girl's jeans unsnapping, the thumb pull past her hips as her panties fell to half-mast. "So nice," he whispered, "so wonderful." Linda's tongue touched the top of his penis, then her lips and mouth closed down, taking him deep, and in gratitude he touched her neck. He could not stop now. He ground his hips down, pressing them into the mattress, until he arched upward, falling deeper into her mouth, voicing just the smallest groan to let her know it had been delightful. Quietly he felt himself rising, his body unlocked, his eyes closing just for an instant. "Now, now, now," he whispered as he emptied inside her, his words combined with the pulse of his penis, his heart knocking toward a stillness that could only be sad. "Oh, you're sweet," he said, his body just short of a full quiver. He lay perfectly still until he nudged her upward. She lay on his stomach, warm and gentle. He combed her hair with his fingers, his face still turned to the window, the sunlight retreating along the sea toward England.

"That was something," he said. "It was really something."

"You were full. I couldn't believe how full you were."

"It's the sea. I'm going upstream."

"It's nice being here, isn't it? I wasn't sure about it, but it's good to be away. Sometimes vacations are so lousy."

"When did we have a lousy vacation? Name one."

"We never did, really. Never lousy. But I didn't like it much when we were in that tent phase. That wasn't much fun when the kids were so small."

"We couldn't afford anything else."

"I know. We're doing better now, aren't we? I like having a little more money. Do you ever miss all the coaching and stuff? All the sports talk?"

"No. No, I don't. And the money was so bad it became demeaning after a while. I was starting to be embarrassed."

Linda pulled higher in the bed. Her right breast rubbed against his chest as she climbed him. He bent and kissed her nipples, both of them, his head moving back and forth.

"You think we'll have anything left of the house money when it's all over?" she asked. "I mean, just even a couple of thousand dollars?"

"If Michael doesn't get enough aid, we'll be right back where we started. Why?"

"I don't know. Maybe we should buy something just for the hell of it or go on a long vacation somewhere. I'd like to go to Europe with you. I'd like to see some of the places everyone talks about."

"Where in Europe?"

"Paris, London, I don't know. Wouldn't it be fun to plan it, though? I'd get the brochures and everything. I wouldn't even care if we were just stupid tourists. I'd still love it."

"I'd like to get you something. I'd like to get you something you really wanted. I'd like to get you something you didn't even know you wanted, but when you opened it, you'd know you always did want it. Do you know what I mean?"

"Of course I do. That's wonderful," she said, turning and kissing his chest.

"We might have a little left over," he said, and touched her hair. "You'll start bringing in some, too. Don't forget that. I'm sorry you've had to go so slow because of Louey. But eventually you'll start piling it in."

"It's going to be a while before I bring in anything. Do you think we'll have a couple of thousand?"

"A little. Kate's coming up. She can go anywhere she wants, but I don't think she'll go Ivy League. I hate to root against her, but at least she'll save us some money."

Brennan put his hand on her leg and rubbed it softly. He felt he didn't want to move at all. It would be easy, he thought, to sleep through until the morning.

118

"The kids are probably starving. We can stay right here, though, if you want to," she said.

"No, I'm okay. I'll get the fire started."

Outside on the porch, the ocean sending a land breeze toward him, he felt solid and sure in all his movements. Somehow it was like being back on his feet after the flu. The air felt good. He drank a gin and tonic and stood near the railing. The radio was on in the kitchen. The lead news story was about South Africa. More blacks had been shot, protesting white rule. Some of the white leaders came on and said they would never hand over the government to blacks. Then there was a report about sanctions from other governments and a reporter from Washington said Congress was divided. No one was ruling anything out.

The radio flicked off, and in its place came the sound of "Star Trek." Brennan heard Kirk say, "On my signal," but couldn't remember the episode. On my signal, what? Beam me up? Beam me down? Put phasers on stun? Maybe Kirk was warming a stone with his phaser on some arctic planet. There was an episode where the men warmed rocks with phasers and kept calling to the *Enterprise* for help. Give us a little more heat, Scotty. Toast the rocks.

Louey came out with a package of sparklers. It was only the second of July. He slid two sparklers out and held the ends in the charcoal pit. One of them caught, then the other.

"Whoopee," Louey said.

"What are you doing them for if you don't like them?"

"I want to like them, that's why."

"You're too old to like them anymore."

"I guess so."

Michael came out in a pair of jams. He wore a hooded sweat shirt but no shoes. His face was tan. Kate pushed out the door behind him, wearing almost the same thing. Her sweat shirt said TEMPLE UNIVERSITY across it. She was already remarkably tan. She had spent the day on the beach while they had been out fishing.

"Give me a sparkler, punk," Michael said.

"Me, too," Kate said.

"You're too old," Louey protested, writing something in the darkness.

"Give me one. Mom bought them," said Michael.

Louey slid one more out, then handed over the package. Brennan watched Michael and Kate take out the sparklers and light them. There was a moment of excitement each time a sparkler caught, but after that the bright light was boring.

"What was Kirk doing?" Brennan asked.

"He went back in time to 1920 Chicago. It was ridiculous," Kate said. "I don't know why you guys think it's such a terrific show."

"He could have altered the future," Michael said, waving his sparkler in zigzag patterns. He made a figure eight and a Z for Zorro. "If you change one event, the whole future's changed."

"Maybe," Louey said. "Maybe it's changed."

"Spock said it was. You don't mess with Spock," Michael said. He reached out and pinched Kate's shoulder in a Vulcan death grip.

Kate said, "Ow," and squirmed out from under his grip.

"What are sparklers supposed to do exactly?" Louey asked. "I never figured that out."

"Just burn," Brennan said.

"I liked those snake things we got one time. The ones that went out like snakes when you lit them."

"There are fireworks over at Seaside Heights on the Fourth of July. They shoot them out at the ocean," Kate said, suddenly going rigid and pretending to conduct an orchestra.

"You guys each light one more; then I've got to put the grill on. Does your mom have the fish ready?"

"Bluefish. How scrumptious," Kate said.

"I still can't believe that shark. That was one of the coolest things I've ever seen," Michael said.

"You should have felt it," Louey said, his sparkler catching and turning almost blue. "I never felt anything that strong before."

"Did it really dip?" asked Kate.

"No, it was like the shark shook the fish back and forth really hard; then it starting swimming with it before it was completely dead. It was something."

"You remember how still it got right afterwards?" Michael asked. "Everybody was a little stunned or something."

"More than a little," Louey told him. "How about those jerks who starting throwing their spoons at him? The captain went crazy."

Brennan finished his drink, shook it at Michael for another, then put the grill on the barbecue. Michael went inside. "Send out the fish," Brennan called in after him. Louey and Kate stood on the top step of the porch and dueled with the sparklers. White flames and sparks jumped off in all directions every time their sparklers hit. Brennan sat on the porch railing.

"I can't believe we have a week like this," Louey said.

"You like it?" Brennan asked.

"I liked fishing today."

"How about you, Kate? You like it?"

"It's okay."

"She misses Jason," Louey said, striking her sparkler twice rapidly with his. "She misses her lover boy."

"He might come down for the fireworks. Could he come over for the day here?" asked Kate, not looking.

"Sure, why not? Invite him to dinner."

"We can check out his table manners," Louey said.

The last sparkler went out. Michael appeared with a drink and a trayful of bluefish fillets wrapped in foil.

"Is your mom coming out?"

"She said in a second."

"You all clean up, okay? It isn't your mom's job to do everything. It's her vacation, too."

"Mom said moms don't have vacations. They simply relocate. That's what she said," Kate said.

"Your mother can have a vacation if you pitch in."

Brennan put the fish on the grill, then sat back on the railing. He took a good long drink of his gin and tonic. Maybe he'd get drunk. He felt like getting drunk. It was hard to wind down after working for forty some weeks. Vacations took getting used to. He took another drink and let the gin burn down. Jason would be down; then Kate would be gone. Michael would find a video-game arcade somewhere and drift off with rolls of quarters. Louey would stick around. Then he and Linda would be just where they started, relocated, on vacation. It felt good but lonely at the same time. That was the thing about nests: Everyone learned to fly at once.

Brennan took a ball high and inside, then set his feet for the next pitch. He watched the metal arm of the machine cock, the ball fall into the hand, then listened while the motor clicked. Suddenly the ball was launched, but Brennan was prepared this time. He stepped into it and brought his hands quickly through his swing. He kept his head in and swung smoothly. The ball hit the bat solidly, in the flesh, but the bat was made of aluminum and didn't give Brennan any reward. The ball flew off into the net, just above the triple sign.

"That's a run," Louey said behind him.

"What's the score?"

"Two to one, mine."

"How many more balls do I have?"

"Three, I think. I lost count."

Brennan set himself again. This time the ball came so fast it was all he could do to foul it back. He swung at the second pitch and hit a dribbler back to the box. The third pitch he missed entirely.

"I hate these bats," he said, stepping out of the cage. "I hate hitting a ball with aluminum."

"It goes farther."

"I still hate it."

Brennan stood for a second rubbing his hands. It was a good day. He smelled the ocean and cotton candy and hot dogs. He always liked amusement parks. He was a sucker for tests of strength, throwing contests, dart games. All his life he'd had a romantic notion of the circus, of side shows and carnivals. He liked thinking about the free-and-easy life, even though it was anything but free from the outside. It was a quarter a chance on most things, fifty cents on others. That had gone up. He could remember playing pinball for a dime at Ernie's Delicatessen in Charlemont. Comics were twelve cents; a pack of bubble gum, five. You could do an entire economic study, he thought, on the rising price of being an eleven-year-old boy. It cost almost triple now for a kid to fill up a Saturday afternoon.

While Louey took a last set of swings, Brennan stood near the railing, looking out at the beach. The sun was bright, and he slipped on his sunglasses. Shades, Daddy-o. Kookie, Kookie, lend me your comb, he thought. The waves were white lines moving at him. It reminded him of a TV set on the blink, or maybe an edge of sand being raked toward him. He liked the ocean but was afraid of it. He preferred lakes and rivers. A lake you could swim in. A lake was friendly; it had no will of its own. The ocean was different. He didn't believe it was possible to get to know the ocean.

Louey came out of the cage breathing hard. Brennan looked him over. He seemed all right, but weak, and Brennan thought maybe they should pull back on some of the activities. Remission was only remission after all. Linda had said she had seen a deep bruise next to Louey's lowest rib, just at the belt line. Brennan hadn't seen it yet. Louey would hide something like that.

"You ready for a swim?" Brennan asked, starting to move toward the stairs that led down to the beach. "It's getting hot."

"I'm ready."

"What time is Jason supposed to be here?"

"I don't know. He was supposed to be down this morning."

"What's Michael say? Is he a pretty good kid?"

"Jason's okay. He's a jock, so Michael thinks he's an idiot. But he's okay. He's not too wild."

"How wild is he?"

"Not wild. I mean, he isn't one of those jocks that drink until they barf every night of the weekend. That's what I mean."

Brennan nodded and started down the steps. He was glad Jason didn't drink until he barfed. That was a relief. Brennan wondered if that was a new scale for things. Bad kids snorted coke, pretty bad kids drank until they puked, and nice kids just chugged beer now and then. He wondered what kind of kid Michael was outside the house or, for that matter, what Kate was like. He had no idea how you were supposed to know. You closed the door on Saturday night and didn't sit too close to the phone. That was the trick. It didn't help to know everything your kids did. He was glad, at least, his kids were smart. Maybe they would escape some of it. The worst torture would have been to have dumb kids who never saw a bad scene forming; to retrieve an idiotic kid from the local police station weekend after weekend and to ride home with some numskull who took his punishment as simply another fine for his stupidity.

Brennan walked along the wooden spur of the boardwalk as far as possible, then stepped onto the hot sand. Somewhere Simon and Garfunkel sang "The Sounds of Silence." Out about a mile from the waterline a plane flew overhead, dragging a sign that said COPPERTONE. Louey trotted off toward their umbrella, leaving Brennan alone. Brennan straightened his shoulders and checked asses as he walked. It was almost too much sometimes to see women this way, their skins wet and brown, their bathing suits stretched tight across their flanks. He passed a blanket of college-age girls, all of them asleep with their heads on their folded arms, their bra straps loose. He imagined the warmth of the sand and the blanket pressing against their thighs. Ho, ho, he wanted to shout, and dive on them, perhaps lie crosswise on them, his body supported by their tan backs, the beautiful dimples just above their cans. He wanted to bathe in them.

The beach was crowded. If it was this crowded on a weekday, Brennan couldn't imagine what it would be like on a weekend. He was surprised by the number of Chicanos and blacks and Puerto Ricans. Walking down the beach was like crossing borders, and as he passed from one group to another, he heard different music, smelled different food. He was conscious of his big Hawaiian shirt, his wide-brimmed hat, his bad-ass shades. He felt like a tourist in his own country, in his own state, and he was pretty sure the others also saw him that way. He had read somewhere that by 1990 eighty percent of the country would speak Spanish. They were pouring in, and Brennan knew as well as anyone else that his world was shrinking. Guys like him were being pushed higher and higher into the sky-scrapers. It was as if they were apes going up into the trees for safety. The world was turning.

Brennan worked his way down to the water and walked in five inches of foam back toward his blanket. The water was cool. The beach was picked clean. There were no shells or pieces of kelp or sticks of driftwood. A few women sat in sand chairs, their bottoms in the water, their faces turned up to the sun. He dodged around them, dodged the kids who came skidding toward him on rubber rafts, and continued on, his hand up to his eyes to spot the umbrella.

He finally saw Louey and Michael in the surf, but there was no sign of Kate or Jason. He cut up past two barbecue grills and found Linda asleep on the blanket. Her back looked burned. He took off his shirt and flipped it over her and headed toward the water. He heard a radio say it was ninety-three. The disc jockey told everyone in Manasquan that they were done on one side and should now flip.

Brennan waded in, taking the first wave on his knees, the second on his thighs. Just before he dove in, he had a quick image of the shark, the white or blue or whatever the hell it was, patrolling under the waves. It could be there. People were killed by sharks in New Jersey. Last year a woman had been killed on her morning swim, fifteen or twenty feet from shore. Brennan imagined what it would be like to dive into a shark, actually to bump into it, or to see it rising from the bottom to attack. A girl on a talk show who had lost her leg to a shark said she thought it was a boy playing a game with her. That was how sharks came, quickly and violently and so unexpectedly that there was no protection. Shock killed people half the time. Brennan looked around at the thousand of bathers and tried to make a mathematical net for himself. He multiplied everyone he saw by two, figuring sharks could hit either leg. Then he dived in, his adrenaline pumping remarkably high, his fists out in front of him in case a shark was awkward enough to get in the way.

When he came up, he was close to Louey and Michael. They were trying to catch waves. Both of them stood in water up to their chests, their heads turned to look over their shoulders. "Hang ten," Brennan said, but they didn't hear him, and so he swam closer, half expecting at any moment to see a fin following him.

"Where's Kate?" Brennan asked when he was close enough.

Michael turned and let a wave go by. Louey swam for it and missed.

"She took off with Jason," said Michael. "They went down the beach somewhere."

"They coming back for dinner?"

"I think so."

Another wave came, and Brennan floated over it. He was cool now and wanted to be in. He moved into line beside Louey and Michael and waited for a wave. The undertow pulled against him, then there was a shift, and the wave started to build. He wondered what he would do if he saw the silhouette of a shark lifting out of the water in the center of the wave. But then the wave was coming on faster, just breaking at the very top, and he dived forward and swam as hard as he could. The wave picked up gradually, and he felt he had it, felt he was in just the right position. He put his hands out in front of him, and the wave clipped at his waist; but he was up and on it, streaking to shore, Superman soaring over Metropolis.

The wave tumbled him a little as it broke, but it carried him into the tidal pools. He stayed on just his arms and found himself in three feet of water. Two or three kids ran in and out of the waves, their jumps high and spastic, their bodies blue and ribbed and pure energy. Brennan imagined himself a shark rising into the tumble of little legs and gobbling, hooking a foot in his mouth and backpedaling into deeper water. Alligators did that. They carried off animals and humans and kept them in their underwater dens until everything went rotten. Resting on his fingers, the sand soft under his hands, the water warm and tight on his back, Brennan could almost imagine the pleasure of it.

Sand grated in his bathing suit, down in the little white mesh trampoline they put in as a jock, and he put one hand inside and tried to shake it loose. He moved out a little and sloshed water up and down over his suit, the salt pickling his scrotum. Then he walked up to the blanket. Linda was awake when he got there.

"Hi, honey," she said, "did you have a good time with Louey?"

"It was great. We played about seventy-five different games."

"Did you see the bruise on his hip?"

"Not yet."

"Take a look at it, will you? When you get a chance?"

"I will," he said, reaching for his sunglasses and a towel. "Are there any peanut butter and jellies left?"

"One or two. You hungry?"

"I'm starved."

Linda dug into an insulated picnic sack and handed him a sandwich wrapped in wax paper. He ate it standing, his body dripping onto the white sand. The peanut butter tasted salty, but good, and he ate the whole sandwich in about three bites.

"Jason arrived," Linda said, rubbing white cream across her throat and bosom. "They went down the beach. He's a cute kid."

"Where did they go?"

"I don't know. Under the boardwalk. Someplace to neck. They didn't want to lay here and listen to us. Would you have wanted to when you were their age?"

"No."

"They'll be back for dinner. Jason has his car."

"Did Kate take a T-shirt or something?"

"You're such a prude, Brennan."

"So?"

"So relax."

He sat on the edge of the blanket. Two little girls ran past, pails and shovels banging against their legs. Beware of sharks, he wanted to say. Somewhere behind him he heard a conga start. The music had a good deal of whistling, castanets, and sand blocks. It was just the thing for an afternoon on the beach. He expected five or six groups of people to stand and begin a big line up to the boardwalk and back. Life as a musical.

He was still thinking about it when Louey came up. The bruise was there, brown rimmed by pale yellow. Brennan felt his stomach recoil. Louey held his elbow in front of the bruise so it was difficult to see. He also had his bathing suit hiked high. In quick calculation Brennan guessed the bruise to be at least double what he could see, an entire iceberg down below the belt. Maybe it was triple, maybe more. He wanted to look at Linda to see what her reaction might be. She hadn't told him it was this big. He had thought it could be something any boy might get, but this was different; this was an

127

organ, or internal, or just the salamander pressing against his son's soft skin. It was possible that it had been getting bigger during the course of the day. That had happened in the past, and now he wanted to turn to her and ask, "Was it like this before?" But Louey stood at the edge of the blanket, in the sun, his lips blue. Michael threw him a towel and Louey brushed himself once with it, then quickly wrapped it up around his waist.

"You look cold," he said to Louey.

"It gets cold after a while," Michael said.

"Louey, you stay out now. We're almost ready to go," Linda said. "Maybe we should start packing up."

"The waves are just getting good," Louey said, his voice trembling.

"Still," Linda told him.

"Waves always get bigger at sunset," said Michael.

Brennan helped Linda pack. They folded the blanket together while Michael stuffed two beach bags with clothes and flip flops and Frisbees. Louey continued to shiver. Brennan touched him with his hand, pretending to brush off sand. Louey's skin was cold, remarkably cold. He brushed him again, just to check, and again he felt Louey's raised skin, his cold, tight muscles.

"You okay?" Brennan asked him. "You're like an ice cube."

"I'm all right."

"I mean, you're really cold."

"I'm okay. The water's just cold, that's all."

Louey hiked the towel higher, his fingers trembling on the knot. Brennan caught a glimpse of the bruise again, but it was only a glimpse. He wondered now if there were other bruises, but that wasn't really possible, since he was practically naked in front of them. No, it was just one. One bruise and a loss of core heat and Louey too sick to pump his blood back into his extremities.

"Put on my sweat shirt," Brennan told him.

"Dad, it's ninety."

"Put it on."

"Dad . . ."

"Listen to your father," Linda said. "You're shivering."

And so it was back. Brennan tried to see the bruise again as Louey dropped the towel and slipped on the sweat shirt. He almost demanded that Louey pull down his suit so that he could see, but that wasn't fair. You had to leave him his dignity. Besides, Brennan knew what he would find. The actual extent of the bruise was the only question. Brennan knew where it came from. He knew what it signified.

"Let's go," Michael said. "It's boiling right here."

"Think of the car," Linda said.

"I hate hot cars. That's the worst thing in the world. You get in and you feel like you never even went swimming the whole day," Michael said, picking up one of the beach bags.

Brennan looked at Louey. Louey shrugged and started walking.

At dinner they heard the first firecrackers going off. It wasn't the big show, just local stuff. Sometimes the firecrackers were close, rattling for a few seconds and disappearing. Other times the explosions came from far away, the sound carrying over the water, the thuds as steady as bombardment. Brennan had never been in a war, but it was this sound he always imagined when people told him battle stories. In time you could probably distinguish each type of firework, but for now they sounded uniformly tedious, like an old electric fan sighing on each sweep of the room. It would be impossible, he thought, ever to become accustomed to the sound. It would never drain into the background noises because its monotony was more insistent than any irregular sound might be. Don't forget, it would say. Here I am.

Brennan drank off the last of his beer. He looked across the table at Jason and decided he liked the kid even more than before. It wasn't easy coming into a family dinner and handling yourself well, but he had done it. He had eaten enough, but not too much; he stood to help with the dishes, but he didn't make a fool of himself by trying to clear the whole table; he spoke when it seemed appropriate but didn't rattle on. He was calm and steady, and Brennan wished Kate had met him ten years from now, when they both were ready to settle down. He was the kind of kid to marry. He was a dray horse, bit-worn and accustomed to carrying things through. Brennan imagined him with big Clydesdale hooves crossed under the table, a smell of oats and hay occasionally springing off his wide shoulders.

"So, you-all going to head over to Seaside Heights?" Michael asked. "You going over for the fireworks?"

"You can see them from here," Louey said.

"If you want to," Kate said, looking at Jason.

It was played so perfectly, the question dangled so sweetly, that Brennan felt himself pulling for Jason to slam down his napkin and say no. Where had Kate learned that? Brennan watched her lean a little to one side, perhaps to send perfume in Jason's direction, perhaps simply to make him aware of her body, her head tilting just enough to let him know that she and he were together, whatever he decided. It seemed so transparent to him! And yet he saw Jason look at her, trying to read what she wanted to do, his good broad shoulders dipping a little to imply indecision. She smiled back at him, then looked down at the tablecloth, embarrassed to be having a conversation with a boy in front of her parents. Jason stalled, his fingers brushing a few crumbs into a mound before him, and finally looked at Michael.

"What time do they start?" he asked.

"In a little bit. Sundown, I guess. As soon as it's dark enough."

"How much can you see from here?" Linda asked.

"You can see everything from up on the porch roof. I was up there looking earlier. I could see the Ferris wheel in Seaside," Louey said.

"I'm just trying to decide myself," Michael said. "I might go over. Franky and some of the guys were talking about coming down."

"Aren't they turning on the Statue of Liberty tonight? That must be on TV," Brennan said.

"The whole harbor thing, yes," Jason said. "My uncle has his boat out there."

"It must be wonderful," Linda said.

Kate looked up again. Come out, come out, wherever you are, Brennan wanted to say. Her tan made her more attractive than ever. She wore a white sweater, the kind with blue and purple piping around the V neck, which made her seem collegiate and preppy. Parent clothes, she called them. But actually they made her look too grown-up for Brennan. She was already older than Michael, older by miles, even though she was just entering her senior year. Five, six, seven years from now, Brennan figured, and he would have a grandchild. It would all start up then, like a disease or a new hobby, and suddenly there would be little kids around the table, fractured conversations, his sons and daughter leaning down to stuff potatoes in tots' mouths. He didn't mind, that wasn't it, he liked kids, but it all seemed too soon. Once you had a grandchild, you were kidding yourself if you thought it meant anything but the other end of the seesaw lifting to show you how far you were sinking.

"We should make up our minds," Kate said.

"I'd like to go if you would. Mike, do you need a ride?" asked Jason.

"Can I have the car, Dad?"

"If you're careful. There are a lot of drunks out on the Fourth."

"Can I go with you?" Louey asked Michael.

"Not if I'm meeting the guys, squirt man."

"I think you should stay in Louey," Linda said. "You can watch them from here."

"Aw, come on. That's a gyp."

"Not tonight," Linda said.

Kate stood, then Jason. Jason pulled her chair out just enough to show he was being attentive. He was good. Brennan stood, too, ready to usher them all out. He looked at his watch and saw the Yankees were already finished, but maybe he could catch the Mets. Maybe the Doctor was pitching.

"Have a good time then," Brennan said. "Enjoy yourselves."

"Thank you, Mr. McCalmont," Jason said. "And thank you, Mrs. McCalmont, for dinner."

"You're welcome anytime."

Then it was over. Brennan grabbed his radio and went out on the porch, happy to sit in a rocker and watch the sky getting darker. He felt relieved for Jason's sake. They might hang around a little before they left, but at least the kid could relax now. He had handled himself so well that Brennan couldn't help wondering if he wouldn't be rewarded somehow by Kate. Maybe tonight he would conquer her bra, maybe dive into her pants. You could use things like dinners as sign-posts sometimes. An under-the-sweater feel, for good behavior. It was terrible to think it, almost perverse, but you couldn't stop your mind from coming up with these things. At seventeen you earned your way down a woman. At any age, really, you earned your way down a woman, journeying eventually into the jungle lands. Maybe it was like *Heart of Darkness* or *Apocalypse Now*, that crazy movie with the natives shooting wooden arrows at the PT boat, old McHale's navy getting it with punji sticks. You went downriver, or upriver, stripping off good behavior as you went along. Kate was enough of a snob to figure things like manners and politeness into the equation. She didn't go for the wild guys, the motorcycle types who spent half their high school careers in auto shop, or the punkers with mandrill-colored hair. She was conservative. She was after a Ken doll.

Brennan flicked on the radio. He had to fiddle with the dial until he finally homed in on the Mets game out of Shea. They were playing the Expos, and they were way ahead. Brennan left it on for the sound. He liked the noise of vendors selling beer and popcorn. A couple of heavy rounds of firecrackers went off, thick and dense, and Brennan looked up in time to see two beautiful blue flares arch out toward the ocean. "Come here, you-all," he called. "They're shooting—" but his voice was cut off by three tremendous explosions, mortar fire, then a big crack as one of the first rockets exploded as it came down. Thuuum, thuuum, thummmmbph, they went, the sound actually compressing the air on the porch for a moment. Somewhere down the street a few people cheered. Brennan called inside again, and this time they all trooped out, the whole family, Kate with her jacket on and new perfume.

"Isn't it beautiful?" she said.

"I'm taking off," Michael said. "I'm heading over to Seaside."

"Can't I go with him, Dad?"

"He's got other plans. Besides, I think maybe you've had enough for one day."

Linda put her arm around Louey and kissed his forehead. Brennan stood up. It was a moment to be on his feet, July 4, 1986, Lavallette, New Jersey. He watched the rockets flinging out at the ocean. For an instant they reminded him of the old Walt Disney show, the one with the castle and Tinker Bell flitting around. Walt Disney was frozen now, waiting for the world to advance enough to be able to retrieve him. That's what they said anyway. Brennan thought that wouldn't be bad, but it would be better to freeze moments, to snap them whole into a block of ice. Maybe put a day from each decade into an ice tray, a bouillon cube, the fixings for soup.

THREE

THREE

B RENNAN drove through Elizabeth, wearing a sweat shirt and gym shorts, a brand-new pair of white wool socks on his feet. It was late August and still warm even now in the evenings, though the days were getting shorter. He kept the window down, his biceps fleshed out on the door. Driving, he felt nervous and a little silly, but he didn't care. He was going to take a look, that was all, and if the league was way over his head, if the guys were too young and vicious, he could back out of it. That was his agreement with himself, the one he had made when he first saw the notice for tryouts. The team was called the Plainfield Red Oaks, a semipro team, part of a league sponsored by local businessmen or something, he wasn't sure. He had taken the flyer down from the wall in one of the Newark schools and pocketed it on impulse. You never knew. But later he had pulled it out, memorized the date and the name of the field, then tossed it away. He didn't want Linda to find it. To get out of the house, he had told her he was going to take a run up in the Watchung Reservation, breathe better air and look at the trees, but he had driven straight this way instead. The Plainfield Red Oaks. The flyer said the team carried sixty guys, which was too many, but maybe that meant people played on a revolving basis. It probably wasn't enough money anyway, not real money. They wouldn't be real professional players, just a bunch of guys either over the hill or young and untrained, but still aggressive as hell.

Brennan looked for signs to Scotch Plains, Fanwood, and Plainfield. It was somewhere up around the Plainfield High School field. Most of the area was black, and for a second Brennan wondered if he hadn't missed something in the flyer. Maybe this was something like the old Negro Leagues before Jackie Robinson, and he was going to show up and be the only white man. A white oak, a polar bear. It didn't matter. If that was the case, he would back off, just drift away, or perhaps stay for a run and then go home. Even if he wasn't the wrong color, he wondered if the Red Oaks would take him seriously at his age. At forty-two the Silver Bullet was tarnished, there was no denying it, but when he played catch with Louey or Michael, it was still there sometimes. He could still throw, still move a little. He was in pretty good shape now, his running up to thirty miles a week, and that wasn't bad. Besides, people were staying in sports longer than ever. There was Blanda a few years back, and the Niekro brothers both playing for the Yankees with whitewalls over their ears. Nicklaus had won the Masters Tournament just this year at forty-six. He had finished with a sixty-five, something like birdie, birdie, bogey, eagle, birdie, birdie, and passed Norman and Kite and everyone else. Nicklaus had cried four or five times, right there on TV, cried because it all was coming back to him, he felt it, and it was there, spring once more, the Golden Bear whacking himself into history. Why not, Brennan thought.

He finally saw the field back behind what must have been a junior high. A few cars were parked in the lot, and he saw two guys, both younger than he, trying their shoes with their feet up on the bumpers. Out on the field, through the rear grid of the grandstands, Brennan heard a ball being kicked and watched it arch upward in a spiral. It was an old sound to him, and as he pulled his car into a slot next to the other players, he felt embarrassed and sentimental at once. He sat for a moment with the window down, the smell of grass coming to him, the shy clatter of cleats on pavement just to his right. He felt ridiculous sitting there, but also moved. There was nothing like sports to bring you back. You couldn't forget the smell of playing fields, or the sounds, or the feeling of doing something right, clean, smooth. No wonder Nicklaus had cried, Brennan thought. Anyone would.

He climbed out slowly, holding his stomach in, surprised at himself for wanting to appear in shape, a stud. He fished his cleats out of the trunk and smiled at the two guys who were still tying their shoes. One was black, the other white, and Brennan was relieved at least that much.

"Red Outs tryouts?" Brennan asked, his tongue playing a trick on him, and he smiled foolishly and said, "I mean, the Red Oaks tryouts here?"

"Right here," the black guy said.

138

The white guy gave Brennan a long look, and Brennan smiled again, then bent to put on his cleats. The shoes were old and stiff as bark. A few clumps of mud were impaled on the bottom cleats, and Brennan tried to remember where he had last worn the shoes. It could have been in college, or even later, on one of the lawn jobs he'd had. A woman up in Summit had a yard that was so steep he'd sometimes worn his football shoes to keep his footing. Maybe that was it. He jammed the shoes on, bending each one to get it loose; then he did a few minutes of stretching. He wondered if perhaps it wouldn't be smarter to run a few laps, then circle in once he got a look at the players. If they seemed too young, he could beg off. Taking laps, he thought, he might get a look at some of the other quarterbacks, too. He didn't want to compete with a bunch of guns fresh out of college. He had a good arm, an accurate arm, but it wasn't a cannon like some guys had. He could throw a long bomb easily enough, that was cake, but laying one out on a thirty-yard hook or square out, that was a pro arm. You couldn't fake a square out.

A whistle went off, and Brennan decided the hell with it, he'd try it, there was nothing to lose. He took a few steps and came onto the grass. It was a wonderful feeling being back on grass in a pair of cleats. It was powerful enough to feel up in his balls. He lifted his knees a couple of times in a quick run in place, then did a few jumping jacks. Suck the stomach in, he thought. Young, virile, the Silver Bullet. He ran once more in place, and then finally looped around the edge of the bleachers, astonished that he could be so keyed up at his age. About twenty or thirty guys were scattered around the field, all of them getting loose, stretching along the sidelines or running easy patterns for each other.

"Hey, take a number, babe," a black man called from over by the bleachers. The pair of guys who had been putting on their shoes in the parking lot were standing next to a small table, writing on a sheet of paper. Brennan looked at the black man and touched his chest.

"Me?" Brennan asked.

"Yeah, you, come on over and sign up," the black man said again. "You going to be an Oak, you need a number."

Brennan didn't know whether to trot over or walk. He suddenly wondered what the hell he was doing there. It was ridiculous. He walked toward the table, rehearsing in his mind what he might say, but the black guy didn't seem to find anything odd about a forty-two-year-old man trying out for the Plainfield Red Oaks. The black man smoked a cigarette, but he wore football cleats and gym shorts. He was twenty pounds overweight, with big, goat shoulders, a wide forehead, and heavy brows. A guard, Brennan decided, a pulling guard, mean enough to bury people when they went down and tried to stop the trap. Mean enough to stick his nose in, yet a little out of shape now. There was something likable about him, something lazy but on top of things. He reminded Brennan of a bear that had just spent the summer getting fat and wise, spending its nights at the edges of streams slapping at fish, its breath clean but tainted with berries, its stomach now pushing it to sleep and winter.

The other men, the guys he had seen in the parking lot, stepped back and trotted toward the field.

"You trying out?" the black man behind the table asked.

"I guess so."

"We don't provide insurance, anything else. We give you some equipment if you play. How good are you?"

"I don't know anymore."

"Who does?" the black man asked, and threw away his cigarette.

"I was worried I'd be a little old."

"Maybe you are. This isn't the Green Bay Packers out here, though. This is just some guys who got together and like the game. We got a little backing from some of the people around, you know, businesses. What position you play?"

"Quarterback."

"Good, we need a couple. They go fast in this league. They take their share of lumps . . . blocking isn't so good, you understand?"

"I understand."

"I mean, people aren't going to do a whole hell of a lot of crabbing on a team like this. They miss a block, they just yell."

"Okay."

"Write down your address here, and then go throw some balls. I'll watch you."

"Are you the coach?"

"Coach Bonow. What's your name?"

"Brennan."

"Okay, Brennan, we'll see how it goes."

Brennan wrote down his address, his position of preference. Another column asked things he never imagined being asked on a football field: Did he have a car to transport players? Any days he couldn't practice? Would his wife be willing to work the snack bar? Did he have any equipment of his own? Brennan checked the appropriate items. He left Linda out of the snack bar brigade.

When he finished, he trotted onto the field, wondering if he had made the team. Was that it? If he mentioned he worked for Riesel, he'd be elected captain, he figured. This definitely wasn't the big leagues, but he liked it. He liked Coach Bonow. He liked being out on an early-fall evening with cleats on and a good grass field. Even if he just stayed for one practice, it would be okay. He just wanted to feel that click, that zing, snap of a ball coming off his fingers. You couldn't describe it. It was like trying to explain to someone what it was like to hit a line drive.

He picked up a ball and did a few finger exercises, stretching his hands to make them supple. Then he moved the ball under his legs, around his back, warming into games he used to play just for fun. Now, though, they got him loose, and he did them more seriously, a Globetrotter, putting on the dog just a little. He did a few knee bends and then finally spotted a big white kid, tall and skinny, who was obviously a receiver.

"Feel like catching some?" Brennan called to the kid, and saw the boy stretch and move over, his wide hands flexing at his sides.

"Sure. We going to do drills? We always did patterns."

The kid held up his hands. Brennan lobbed a pass to him. The kid took it in with his giant hands and tucked the ball in, a reflex of training, then lobbed it back.

"I don't know. You new here?" Brennan asked.

"Yep."

"Me, too."

"Where'd you play? I mean, when you played," the kid asked.

"I played at Temple."

"Down in Philly? Shit, we killed those guys. I played at BC for two years."

"Your last two?"

"No," the kid said, "knee. Fucking lateral miniscus. Changes your plans."

"Were you counting on the pros?"

"I was thinking bonus, baby, that's what I was thinking. Now, hell, it's all gone. I just thought I'd come down tonight and see."

Brennan tossed him the ball again, a completion, two for two, a hundred percent. He could throw to this kid all day. There were some people who made catching the ball a thing to watch. This kid was like that. He was big and wide, a web, and you could crank away and the ball would always be caught softly. He would make you look good. Other guys caught the ball just as efficiently, but it wasn't a pleasure to throw to them. Flankers and split ends a lot of times were the worst. Tall, wingy kids who were always so intent on getting gone, on speeding, that the ball was just secondary to them. They never seemed grateful, somehow, when you got it to them. Brennan liked tight ends. He liked throwing to meat.

Ten minutes later Bonow came out on the field. He blew a whistle and waved everyone in. "Take a knee, take a knee," he said as each group came to him. Brennan knelt to Bonow's right. He plucked a few blades of grass and sucked them, tasting dirt and fertilizer and lime. Bonow looked at a clipboard.

"Now, listen," he said. "We want to take this nice and easy tonight. We're not all in the best shape—"

There was a laugh here. Bonow smiled his weary smile, then went on.

"We're going to split up into two squads, offense and defense. I want to avoid us playing both ways if we can. I want the offense to start wearing white T-shirts or sweat shirts, something white. The defense can wear anything dark, red or blue, I don't care, just dark. We've got to be able to tell you apart."

"We get jerseys?" someone asked.

"If you show up to enough practices, yeah, you get jerseys. Now, tonight we're going to be doing basic things. Everything's simple. Our offense is simple and our defense is simple. We don't want anything complicated. I don't want to worry about first string and second string either. Everybody will get a chance to play. Injuries, weddings, bar mitzvahs, you name it, you never know when you're going to play. We play nine games up through Thanksgiving. It's just like a high school schedule. There aren't any play-offs, none of that crap. If your team wins the league, you get a trophy."

Bonow checked his clipboard. Before he started in again, he asked, "Any questions?"

"How many people do we get at games?" a big guy asked.

"A thousand or two. Not as many as a good high school team."

Bonow looked around once more, then looked down at his clipboard again. He took a deep breath. Brennan found himself liking this man.

"Now, I'm just going to say one thing before we start. This isn't supposed to be inspirational; it's just the way it is. The reason we're out here, the reason I'm out here anyway, is that I grew up playing football. I played it every fall all my life. It's a game you can get too old for, and maybe I'm there already, but sometimes I still play pretty well. What I'm trying to say is that there are some tough kids here and there are some old guys here, but there isn't much chance of anyone jumping from here to the Giants. The scouts come once in a blue moon; I've had three guys sign on with the NFL, and they were mostly fill-in people, guys on the suicide squads, you know. So, if you're here to make a name for yourself or to prove how bad-ass you are, we don't need you. We're not out to play rough or dirty or to win a bonus. We're out here to do a few things well, have some fun, and play a game we all love. Is that clear to everyone?"

Everyone said, "Yes," in that team voice that Brennan remembered so well. Yes, Coach. Of course, Coach. But Brennan was happy with the speech; it couldn't have been better. He switched knees and waited. After a few more announcements he was sent off with a group of backs and ends. He trotted off, loose now, sweat starting on his back.

His legs felt good and strong. He shifted from side to side, getting his ankles limber. He couldn't wait to throw.

Brennan walked to the bar and put down money for a pitcher of Pabst. The bartender, a big, fat guy with a red face, a heart attack ad, took the empty pitcher and money at the same time. "Again?" he asked, but it was just to make conversation. Brennan nodded. He read the notices posted on the wall while he waited. Need twenty guys to go to a Yankee game, July 7. Need six guys to fill out a bluefish charter, July 23. Legion picnic, July 4. Above the notices the Mets went into the seventh inning. Time for the home team to stretch. Someone down the bar said, "Go, Mets," and another guy said, "The Amazin' Mets," just the way old Casey Stengel used to say it. Brennan listened to it all, feeling good, feeling stiff and brittle, but on top of it. His legs trembled and his back ached; something deep in his left buttock felt strained or pulled. The feeling was okay, almost welcome. A few more beers, and it would be gone, Brennan knew, at least put off until tomorrow. What he wanted to do now was play a couple of games of pool, drink a little more, then head home.

The bartender came back and slid the pitcher to him. "Thanks," Brennan said, and left a fifty-cent tip on the bar. Back at the table he lifted the pitcher over the big white kid and set it in the center. Bonow was saying something about the offense, but no one was paying attention. The big white kid, his name was Webb, kept trying to work BC into the conversation. He wanted to tell everyone who he was. Brennan sat next to him. Webb filled his own glass immediately, then Brennan's.

"You feel like shooting some pool?" Brennan asked Webb. "Just some eightball?"

"Sure. You have any quarters?"

"I think so. Yes, here we go. You want to play?"

Brennan stood. He gave Webb a quarter and let him rack the balls. Brennan went to the wall and selected a cue, rolled it on the table, then chalked it. He used to be a good shot, but now, when he went to break, he miscued and sent the ball off at an angle, the cue ball finally coming to rest against the pack.

"You want to hit them again?" Webb asked.

"No, go ahead. You break them. I'll rack again."

Brennan had just lifted the rack off the table when Webb's ball came, smack, and the balls broke in every direction. Two went in right away, too fast for Brennan to catch their numbers, but Webb stood and came around.

"Stripes," he said. "I got stripes."

"Okay."

"Stripes are highs. You shoot lows."

"Got it."

"I used to play a lot of cue," Webb said, lining up his shot, then snapping it off hard and fast, too hard for a good player. He sank the fifteen, but bounced the cue around until he left himself blocked.

"Tough one," said Brennan.

"Eleven in the side, on the bank."

Webb missed by ten inches. He left Brennan down at the far end of the table, out in the pastures. Brennan lined up his first shot, let his breath out, then tapped. He put in the three, the five, and the four before he missed.

"You throw a nice ball," Webb said, bending to take his next shot. "You don't try to knock a guy's shoulder pads off."

"You catch the ball nice."

"I have pretty good hands. Pretty"—he rammed in the ten—"good, most of the time."

"How did you do the knee?"

"Hit on the line. One guy hit me from one side, the other from the other side. Wham, wham, it went back and forth, and then kapow! the whole thing went out. You could hear it. I screamed my head off."

"They hurt."

"You got a knee?"

"No, I've just seen enough guys. I can sort of imagine."

"You can't imagine," Webb said.

Then the guy who talked like Stengel over at the bar shouted, "It's gone, no way, José, sayonara."

The bartender rang a bell and called, "Strawberry."

"Metsies are amazing," the Stengel guy yelled again.

Webb missed on his last stripe. He left Brennan set up. Brennan knocked in the first two balls smoothly; but then his rhythm deserted him, and he missed the next one by a foot. Webb knocked in his last stripe and sank the eightball on an easy corner shot.

Brennan played four more games with Webb, lost three, but won the last. He said good-bye to Bonow and the other guys at the table. "Webb, see you next time," Brennan called. Then he was out standing in the parking lot of the Garwood Rest, pebbles digging into his soles. His legs were stiffer now. As he climbed into the car, he grunted from the pain in his buttock. He would have to hide it. He had called Linda and said he'd run into Freddy and they were going out for a beer. But he wouldn't be stiff after a beer with Freddy. He figured he'd go to a couple of practices and see what was what before he said anything to her.

At a light he tried to stretch. His buttock contracted on its own and his legs shook. He tried to imagine what he would feel like if he went through a scrimmage or a game. He wouldn't be able to move. Nothing bounced back. Everything now was polishing the furniture—this wasn't new wood. He wondered how the old guys did it, not the Niekros, but the guys like Blanda or Gordie Howe. How did they stay in it so long? It was all will, it had to be. Will and reflexes, but mostly will.

He pulled into the driveway and almost rammed Jason's car. Two heads were caught in his lights, and he watched Kate and Jason pull apart. A library date, nooky afterward. Brennan backed up and let Jason pull down the driveway; then he went past. He put a hand to his lips and blew them both kisses, knowing Kate would die, simply perish, but what else was he supposed to do? He didn't want them to think he was going to be blind to everything. He wanted them to be wary, reluctant to jump out of garments, shaky because they could be caught at any minute. Good American teen-agers.

He had trouble getting out of the car. He stood in the center of the driveway and stretched. Moths stirred around the floodlights in back. The light shone into Linda's garden, and Brennan saw two eyes looking back at him. At first he thought it was a dog, but then he made out the form of a raccoon. It waddled a little farther into the garden and stared at him. It was probably into the tomatoes. It came almost every night, and the only thing Linda did to prevent it was to tie mothballs on some of the cornstalks. The mothballs didn't do any good, but she had read it somewhere in a gardening book and wouldn't let the idea go. The raccoon had a smorgasbord every night, yet there was still enough to feed fifty people. They had tomatoes lined up on all the windowsills and beans frozen in the box downstairs. Acorn squash, peas, lettuce, radishes, everything now went into freezer bags—no more canning; that was a lost art—to sit and wait to be eaten. White bags, frosted and mysterious, labeled by Linda on a piece of adhesive tape. "Lima beans, 1 serving." Survivalists, Mormons, and the McCalmonts, he thought, would be left on the earth together after the big blow.

Brennan went inside, really feeling the beer and the exercise now. Linda was in bed, reading a pamphlet on land taxes. He kissed her hello, then went down the hallway to Michael's room. Louey and Michael were playing Plazmania. It was a game Brennan liked. You had to guide a ship up a blood vein and deliver a shot of adrenaline to the heart patient. As you traveled the heart fribrillated and the EKG started to slip. When you saved someone, "The Stars and Stripes Forever" played. Brennan wondered what the hell Louey thought about it. Louey's own blood wasn't in such great shape. The platelets were failing again, and he had been back to the doctor twice. Everything was slowly kicking into gear, the leukemia coming back in small bruises that spread from the initial bruise Linda had seen on Louey's hip. Louey's eyes were bagged and circled by black, and the strange stiffness had returned to all his joints. He was scheduled for another round of chemotherapy. The salamander was back.

"Drs. Kildare and Casey," Brennan said, sitting on Michael's bed, then lying back. "Almost time for bed."

"Hi, Dad."

"Who's saved more dying patients"

147

"Michael," Louey said.

"The guys at Brown play Plazmania?" Brennan asked. "I want to know if we're going to spend our money on the right kind of education."

"Plazmania is a universal language," Michael said.

"So's pig Latin," Louey said.

Downstairs the door slammed, and Kate called up the landing. "I'm home," she sang.

"Who cares?" Louey and Michael sang together.

Kate came running up the steps. Brennan heard her throw her purse on her bed. She came through the door and said, "Airplane rides."

"No way," said Brennan. "I'm too old."

"You are not."

She climbed on the bed and stood at the bottom. He lifted his legs and put his feet on her hips. They were wide hips now, a woman's hips. He felt the bones under his toes, but she leaned forward and grabbed his hands. "Ready?" she asked. "One, two, three . . ." Then she jumped forward, and he took her weight on his legs, her hands linked in his. She made a flying sound in the back of her throat and pretended to zoom down and change direction.

"Airport control, airport control, we can no longer support you," Brennan said in a pinched voice. But he held her, swooshing her around, the Silver Bullet in August at the start of football season.

Everything about the place was expensive. That's what Brennan thought as he walked down the hall of the Providence Ramada Inn to collect ice cubes. Brown was already costing him money. Eighty bucks a night for a double. You could buy the sheets for eighty bucks. You could buy a new mattress and hire guys to drag it upstairs for eighty bucks. For the eighty you got to walk around searching for ice cubes, nobody served anything anymore, and watch a huge color TV that didn't come in half the time unless you stood with your foot on the trash can and used your body as a conductor. Brennan had watched a tight game between the Yankees and Red Sox that way, touching the trash can each time a pitcher threw the ball, while Linda lay on the bed and read a thriller. Eighty bucks! Brennan dug in the ice machine and came up with flecks of frost on his forearms, the bucket full. He headed back down the hall, a headache beginning. He thought once about calling off the dinner with Michael, telling him they would stop and say good-bye tomorrow, but that wouldn't do. There had to be one last festivity to the tune of sixty or seventy bucks; then they'd let Michael go off to his dorm while they came back and slept. Brown was expensive. The whole place was expensive as hell.

He backed through the door with the ice bucket out and passed Linda, who stood in front of the long mirror on the bathroom door adjusting her make-up. The bathroom smelled a bit of dope. "Bar's open," he said, and carried the bucket to the queer little table they had next to the window. Brennan hated tables like that. All the brochures had men in business suits sitting around these tables, yellow notepads out, a plastic bronze-colored coffeepot at their elbow, apparently holding a conference. Didn't the business have an office? is what Brennan always wanted to ask. Didn't they have anyplace better to talk over deals? Besides, the chairs they gave you were like sit-up boards, you had to keep your stomach tensed the whole time if you wanted to reach the paper, but who noticed in the brochures? The guys would talk with these congested voices, squeaking at each other, turning red or huffing big sighs and falling back in the chairs.

"Is the scotch open?" asked Linda, leaning close to the mirror and doing something to her eyes.

"It will be in a second."

"I still can't believe we're old enough to have a son entering college."

"I still can't believe we're expected to pay."

"What's money for if not this?"

"It's for my retirement," Brennan said, sitting and twisting off the cap of the scotch. He poured two fingers of booze in each glass. "It's for me to play golf for the last ten years of my life."

"Oh, you're just being cranky," Linda said, dabbing her eyelashes.

"Nothing about fifteen scotches won't help. I tell you, though. This is some racket these Ivy League schools have going. I mean, can their education be that much better? Is that really it? I think the whole thing's connections. They grab a bunch of the most talented kids, throw stuff at them for four years. Then they let them loose on the world and the kids go on to do all sorts of wonderful things and the school gets the credit for it. The way it pays off is that you have a contact with the other kids, so that if Billy becomes a lawyer, you can call him up and get a job, too, or find out where they're putting in a new road. . . . It kills me."

"You're jealous. You went to an average school, so you're jealous."

"I went on scholarship. I didn't cost anyone anything."

"Rah, rah."

"I played football. I count that as working my way through college. On today's market a football scholarship's worth around thirty thou. Christ, it's about fifty thou at Brown."

Linda came over and picked up her drink. The mascara pencil clinked against the glass. She lifted a toast. "To Michael. We saw him well launched," she said.

"I'll say."

Linda took a drink and he followed. She touched his shoulder for balance, her stockinged right foot coming up to rest on her left calf. A flamingo.

"Are you really grumpy? Is the money really bothering you, sweetheart?"

"I don't know."

"He might get some help. The dean even said so."

"It's the Ivy stuff, too, a little. It makes me want to brag about being working class or something. I don't know. It's silly. I want to shock some of the people around here, and then I realize it's just defensiveness. I keep thinking these people don't deserve it. They're the only ones with all the cards, and they get to keep the pot too."

"Michael's not like that."

"No, but maybe he'll become like that."

"You worried you're losing him, honey?" she asked, and bent to kiss his cheek. "Is that what's behind all this? Honey, they all leave."

"I know."

"Michael's done the most with his talents. He's a very talented boy."

"I know."

"Don't worry about the money. We're okay. It's going to be tight, but we'll get along. I'm just sorry I'm so slow getting started with the real estate."

"I'd rather you spent the time with Louey."

"That's what I thought. It will work out, believe me."

Brennan shrugged. Linda kissed him once more and went back to the mirror. As he sat in his chair and watched her, he had half a notion to throw her down on the bed, just tumble her, and dive in. Panty hose, bra, slip, maybe a teddy. He liked dressing a woman down, stripping her bare, pulling at cloth. That cloth got to you, you couldn't resist, it was all so female. He wanted to wade into the underwear, strap a bra over his head like a pilot's helmet, rub his cheek against her slip. It always happened this way. You were hit by passion when you had two minutes before stepping out the door, and then you had to explain to your wife that it was the whole preparation, the whole ritual that had excited you. How nice to rip it all apart, to get inside. The Prince of Playtex.

He knocked back one drink, had another short one, then stood as Linda came back out of the bathroom.

"Ready?" she asked.

"All set."

"Listen, honey," she said, moving across the room and putting her arms around him. "Don't worry. Enjoy this last night. Your son is going off to college. This is it."

"I will."

"Promise me?"

"Sure."

"Okay, let's go. Michael will be waiting."

He drove through Providence, down Benefit Street past RISD, then up the hill onto the Brown campus. He spotted the college green to his left, just where he had expected to find it. It was a beautiful green, he had to admit that. You expected Fred MacMurray to come hopping out at you with some sort of sweater and elbow patches, the newest batch of Flubber under his arm. As Brennan parked the car, he saw students hustling across the green, cold already or maybe only hurrying to get to the cafeteria. They could have been going to a sock hop, or a pep rally, the place was that quaint. You get what you pay for, Brennan thought. That was the truth.

He held Linda's arm as they walked across the green. Brennan had to stop once to reconnoiter. There was a chapel, a student union, and down below it all a statue of Marcus Aurelius. He took the left cross where the sidewalk came together, hoping it led up to the dorm. They weren't even halfway to the building when Michael came to meet them, probably ashamed, Brennan thought, to let anyone know he had parents.

"You fit right in here," Linda said, kissing Michael. "I would have walked right past you."

"This place is really neat," Michael said, stepping back, his preppy tie already skewed just enough to make him look like a Kennedy. "The dorms are great. My roommate is this black guy from Chicago. He's really sharp."

"What's his name?" Linda asked, taking Michael's arm and walking between her two men. Her two men. Brennan knew that thought was in her mind, but what the hell, why shouldn't it be?

"His name is Johnny. He's neat."

"What's he do that's so neat?" asked Brennan. "Has he taught you to break-dance yet?"

"No, right now we're just up to talking about offing Whitey, Dad. Break dancing is second semester."

"Make sure you learn how to spin on your head and pick out the best cardboard. You're going to have to work sometime. Maybe you can spin on your mortarboard at graduation."

Brennan felt Linda squeeze his arm. What the hell, Brennan thought. It was just money. He tried to let his body relax. He took a few deep breaths. It was New England air. It smelled of granite and pine and maybe the scent of old leaves raked into a wool blanket. For a second he smelled the Deerfield River, the coolness under the birches as he sat beside them, waiting for the evening hatch. He pictured the first

152

trout coming up, puckering the water, lipping the duns, and diving back down into the wedge of the current. He liked to fish in the evening with the insects thick, the fish quick and hungry before nightfall, the air turning soft and the sound of houses up and down the river closing into night. But the house, of course, was gone. He thought of that as they crossed the middle of the green, stopping once to admire the tall spire of the chapel against the autumn moon. "Beautiful," Linda said, but his house was gone, the $43,000 already pared down to thirty-one. Twelve thousand dollars, what was that, a roof, a porch, maybe a new basement? It was slipping away, that was the thing. Once you turned property into capital, it was too easy to spend. When you knew you had it, you smeared it around, but a house would have stayed there, his memories in the wood and dampness, his whole boyhood floating by on the river.

Brennan let Michael help Linda into the car; then he drove them all back down Benefit, past RISD. He worked his way out to the Providence River, caught a glimpse of the building downtown that looked exactly like the *Daily Planet*, then pulled into a sort of mall area being renovated along the shoreline. The buildings were all brick, with names in colonial gold etched into burnt wood placards. The Gupper, the Blarney Stone, the Middle Way. On a tip from one of the tour guides at Brown, Brennan had made a reservation at the Blarney Stone. Now, as he led Michael and Linda to the restaurant, he heard the wail of Irish fiddling and a microphone flare wide with static. Opening the door, he smelled smoke and congestion and burgers.

"Faith and begorra," Brennan said, "it's a little piece of the old sod."

"Three under the name of McCalmont," Linda told the hostess who greeted them at the door.

It was the kind of place Brennan didn't like, but in which he felt comfortable. Walking behind the hostess in single file, Brennan brought up the rear. Behind him the fiddling started once more, this time riddled with a penny flute. Brennan watched a few people begin to tap their tables, others begin nodding. Everyone was heading out to sea, heigh-ho, and a pint of rum for every man. Brennan wondered how you danced to this kind of music. Maybe a jig or the sort of thing where you licked your fingers and slapped your heels. Actually it was the kind of music that made you want to pull a rope with fifteen other guys, but here in Providence, Rhode Island, there wasn't much to swashbuckle about.

"Your waiter tonight is Mark, and here's your menu," the hostess said, moving around the table and placing a menu by each plate. "May I bring you a drink to start with?"

"Two scotch and waters, and what will you have, Michael?" asked Brennan, suspended awkwardly between his chair and a standing position. Somhow he didn't feel he could sit until the hostess left.

"A beer. A Heineken," said Michael.

"You heard the man," Brennan told the hostess.

"Enjoy your meal," she said, and went off, the sea chantey making her appear to roll with the ship. She hadn't even asked Michael for proof of age.

Brennan took his napkin and flattened it across his lap. He wanted a piece of bread with butter, but it wasn't on his diet. He was at playing weight, a veteran of five practices with the Red Oaks, one of Bonow's offensive coordinators.

"So tell us about the dorms. Did you settle in okay?" asked Linda.

"Oh, it's better than I thought it would be. The rooms are pretty cool . . . well, you saw them, you know. And Johnny's got an amazing stereo with about six crates of records. He's really neat."

"I'm glad you hit it off," Linda said.

"I was worried at first, you know, him being black and everything; but he told some jokes right away, and he said he was shocked to find so many whites at Brown. He's got a good perspective on it. I don't mean like he had a disease. I just mean he knows he's black in a white place."

"Do you have everything you need?" Linda asked.

"I need to pick up some stuff, but I can do that tomorrow. I forgot my deodorant and things."

"We could go out after dinner."

"No, that's okay. There's a grocery store right down the street, someone said. Out on Angell Street. It's no big deal."

Mark, the waiter, came with the drinks. He introduced himself, served the drinks around, then stepped back and said, "Can I tell you about tonight's specials?" Without waiting for an answer, he went down a long list with lots of sauces. Linda asked him to back up once or twice. Mark explained the white sauce on the baked Boston scrod, and finally disappeared, rolling back to the galley with the rest of the swabbies.

After he was gone, Brennan realized Linda was waiting for him to make a toast. Michael must have been aware of it, too, because he was pretending to look around the bar, stretching a little in his seat to glimpse the band. Brennan raised his eyebrows and made a little pout with his lips, trying to see if Linda would lay off, but she nodded slightly in Michael's direction. Brennan reached for his glass and suddenly felt off-balance. He wondered what you said at moments like these. Keep it light, he thought, never a borrower or a lender be. But at the same time he saw Michael look at him, his father, and he realized it all was there, all the father-son feeling that had ever been between them.

"To Michael, my son," Brennan said, lifting his glass, his breathing hard, his face heated. "You've made me very, very proud of you."

Brennan touched his glass to Michael's, then to Linda's, and finally reached across the table and hugged Michael. "I love you," he whispered to Michael. He kissed the boy's cheek once, twice, afraid to let him go. Good-bye, my baby, he wanted to say. Don't forget me.

Brennan knew he looked good in the Bermudas he had chosen. They were tight around the waist, a little flared in the legs. They were made of khaki, ordered from L. L. Bean or Patagonia, one of those outdoor places, and they made him feel like Rommel. With his Lacoste shirt, his stomach flat, his legs in running trim, he felt good. No, he felt great, better than he had in years. Bending to put more beer in the big ice tub next to the liquor table, he no longer felt his belly hang like an opossum sac. No more Crisco, fat in the can. No more anything but muscle and fiber and a fucking fighting machine. You could sweat off years, that was the amazing thing. He wanted to squat around a fire like a Bushman and head off over the Sahel for game. He imagined he could trot all day, stopping only to drink water out of an ostrich shell, or a gourd, or a goat bladder; he could taste the heat and dust in the water.

He threw three more beers into the big tub, flicked some water at McGregor, then gave the backyard one more look. It was okay. Linda had given her garden a trim, and it looked like a kid with a crew cut—clean and sharp. The rest of the yard was as good as it got. He had cut the lawn, edged the flower beds, hacked off a few dead branches on some of the maples in back, and set up the bar. The bar was a white tablecloth over a card table, but the booze was there: two bottles of scotch, gin for that Lilly with the cigarette voice, a few bottles of white wine, more in the kitchen, a half gallon of vodka, orange juice, mixers, and beer. If people wanted something else, they could screw themselves. There was enough there to get everyone blasted. Besides, it was a perfect night, absolutely perfect. Rain wasn't even a possibility. Seventy-five degrees, a breeze puffing up sometimes, enough to get the women in sweaters. He had staked out the giant Roman torches Linda had inherited from her mother. They were shoulder-high pots on metal poles. Their smoke was heavy and black, like heat coming off asphalt, but they shed light and killed bugs. Even now, surveying the yard, he saw a few moths flash up in flame. He thought of those Indian women who threw themselves on their husbands' pyres—what was that called?—in a final act of love and devotion. Suttee, or sutrea, something like that. Linda would know, he thought. He made a mental note to ask her.

He crossed the lawn and went up the back stairs, careful as he came through the door not to disturb the caterers. The caterers were three women, all of them around thirty, who had been through divorces and ended up in a kitchen together, making hors d'oeuvres. At least that was the rumor, and Brennan believed it. Now, as he entered, two of them looked up with hopeful eyes, while the other had something sizzling and half on fire next to the stove.

"You're really cooking," Brennan said. It was ridiculous, he knew, but he felt funny about having these women working for him. He wasn't paying them much, since they were new at the game, thankful for whatever work they got.

"It got a little hot," the woman at the stove said.

"Please help yourselves to anything you need or want. This is just friends."

"Thank you," one of the other women said. She was very pretty, in a thin, tired way, and Brennan had to catch himself before he invited them all to the party.

"Do you need anything?" he asked.

"Not right now, thanks."

"Okay. I'm going to hook up the music. Any requests?"

"Just pretty," the thin, tired one said. "No slam dancing."

"You've got it," Brennan told her, pleased to be flirting and the sun still up. He went into the living room and moved the two stereo speakers to the window fronting the backyard. He balanced them against the screen. It wouldn't be great stereo, with everything coming from one place, but he just wanted to drift the music over them anyway. He selected an old Glenn Miller record, a collection of his greatest hits Brennan had sent for one night when he saw the ad on TV, and put the needle down. Immediately the wonderful trumpet started playing, a song Brennan had heard a thousand times but had no name for, and Brennan danced slowly around the living room, his right hand on his belly, his left out to hold his partner's hand. The music made him think of World War II, and he pictured himself dancing with a beautiful blond British girl, her hair up in a net, her blue suit patriotic and faintly frumpy. Maybe he was a pilot, wearing a leather fly jacket, and this was it, shove-off time, a last dance before another raid on Germany. The trumpet played, and he kept dancing, the smells of the backyard soft and warm. Summer was over tonight.

When the record switched to "In the Mood." he went upstairs to hustle Linda along. She was dressing in front of the mirror. She wore a peach sundress from Laura Ashley, which made her look sweet and innocent and not quite real. He wondered if she had already smoked her joint. She turned when he came in and said, "You can't wear the Bermudas."

"Why not?"

"Too informal. Why don't you wear your Brooks Brothers slacks?"

"I'll look like every other guy here, that's why. I look like Rommel in these."

"Like Rommel? The Suburban Fox, Brennan McCalmont. It's too informal."

"I thought there was a rule the hostess could wear anything she wants. Can't the host?"

"No, the host has to wear anything the hostess says. That's the real rule."

"They really look bad?" Brennan asked, moving next to her in the mirror. They looked good to him, but he could see what she meant. "I think they look boss."

"They look like you should be carrying a riding crop."

"What's wrong with that? I think that's okay."

He went to his closet, pulled out the Brooks Brothers khakis, and shucked his Bermudas. He put on the khakis, pleased at how they fit his tighter waist. Below him, the music switched to "Chattanooga Choo-Choo."

"How are the caterers getting along? Much better," she said, looking at him, then back to the mirror.

"They're doing okay. One of them had a frypan on fire when I went through the kitchen."

"I'm glad we could give them work."

"So am I. They look so beaten, though. I'm afraid they're going to cry if their canapés don't come out right."

"They'll be fine. It's a new trend. A lot of women are starting their own businesses. They're using what they know. It's smart, I think."

"I should get downstairs. People might start showing up. It's almost six."

"What's it like outside?"

"Still warm. Sweater weather later on. It should be a pretty party. Will you dance with me later?"

"Are you on my card?"

"Put me on, okay?"

Outside again, he grabbed a beer from the ice bucket and popped the top. He strolled next to the garden, checking the last growth. Everything was a little gone now, the peppers wrinkled, the tomatoes picked apart by birds, the wire fans of beans toppled and bent. The pumpkins, though, were shooting out through the lawn. Linda had nipped back some of the smaller gourds so that a big one at the end of each vine would become larger. It had worked, and now the garden was pumping its last energy into the pumpkins, fattening them up for October.

He was still by the garden when Phil and Margaret Dedich came up the driveway. He heard Margaret's heels but pretended to be absorbed by the pumpkins, allowing them the drop on him. He looked up finally and waved his beer. Phil Dedich had on a pair of Brooks Brothers pants identical to his own.

"You're loyal friends to be the first ones here," Brennan said, walking across the lawn to meet them. "Happy Labor Day."

"God, you're looking fit," Phil said. "You look great."

"I feel great. Hi, Margaret."

Brennan kissed Margaret's cheek and shook Phil's hand. Margaret wore too much make-up.

"Let me get you something to drink," Brennan said. "We've got everything set up out here."

"I'm going to run in and see if Linda needs anything; then I'll be out," Margaret said, then leaned close to whisper in Brennan's ear. "How are the caterers?"

"They seem okay. I haven't tasted anything yet."

"I've got a story about them. I'll tell you later."

"Okay. Linda's upstairs. You know the way," Brennan said to Margaret as she went inside. "Phil, you want a beer?"

"No, I'm going to drink some scotch. You have enough?"

"I've got loads of the stuff. You want it with a little water?"

"Just ice."

Brennan put ice in a glass, splashed in some scotch, and handed it back to Phil. Phil raised his glass.

"Jesus, your yard looks nice," said Phil, taking a drink. "I've got some sort of blight on mine . . . brown spots and this spider mite stuff, or something. You got to keep up the land for the resale."

"You thinking of selling?"

"No, but I've played around with the idea of putting the house on the market at a big price and seeing if anyone bites. I got a guy at work who's done that with his last three houses. He had takers every time."

"But you've got to keep moving," Brennan said, taking a little more beer.

"So? You get ahead enough and you can buy another house, an extra house. That's how empires are made."

"How come everyone I talk to knows all these tricks and everyone I know is still in my tax bracket?"

"No guts, that's why. I'm the same way. You got to be willing to risk it all. I'm too chicken."

Brennan heard his name called and turned around, expecting people coming up the drive. It was time. But when he looked, no one was there, and it took him a second to see Linda up in the window. "Brennan?" she called again, and this time her voice was worried.

"Linda? What is it?"

"Could you come up here, please?"

"Right now?"

"Right now."

Brennan turned to Phil. "Make sure everyone gets a drink, will you, Phil? I'll be back."

"No problem."

Brennan trotted up the stairs, smiled at the caterers, then took the flight to the second floor two steps at a time. Margaret sat on their bed, a glass of white wine in her hand. Linda had just hung up the phone.

"What is it?" asked Brennan.

"That was Mrs. Kane. Louey wants to come home. Or rather, she thinks he should come home."

"Why?"

"The boys at the sleep-over were being rotten to him. They were on him about his hair. They all ganged up."

"The poor kid," Margaret said.

"It's nothing big. He's just not having a very good time," Linda said. "And I think he's embarrassed to come home because of the party."

"Why would they kid him about his hair?" Brennan asked. "What a group of little pricks."

"They're just kids."

"Before he was sick, he was the fucking star of that group."

"I know, honey. But I think for tonight maybe you'd better run over and get him. Okay? I'll go down now, and Phil and Margaret are here. He's not really with the group over there, and the rest of the night will be pretty rough on him."

"I'll get him," Brennan said.

"The poor baby," Margaret said once more.

Brennan hustled down the steps. He felt sick, and he knew it wasn't something that was just going to pass away. Picked on for his hair. He pulled open the front door and went out that way, not bothering to tell Phil what he was doing. Fuck it, he thought. Fuck the little bastards. What he wanted to do was wring their goddamned necks. Yes, kids were cruel, so maybe you should be cruel back. Who gave them the right, that's what he didn't get. A year ago Louey would have handed them their lunch. Hell, a year ago he was the kingpin, the head guy in his whole age bracket. He had scored fifty-seven points in Little League football, and that was even after the coach had stopped giving him the ball in the fourth quarter. He was unstoppable, the Galloping Ghost of Westfield, Famine, Pestilence, and War.

The Atwaters were pulling up in their gigantic Bronco as Brennan reached his own car. Jim Atwater tapped his horn, and Brennan waved his hand. "Ice," he called. "Be right back." He pulled open his door and kept the windows up, sitting in the heat just so he wouldn't have to say anything else. He pulled away quickly, letting them think he was anxious to get the ice, his tires turning the loose gravel at the edge of the lawn.

He drove down Prospect, over toward Franklin, then took a right onto Effington. The houses all looked the same, wide and tall, with big porches around the bottom floor. He saw a pack of kids running down the street and slowed to see if he could spot Louey, but the kids were too young. He pulled the car to the curb and got out, sweat now pooling in the middle of his back. He didn't know the number. He remembered it was gray, he thought, but he wasn't even sure of that. Gray with white trim. He walked after the kids and caught up with them as they grouped around a four-square board chalked on one of the driveways.

"Which house is the Kanes'?" he asked. "Any of you know?"

"Over there," a little girl said. She pointed. "The gray one."

"Thanks."

Brennan crossed the street. He stopped at the bottom of their steps and took a deep breath. Up on the top floor he heard some kids shouting. More kids yelled out in the backyard, and Brennan remembered this was supposed to be a big sleep-out. Mrs. Kane, a dark, serious-looking woman, came as soon as he rang the bell. She pushed open the screen and gave him a nice smile, a good smile, which tried to say she sympathized.

"Hello, Mrs. Kane, is Louey ready?"

"He's out in the kitchen with me. I'm very sorry."

"Does he know you've called me?"

"Yes. He didn't ask me to, but I thought it was the right thing. He's very upset."

"Okay, thank you. Can I see him?"

Brennan followed her through the dining room. She slowed a little as she came to the kitchen. Then she stepped to one side and Brennan saw Louey. He sat at the kitchen table, looking out. He didn't turn his head when Brennan came into the room.

"Louey?" Brennan said.

Louey nodded but didn't look away from the window. Brennan thought about making up something, pretending to need Louey at home, but decided against it.

"Come on, Louey, let's go home."

Louey stood. He didn't look left or right. He didn't look down either. He walked straight ahead. Brennan saw he had been crying. His cheeks were red and stained.

Mrs. Kane handed Brennan Louey's sleeping bag. "I'm so sorry," she repeated, but Brennan couldn't say anything. He took the bag and put it under one arm and tried to smile. He followed Louey out onto the porch, out into the warm summer evening. He started down the walk after Louey, but then he heard the whistles above him. Brennan looked up. The sun had turned the screens golden, but he could just make out the faces upstairs, the five or six boys' heads pressed together to see out. "Loueeeeeeyy," someone called, and another boy made a kissing sound. A few of the others laughed, and one blew a kazoo to the tune of "Popeye the Sailor Man."

Brennan was about to say something when Louey turned in the center of the yard and gave them both fingers, jabbing them forward and back like pompom guns. He shot them the fingers and started to scream. "Fuckers, fuckers, you fucking bastards," he screamed, spit dripping down his chin. His eyes filled, the veins in his neck standing out like pieces of blue twine. "You fucking bastards, I hate your fucking guts," he shouted, pumping his fingers at them, while the boys upstairs made a big wooooooo sound and started to laugh. But then Louey screamed again, "You fucking assholes, you fucking assholes," and this time it was hysterical, and even the boys heard the change. They stopped jeering and pulled away from the window, while Louey stood in the center of the yard, his soul empty, his arms open to them.

"Come on, Louey, let's go home," Brennan said, taking a step toward him.

"I hate them," said Louey, but he didn't look at Brennan. "I'll kill them."

"Shhh, let's just get going. They're jerks."

"Fuck them."

"Stop that language."

"Fuck them and fuck you."

"Louey, stop swearing."

Louey turned and went to the car. He climbed in and said nothing as Brennan tossed the sleeping bag into the back seat and started the motor.

Halfway home, Brennan reached over and touched Louey's knee, but Louey jerked away. Brennan left his hand on the seat next to his son's leg. He glanced over several times to see if Louey was crying, but Louey just kept staring out the window.

"Listen," said Brennan, "this party is no big deal. You can go up and watch TV and no one will bother you. I'll come up and see how you're doing a little later."

Louey nodded.

"Those guys don't know any better, that's all," Brennan went on. "They're too immature to understand. Don't start hating them just because they're too young to see things right."

"I'll hate who I want."

"I know."

"I hate them."

"Okay."

"Don't tell me who to hate and who not to."

"Let's just drop it, okay? Sometimes you have to let things go."

"I don't have to. I'm going to kill them."

"Okay."

Brennan parked on the street. The driveway was filled with cars. Louey climbed out as fast as he could and made it to the front door even before Brennan was halfway to the house. Brennan carried the sleeping bag up the front stoop and went into the kitchen.

"You going to get us all to sleep out? Is this a sleep-over?" Pam Samuels asked. She stood by the washing machine, talking to one of the caterers, the dark, matronly one who seemed to be in charge of the cooking. Pam wore a red, halter-necked dress and carried a fizzy drink, probably a GT.

She came over and kissed him, and he smelled gin and suntan lotion. Her skin felt very warm. She had a soft, boneless feeling that made him wonder how many drinks she had already taken.

"I just joined the Boy Scouts," Brennan said.

"And you're prepared for anything?"

"Anything," Brennan said, throwing the sleeping bag into the closet next to the bathroom. "How's the party going? I had to run an errand."

"It's wonderful. A perfect night."

"It filled up, didn't it?" Brennan asked, looking over her shoulder to the backyard. The dimness made the guests' pastel clothes seem brighter. Most of the yard was filled with people.

"Everyone's here. It's the social event of the season," Pam said, her arm slipping around his waist, her right breast punctured on his ribs.

"Did Ed Koch make it?"

"He's around somewhere."

He leaned back a little, using her arm as a backrest, and looked at her. She was tipsy all right. Her eyes were shiny and quietly dazed. Brennan tried to remember if there had been another party before his, an afternoon kickoff, but he couldn't recall one. Maybe she had been to the country club, or maybe she had knocked back a few at home, he didn't know. But looking at her made him conjure up the sauna, and he pictured her suddenly in a white towel, sweat streaming down her shoulders and thighs. Steamed chicken.

"Now, am I imagining it, or is your arm around me pretty tight?" he asked her, his voice low so the caterer wouldn't hear.

"It's pretty tight."

"It feels good."

"It's a night to feel good."

"We hoped everyone would feel good tonight."

"I do."

"Well, listen, write me onto your dance card, will you? I've got to put on more music. Will you dance with me later?"

"Sure I will."

"Fast Freddy won't mind?"

"He's not the possessive type. *Au contraire*."

"What's that mean?" he asked, but she simply moved off, pushing through the screen door. The quick glimpse he got of the yard might have been someone else's party. He heard people talking and saw lamps flickering, but it was like watching a documentary.

"Do you have everything you need?" Brennan asked the caterers.

"We're doing fine in here. Nice party."

"Thanks."

Brennan went into the living room and slipped off the Glenn

Miller. No one had bothered to change the music. He put on a stack of three records. No rock because he hated to see people his age dancing around to rock and roll. He put on Sinatra and Billie Holiday and the sound track from *The Wizard of Oz*. Then, for the hell of it, he put on Dean Martin.

Back in the kitchen, he grabbed himself a beer. He pushed open the screen door, and suddenly a couple of people saw him, turned, and began clapping. Fast Freddy Samuels yelled above everyone else, "I lost, I didn't think he'd show," making Brennan raise his beer and take a bow. The music came on behind him, Frank, the Jersey boy, singing "New York, New York," and Brennan had to fight not to walk down the steps in time to the beat.

"Hi, honey," Linda said, hurrying over. "Is Louey okay?"

"He's all right, I guess. He's upset, though."

Margaret Dedich came over.

"Is he okay?" she asked, just hearing the end of what Brennan had said.

"He's okay. It was bad. The kids were bastards."

"Those hideous little creatures," Margaret said.

"I'll go up and see him," Linda said.

"Maybe you should. But don't push anything on him. If he wants to be alone, let him be."

"Okay."

"Tell him I'll be up later."

"All right."

Linda left, and Margaret slipped her arm through his. "I'm so sorry. Not much of a way to begin a party, is it?"

"No, it wasn't."

"Well, try to cheer up. It's really a lovely party."

"What was the story about the caterers?" Brennan asked, taking a long drink of beer. He didn't really care what the story was, but he wanted Margaret to talk for a while.

"Oh, it's pretty involved," she said, taking a drink. "The good-looking one, the one all the men are flirting with here, she was married to a stockbroker in New York. He was with Sutter and Peabody or one of those firms. I guess he had a seat on the exchange, or something. . . . Anyway, money wasn't a problem."

Jim Atwater came up just then and lifted his glass of scotch at them. "Fine party, Brennan," he said. "How did you get that pumpkin so goddamn big?"

"Wait a second, I'm telling Brennan the scoop of the season," Margaret said.

"The good-looking caterer was married to a stockbroker," Brennan told him. "That's when the commercial came."

"That's right," Margaret said. "Anyway, it looked like a wonderful marriage . . . money, cars, two houses, they had one of those houses up in Maine that wade into the ocean and have screen porches around them."

"Wraparound porch?" Atwater asked.

"Yes, wraparound. And a boat, a sailboat, that had some sort of beautiful name."

"Like the *Daddy Long Legs*," Brennan said.

"Like *Duckmobile*," Atwater said, smiling.

"No, like the *Laura Lee*, or *Enchantment*, or something like that."

"So what's the punch line?" Atwater asked. "We know they're headed for a fall."

"The punch line is that one day this woman, who is now catering Brennan's party, came in to find her husband having tea with another man. The tea wasn't just a tea, though. It was a perfect ladies' tea, and both men were dressed like middle-aged matrons."

"They were what?" Atwater asked, laughing.

"Dressed in conservative suits and hats with lace on the top . . . as I live and breathe, it's the truth," Margaret said, finishing the story quickly, Brennan knew, because she saw them both looking at her. She raised her hand and stared back.

"Scout's honor?" asked Brennan.

"Scout's honor."

"So, let me get this straight. They were having tea and doing what? No hanky-panky?"

"No, I guess that was it. Or maybe it wasn't it. But imagine seeing your husband with his five o'clock shadow underneath one of those little veils. Then, to cap it off, they wanted her to join them."

"For tea?" Brennan asked.

"Yes, for tea."

"You know, my aunt Ruth once answered the door and saw this nun standing there selling Christmas wrapping paper or something, and when she pulled open the door, she realized, just as she was getting ready to open the screen door all the way, that it was a man dressed up in a nun's habit. She just saw the whiskers," Atwater said.

"Nuns have whiskers," Brennan said.

"No, I mean, this guy really had them. He was wearing pancake make-up and probably had a shrunken head under the skirt of his gown."

Linda came down then. She shrugged and came over.

"He's okay," she said. "I think he had a cry, but now he's okay."

"Who had a cry? Is the caterer's husband here?" Atwater asked.

"Don't butt in," Margaret said. "This is serious."

"Louey," Brennan told him, taking a sip of beer.

"Oh, I'm sorry."

"Growing pains," Brennan said. "You want to dance, Linda? Let's get this place hopping."

"Okay."

Brennan walked Linda out onto the lawn and turned her into his arms. It took him a second to adjust to the length of the grass. He felt awkward and had to listen for the music, but he was aware of a few people clapping, a few more couples joining them. Sinatra was singing "My Way," which Brennan could never listen to without feeling he was being conned. He closed the words out of his mind and pulled Linda tight. She seemed tired and a little nervous. He was happy to find he liked dancing with his wife even after twenty years.

"I think you should go up in a little," she said in his ear.

"I will."

"I think he didn't like you seeing it."

"You think that's it?"

"It's everything."

"I guess so."

168

"It's a nice party, though, isn't it?" Linda said. "They all seem to be enjoying themselves."

"It's a great party. Margaret just told me the caterer's story."

"She told me, too. It's a nightmare, isn't it? They wanted her to join in," Linda said.

"No. They wanted her to be a boy. They wanted her to wear a derby."

"Do you know what the caterers are called? Their name? It's Ladies of the Night. Do you think that's a little weird?"

"Maybe a little. It's catchy," Brennan said.

"They're doing a good job, though. Really good."

The music changed, and suddenly the Munchkins were singing about Munchkinland. Brennan hadn't remembered this part, but a few people started laughing.

"Maybe I'll run up," Brennan said.

"Go ahead."

"I'll be right back."

Brennan jogged up the back stoop, took a beer from the refrigerator, then jogged up the rest of the stairs. He passed Kate's room and tapped on Louey's door. The TV was on, tuned to a Yankee game, and Brennan heard Phil Rizzuto shilling for the Money Store. Louey was in his pajamas, lying on top of the bedcovers.

"You settled in?" Brennan asked when he came through the door.

"Yes," Louey said, not taking his eyes from the TV.

"Who's ahead?"

"Yankees by two."

"Who's pitching?"

"Guidry."

"Any homers?"

"Mattingly hit one earlier. Some guy hit one for the Twins."

Brennan sat on the bed and opened his beer. He tossed the ring away in the wastebasket.

"Maybe I'll watch an inning with you," Brennan said, taking a sip.

"You don't have to, Dad. I'm okay."

"I know. I'll watch a half inning."

169

"Yankees are out in the field."

"So, I'll watch Guidry pitch."

Louey was quiet for a second. The commercial ended, and the broadcast came back to the catcher throwing down to second. Brennan watched Guidry get two men on ground balls. The game seemed boring. He took a little more beer, then touched Louey's arm.

"You want to do me a favor?" asked Brennan. "You can't tell Mom."

"What?"

"Give Michael a call tonight."

"What for?"

"Just to see how he's doing. I can't call him on a Friday night like this or he'll get all huffy about us checking on him. Maybe you could just call him and see what classes are like, that sort of thing."

"You really want me to?"

"Sure. Just dial direct. If he's not there, so be it."

"Where's the number?"

"Mom has it in her bedside table. Give him a call after the game if you feel like it."

"Okay."

"His roommate's name is Johnny."

"Okay."

"I've got to get downstairs."

"All right."

"You hungry?"

"No."

"Okay," Brennan said, and stood. He went out the door without saying anything else. He drank most of his beer going back to the party.

Brennan sat in the car, waiting for Louey and thinking about Lourdes. The idea had come to him a few days ago while he was at work, and he hadn't been able to get rid of it since then. Whenever he closed his eyes, he had the image of a small girl and boy standing on a hillside, the Virgin Mary appearing above a bush. Dig here, Mary had said. And with the whole village standing behind her, the little girl had dug and a spring had come up through the soil. Brennan remembered that part best, he didn't know why, but he had to admit now it didn't seem so far-fetched. Hollywood or not, people still claimed miracles. Last night he had gone into Michael's empty room and taken out a map of France and spent a half hour trying to spot Lourdes. He had found Paris and Chartres and Lyons, Dijon, Marseilles, and Bordeaux, but either Lourdes wasn't listed or it was in another country. He looked up the town in the index, but the book was a world atlas and didn't have Lourdes. He had come close to bringing it up with Linda. He had wanted to carry the atlas in to Linda and sit with her on their bed, going through the names, maybe dividing France into quarters and examining each section bit by bit. If he could just look at the town on a map, he thought, maybe he would have some feeling about it. He used to do that as a kid. He used to look at maps of Canada and imagine what it would be like to have a cabin way up there, up where there were still endless lakes and moose and perhaps even caribou. But this was different. At work he had called TWA and asked for the price of a round-trip ticket to Paris, just to see, and the woman had told him it was $970. That made it close to $2,000 just for air fare for both of them, plus you had to add on whatever it cost to take a train or bus to Lourdes. Figure $3,000 when it was all done, there and back, which wasn't much if miracles really happened. That wasn't anything.

He was still thinking about it when Louey came out, wearing his sweats and a big Windbreaker. He also wore a wool cap with a N.Y. Giants emblem to cover his head. He was losing hair again. He walked down the steps in that same awkward manner, turning to go down sideways, his legs weak, his balance shot. The remission was ended, gone with summer, and watching Louey now, Brennan wondered how they had ever believed in it. Dr. Breisky had Louey scheduled for another session of chemotherapy in a week.

Louey climbed into the car, struggling with the door. Brennan wanted to reach across and hold it open for him, but he forced himself to leave it alone.

"Where we going anyway?" Louey asked as soon as he was inside.

"You'll see."

"I don't feel like going anywhere."

"You'll like this, believe me."

Brennan didn't say anything more. Louey leaned against the door. At a stoplight in Scotch Plains Brennan looked over and thought Louey was asleep, but Louey smiled a little and looked the other way. It was Saturday, and the streets were filled with people shopping.

"Are we going to a store or something?" asked Louey.

"No, you'll see."

"I hate shopping."

"So do I."

"Not as much as I do."

"Quit being so sour. I said I'd show you something you'd like."

"But you're making such a big deal of it."

"Hey, Louey, relax, would you?"

Louey looked out the window again.

Brennan turned into the parking lot behind Plainfield and slid in beside Bonow's junked-up Datsun. A few guys were dressing under the bleachers. Bonow stood in the center with boxes of equipment spread all around him. Helmets and shoulder pads, pants. The pads for the pants were littered on the grass like bones. Brennan waved to Webb, who was digging through a box of some kind.

"What's this?" Louey said, not lifting his head. Brennan knew Louey was curious but didn't want to show it.

"My team. The Plainfield Red Oaks."

"Are you serious?"

"We've only had about five full practices. We've got a scrimmage today."

"And you're playing?"

"Why not?"

"Aren't you a little old?"

"George Blanda played when he was older than me."

"Yeah, but that was for money and stuff."

"It's just for fun. I just wanted to play a little more."

Louey lifted his head. Brennan suddenly thought maybe this was a bad idea. Maybe it was unfair to play when Louey couldn't. Besides, he didn't want Louey to think he was being brought along to be a mascot or a water boy or any sort of crap like that. Brennan didn't know why he had brought him along exactly, but it wasn't to be an inspirational little sidekick. If it was anything, it was just that Brennan wanted to show Louey what it was like to play. He figured if he could just have a good series, maybe a whole quarter of playing well, that would be enough. If he could do that, he would quit right then.

"I've got to get dressed," said Brennan. "You're on your own. I just thought you might like to watch."

"How long have you been doing this?"

"Since we got back from the shore. August or so. Your mom knows, but I didn't tell you kids because I wasn't sure I was going to stick with it. I figured you'd kid me, too. Come on out and watch if you feel like it."

Brennan climbed out, wondering what he would do if Louey decided just to sit in the car. He crossed to the bleachers. "There he is, there he is," Bonow said, waving and pointing to the equipment all around him. Bonow wore a bright white pair of pants but no jersey. He smoked a cigar in a bone holder. He smelled like the racetrack.

"You guys are serious about this scrimmage, aren't you?" Brennan asked. "I mean, you're going to go through with it."

"Why the hell not?" Bonow asked, laughing.

"Just wondering. You have any quarterback shoulder pads there?"

"Is a quarterback asking?"

"Where's Lenny?" Brennan asked, looking around for the young kid who played quarterback ahead of him. "Is he going to show?"

"Who knows? I was going to put old Webb in for a quarterback. Bet he could throw."

"Damn straight," Webb said, trying on helmets. The one he had on had a face mask gridded for a linebacker or lineman.

Brennan dug in the box next to Bonow and came up with a pair of pants that had a "36" inked on the waistband. He took knee pads and thigh pads, stuffed them into the slots, then pulled the pants on over his gym shorts. The pants clung to his legs, and the pads dug in a little; but they felt good. His legs felt solid in the pants. He lifted his legs a couple of times and pounded the pads with his fists.

173

"Is that your boy in the car?" Bonow asked.

"Yes. His name's Louey."

"Tell him to come on out."

"He's been sick."

"Is it okay for him to be out? Good fresh air won't hurt him."

"He'll come out when he wants to."

Bonow kept looking over at the car. Webb looked over too, his horny face mask birdlike. Fleming and Glass trotted around the corner of the bleachers. They both were backs, both black, and too good really to be playing with the rest of the squad. They were already dressed in the red and white jerseys and wore helmets that seemed to fit. Glass had a mouthpiece that dangled from the lower bar of his face mask. They both had their ankles taped, the tape worn like spats over the top halves of their shoes.

"What's happening?" Fleming asked Bonow. "We playing this tilt or not?"

"We're playing. We start cal at two."

"It must be two already," Glass said.

"Quarter of."

Brennan found a small pair of shoulder pads next to Webb and laced them up. They fit okay, almost too tightly, but he practiced throwing and found they gave his arm enough room. He wondered whether he should put on rib pads, then decided against it. That was a new thing, rib pads, and he didn't think he would be comfortable with them. You could only bundle yourself up so much. He found a helmet that fit on his first try. It was a seven and a quarter. It had a halfback's face mask on the front, with a little loop between the eyes to keep anyone from wedging a forearm inside. All he needed now was a jersey, and he asked Bonow what number he could have.

"Whatever you like. We got single digits, we got the teens. What do you want?"

"You have fourteen?"

"Fourteen?" Bonow asked, bending to dig in the box. "Is that a fourteen or sixteen? Fourteen," he said, yanking out a shirt. "There you go, sports fans."

"I was always number fourteen in everything."

174

"You and about a thousand other guys. Try it on, see if it fits. Go ahead."

Brennan shrugged the jersey over his head, then turned to let Bonow pull it over his shoulder pads. He buttoned the tail under his crotch and pulled up his pants once more. He felt clamped together and tight. He smacked his shoulder pads a couple of times and looked over to see if Louey was watching. Louey looked away. Maybe, Brennan thought, he looked ridiculous standing there in a uniform. Maybe it was all wrong. But he felt he had to go through with it, at least for one day, at least until he was sure Lenny would show up. It wouldn't be fair to the other guys to leave right now, and besides, it felt good, he felt right being in a uniform again. It didn't go away so easily. That was a lie. The skill left, maybe the body slipped; but that feeling, the sense of being about to go into a game, stayed with you. Even now, standing behind the bleachers, Bonow still smoking, Brennen felt nervous. The Silver Bullet, Brennan McCalmont, forty-two years old.

"You're a fighting unit, Pops," Bonow said. "You're a piece of fighting material."

"I think my boy over there thinks I look absurd."

"So? Kids always think you look absurd. What do you think they look like? Do what you want, that's what I say. It's your life, too."

"You got a helmet that fits?" Webb called over. "I've tried on every damn thing here."

But Bonow didn't answer. He took a couple of steps toward the car and shouted to Louey, "Hey, kid, your dad's out here risking his life, and you're sitting in the car like a sissy. Get out here."

Louey shook his head.

"He's got leukemia," Brennan said quietly.

Bonow looked at him, nodded, then began walking over to the car. Brennan almost told him to stop but then decided to stay out of it. He trotted around the bleachers, looking back when he got to the other side. He couldn't see much except Bonow leaning on the car, his cigar sending up a puff of smoke every now and then.

Brennan pumped his legs a couple of times, trying to get them loose. A few guys yelled over, but in their helmets and uniforms he wasn't sure who they were. Everyone had a great build in football uniforms—wide shoulders, narrow hips, muscular legs. He recognized Mussman, the center, and Glenon, the tackle. The rest of the guys he knew just by their shapes. He nodded to everyone, still looking for Lenny.

A whistle went off, and Brennan jogged into the end zone for calisthenics. He lined up behind two other backs, guys who had shown up only at the last practice. Mussman led the exercises. That was good because he was too out of shape himself really to kill them. Brennan did fifteen jumping jacks in unison with the others. Then he fell on his stomach and did twenty push-ups, twenty sit-ups, and a minute or two of neck bridges.

He had a sweat going by the time they were done with cal. When Bonow came around from behind the bleachers, Brennan expected Louey to be somewhere behind him. Louey wasn't around, but as Bonow jogged closer, he made the okay sign to Brennan. Brennan opened his hands to ask what it was, but then Bonow shouted and called them all together. He told them they were going to scrimmage only for a short time, just enough to get them used to hitting again. He didn't want anyone twisting an ankle to bring down a ball-carrier. No crack back blocks, no excessive cut blocks. Stay off people's legs. When he finished, there was a little yelling from some of the guys. Brennan jogged over to Bonow.

"Did you talk to him?" Brennan asked.

"Yeah, he's just having a little cry. He'll be out."

"Is he okay?"

"Like I said, just a little cry. You get ready. He wants to see his dad play."

"Did he say that?"

"Fucking ball have to hit you between the eyes? Go ahead and warm up. You're our quarterback today."

Brennan looked at Bonow once more, then jogged off to throw with Webb.

"Where's this Lenny kid?" Brennan asked Webb when he found him. Webb had a ball and was tossing it up in a lazy spiral. The helmet Webb had finally found was too small for him. It fit way up on his forehead.

"Someone said he quit. He didn't feel like playing."

"Christ, I don't want to be the only quarterback."

"Looks like you are."

"A team can't have just one quarterback anyway. I could get hurt."

Webb shrugged. Dressed in his uniform, Webb looked intimidating. He was six-four or five and probably weighed about 240. His face mask was too gridded for a tight end, but Webb didn't seem to mind.

"You want to throw?" asked Webb.

"For a few minutes anyway."

Webb backed off, and they played catch. A few women had moved into the stands, collected there in bright afghans next to plaid thermoses. Brennan looked for Louey but didn't see him. He didn't think Louey could be sitting in the car still. That wasn't like Louey. Then, just as he was thinking this, he finally saw Louey way up in the stands, a small blue spot on the visitors' side. Brennan waved, but Louey made no sign of recognition.

A whistle blew, and Brennan heard Bonow's voice. "Let's get this going. First offense, over there. First defense, down here."

"Who the hell's first offense and defense?" someone yelled, but the group broke into two fairly even packs. Brennan jogged after the the offensive group, still looking for Lenny.

"We're going to run a series now. It's going to be live. Remember again, take it easy on people's legs. Some of us aren't as young as we used to be," Bonow yelled.

That was it. Brennan looked around once more, checking to make sure he was the only quarterback. No one told him he was first string, no one said he was the man, but who else was there? He suddenly felt very sick and nervous. He knew the plays well enough, probably better than most of the guys, but he had no real feeling for the offense. It was a pro set, with a flanker wide, a split end, and two set backs. That was just the basic formation. From there you could move the halfback, set him out twins right or left, flex him with the tight end, send the fullback out on a curl at the linebacker, go balanced or unbalanced right or left. Brennan decided right away he wouldn't call anything fancy. He looked at Bonow, who was struggling into a pair of enormous shoulder pads. Bonow said in a voice choked by the pads, "You're the man, Pops."

"Where's Lenny?"

"He may not show. He's a little bit of a prima donna. We got another kid who's going to come next week. Just keep it simple today."

"Okay."

Brennan called Mussman over to him and took a few snaps. Mussman had a big, soft can, the good kind for quarterbacks. It was easy to ride Mussman with the back of his hands, taking the ball smart on his top right hand. He took five snaps, getting the feel of Mussman's first steps. You had to get along with your centers, and most of them that Brennan knew were just like Mussman. Big and strong and faithful. Except for quarterbacks, Brennan always found centers to be the smartest players on the field.

"Okay, okay, let's go," Bonow yelled, finally fully dressed. His stomach was flabby under the jersey, but he still looked strong. His neck was muscled. He wore a white neck collar under his helmet, which made him even more streamlined. He looked like a torpedo.

Brennan stepped into the huddle. It was an old feeling. He saw the eyes of a lineman look at him, and there it was suddenly, the feeling of being a quarterback. Being in a huddle always reminded him of being in a stable, and he thought of the linemen as thick-sided cattle, their eyes lazy and calm. He spit in his hands and rubbed them together. "Back right, flanker right, forty-seven boom, on two," he said, and looked up to see Bonow nod. Brennan repeated the call; then there was a loud clap, and the huddle broke. Someone whistled, and one of the linebackers across from him yelled, "Flanker right, flanker right," and a cornerback called, "Robber, robber." The defense had little red pinnies over their jerseys, and Brennan took a second to see how they were set up. Gap defense, or at least it looked that way, the cornerbacks probably in a zone. "Here we go, baby," someone shouted, and someone else said, "Fucking A." The offense line stood with hands on knees until Brennan put his hands under Mussman's wide ass. "Down," he said, and the line went down into its stances. "Hut, hutt-hutt," Brennan yelled, and then the ball was up in his hands and he moved back and away, turning slightly and bringing the ball into his left hand. Smooth, he thought, a matador; but he had gone back too far, or Glass had come in too tight, and Brennan had to dodge away and slap the ball awkwardly into Glass's stomach. Pulling away, Brennan felt his shin swack against Glass's shin, but Glass kept moving. Brennan brought his hands up high, continuing a roll-out fake, and watched Glass cut in behind someone's block and squeeze through for about two yards. Glass gave a second burst once he was hit and scrambled forward for two more yards, a shout going up among the guys stand around. "Good second effort, good effort," someone yelled, and Brennan brought his hands down, his shin forgotten, the smell of dust and sweat and mouthpieces still fresh after all these years.

Riding in the nonsmoking car on the old CNJ, the industrial waste around Newark slowly disappearing, Brennan closed his eyes and pictured his old house, the $43,000 boiled down to $31,000. Spring ahead, fall back. Michael had a job at the local movie house, taking tickets, but there were still books, still recreation, still beer. Kate needed dresses, back to school clothes, she was a girl, it was important to her, and Louey needed all his medical stuff, his prescriptions and special pills that seemed to pile up in amber pyramids inside the medicine cabinets. It was all supposed to be covered, of course, but it never was. They always found a way to milk you a little, ten bucks here, five percent of the costs there, nickels and dimes. The money went; there was no stopping it. It got so you couldn't do anything, couldn't order an extra beer at lunch, without thinking of what it cost. He could see figures in his checkbook, the balance dwindling, the dull black numerals on his calculator shrinking to zero. He wondered again whether he should have sold the house. Lately he had felt like a traitor. You don't just sell places that mean something to you. Besides, even with the money from the house, he wasn't sure they could swing college and medicine and everything else. It probably would have been better, he thought, to do what he had first imagined doing with the money—plunk it down on a painting, or a piece of art, and see who nibbled. Transfer it from one solid thing to another, that was the way to go, that was the way the big boys made money. You didn't touch money because then you lost it. You used money like rocks in a stream, he thought, jumping from one to the next, that was all. You just hoped the rocks got bigger.

But that was just money. As he hit Cranford, one town away from Westfield, he was close to dreaming. He pictured himself in the Red Oaks backfield, Fleming and Glass behind him, Mussman's fat ass comfortable as a stump in front. There was one play he recalled, a short slant-in to the flanker, Ross, and he pictured himself now, straightening onto his toes, the ball high, the linebacker trying to read his eyes. Then, with a quick curl, all wrist and flick, the ball was there. It snapped off his finger just right, the twine of the laces almost knicking his middle finger, then took off in a tight spiral. It went past the linebacker's hand, went by in a blur, then it hit Ross in the pads, snap, just as Ross was hit by a free safety. First down, ten to go, get out of Dodge, suckers. Losers walk.

Brennan opened his eyes as they came into Westfield. He pushed out of his seat, almost forgetting his briefcase and the brown bag containing the presents he had bought for Louey. Men clogged the aisle, and he stood staring at the white back of another commuter. The briefcase was heavy in his hand, his head still filled with sleep. He heard the door snap open and smelled rain and cold. Someone had a cigarette going out on the platform, and Brennan saw an orange flash go by against the windows as he threw it away. "Watch your step," the conductor called, and Brennan started forward, marching a little without meaning to, his briefcase and bag held next to his hip.

Kate was waiting in the station wagon. She started to slide over to let him drive, but he waved her back. "I pay enough insurance for you, you might as well crash it sometime," he said, sliding in on the passenger side. He leaned across the seat and kissed her cheek, smelled shampoo and maybe cigarettes, Juicy Fruit, and perfume. She had the radio tuned to WNEW FM. Madonna sang "Living in the Material World."

"Hi, Dad."

"Hi, sweetie,"

"You look tired."

"I am. I'm living in a material world. I'm going to dress up in widow's clothes and sing about it."

"Dad, they aren't widow's clothes."

"What are they? Madonna wears clothes that little Italian ladies wear to church. She just fills them out differently."

"She doesn't always wear black."

"No, sometimes she wears a wedding gown."

"So what did Billy Haley wear?"

"Bill Haley. You don't call a gone cat like Bill Haley Billy Haley."

"What did he wear?"

"A striped sports coat. It was way out, man."

"Like a Dixieland player?"

"Sort of," Brennan said, slipping his briefcase in back. "Mom still up at the hospital?"

She didn't answer at once. She sat behind the wheel with a straight back, her hands at two and ten. She seemed uncomfortable trusting the mirrors, so Brennan turned against the wrap of his raincoat and guided her out.

"Go ahead, go ahead, they'll let you go."

"I see them," Kate said.

"Good."

"Mom wanted to stay at the hospital, so she asked me to pick you up."

"You want me to drop you back at the house?"

"Are you going to stay long at the hospital?"

"I don't know. How's Louey doing?"

"The same, pretty much."

She stopped and waited for the light across from Ferraro's. Brennan smelled pizza. He tried to decide if he was hungry. There was a McDonald's out on North Avenue, and he could get a bag of burgers for the ride up. "Did you have dinner yet?" he asked, but it was too late to divert her. She went across the intersection at a stately pace, a Bentley or a Rolls with two dowagers in back.

"You want dinner?" she asked when they were clear of the intersection.

"I thought we could go through the McDonald's slot. Have you had anything?"

"No."

"Come on then, I'll buy you dinner. We can eat on the way up."

She circled the block, going past Z's Stationery, the Quimby Street Book Shop, and the new bagel shop, then took a left back onto North Avenue. She drove like her mother. In fact, sitting in the patter of oncoming headlights, she looked like her mother, perhaps ten or fifteen years ago, but still the same shape and form. She could have been a mom herself sitting behind the wheel. She drove with that straight-backed style some women have when they aren't sure or they're too short for the wheel, her uneasiness given away by her hands, too careful on the sides of the steering column. Zip it up, he wanted to say to her, but he knew she wouldn't. This was her pace.

"So what did you learn in school today?" he asked. "Tell me how you're smarter today than you were yesterday."

"I don't know."

"Come on, you must have done something."

"All we do is watch videos. The teachers hate us. They just like to plug us in for forty-five minutes and get us out of there."

"So you watched films?"

"We watched this thing on African wildlife. Life on the Serengeti, or something."

"And?"

"And it was okay. They showed a leopard going up into a tree after a baboon. Then they showed lions snapping meat off a dead gnu. It was disgusting."

"What class was this for?"

"Biology."

"So, at least it was interesting, right? At least you learned something."

"I guess so. Mr. Remmels told us this gross story about oxbirds or something, I forget the name. They live on the parasites that gather in all the cuts on a rhinoceros's back. It's supposed to be symbiosis, like the fish that live in the poisonous coral, but the thing is, the birds not only clean the rhino's skin, they also make sure to peck the rhino up a little more so that more parasites get into the wounds. It grossed everyone out."

"You mean the bird sort of farms the rhino?"

"Oh, Dad, that's even grosser to think of it like that."

"How else should you think of it?"

"I don't know. Anyway, the rhino wallows in mud so that the sores are covered, and that helps, I guess."

"How long did the film take?"

"About a half hour or so. I thought it was going to be barfsville when Remmels started going on about the birds pecking the rhino."

"Not the dreaded barfsville."

"The one and only."

Brennan sat back, relaxing finally with Kate behind the wheel. They passed the factory in Garwood, then turned into the McDonald's driveway. Sting came on, singing something Brennan didn't recognize. It was probably a hit even though it was a lousy song. Kate pulled up in front of the little microphone and ordered hamburgers and French fries for them both, extra ketchup, and two milk shakes. Brennan noted she no longer seemed to be counting calories.

"How's Jason?" Brennan asked as they inched forward to pick up the hamburgers. He dug for his wallet and handed Kate a ten-dollar bill.

"He's okay."

"I haven't seen him around much."

"He's got football practice about every minute."

"They going to be any good?"

"I guess. He says so. I don't know."

"You sound a little cool on him."

"Not really," she said, leaning out to pay the girl who handed them a bag of hamburgers. "Thank you. Is there ketchup in there?"

"Yes," the girl said.

"Okay, thank you."

Kate placed the bag between them and pulled away, heading back down North Avenue. She picked at her French fries whenever she had a relatively straight stretch. He looked at her now and then, thinking how beautiful she was becoming. Brennan wondered if he was supposed to pursue the question about Jason. Maybe he was supposed to probe her to find out how she felt. That was the thing with girls, with teen-agers, that he was never quite sure about. Did they want you to know their business or not? With Michael it was never an issue. Michael was a computer head and probably a virgin. But with Kate he wasn't positive he wanted to know. What if she turned to him and said she and Jason were having problems sexually? What if he got his wish and she was frank with him? He fished into the McDonald's bag for a few French fries and smiled at Kate. Let her start it, he figured, but she simply dug in for her own French fries.

"Can you put some ketchup on them?" she asked, her eyes intent on the road.

"Sure," he said, peeled open the bag, and spread out the hamburgers on their waxed paper. He bit into the ketchup sack and squeezed out two puddles onto the fries.

"What's in the bag?" Kate asked, nodding down at his feet.

"Some stuff for Louey. You'd like it, too. Here, let me show you."

Brennan dug in the bag and came out with a paperback copy of the *Guinness Book of World Records*. He flipped the book open and read the first thing that caught his eye.

"What's the longest voluntary underwater stay?" he asked her, eating a bunch of French fries. "I mean, without breathing apparatus."

"You mean, just staying under?"

"Yes."

"It must have been a pearl diver."

"No, it took place in the swimming pool of the Bermuda Palms at San Rafael, California."

"I don't know. Five minutes?" Kate guessed.

"Not even close."

"Three minutes?"

"The other way."

"I don't know."

"Guess."

184

"I thought there was brain damage after about eight minutes."

"I did, too. You want one more guess?"

"Ten minutes," Kate said.

"Thirteen minutes, forty-two and a half seconds."

"And he lived?"

"I guess so. What's the record for sword swallowing?" asked Brennan.

"No idea."

"Thirteen blades, twenty-three inches long. The guy's name was Count Desmond."

"How ridiculous."

"Louey will like it, though. It's got a whole section on sports," Brennan said, tossing the book back in the bag.

The Watchung Reservation gave way as they drove higher in the mountains, up toward Summit. Brennan spotted Overlook Hospital when they were still a few miles away. The hospital was high and white and looked out on the woods. On clear days you could see New York City.

Brennan carried the paper bag as they piled in the elevator. Just as the door was closing, a nurse pushed the hold button while another nurse wheeled in an old man in a wheelchair. The old man had an IV tube dangling from the apparatus above him. Everyone was quiet going up. Next to him, Kate put her hand through his arm. He squeezed it tightly against his side.

Brennan stepped out on the fifth floor, passing by the old man in the wheelchair, careful not to hit his tube. Kate didn't let go of his arm. She hated hospitals. Everyone hated them, but they got to her more than most people. Brennan had seen her start to shake at the sight of someone being wheeled off to the operating room. "You okay?" he asked. She didn't answer, but she didn't let go either. They passed the nurses' station. Linda knew most of the nurses' names by now, but Brennan knew only a few. Tonight he was lucky. Mrs. Riggins was on the desk. She was a short, dark woman with square shoulders and big hips. Her uniform was always starched and bright. She wore her reading glasses on a small chain around her neck.

"Hello, Mrs. Riggins," Brennan said, smiling, though suddenly weary. "How are things tonight?"

"Pretty well, thanks," she said, looking up, her head cocked at an angle as if she were looking over her reading glasses.

Mrs. Riggins handed him a large wooden key that said VISITOR ROOM 504 on it in block letters. Brennan thanked her and walked with Kate down the corridor, conscious of his shoes striking the linoleum. He tried to get himself right, tried to picture Louey before he actually stepped inside. You never knew from one day to the next how he would look, what new tube had been inserted, so you had to be prepared. You couldn't just say, "You look great, Louey," because that was bullshit and Louey saw through that kind of stuff. Brennan knew he had to have a balance.

He stepped around the corner, stepping heavily to let them know he was arriving, his hands turning the top of the paper bag into a tight, braided roll. He made it a rule never to look at Linda first, never to let their eyes meet, because he knew she might not be able to cover her feelings. This time, though, the curtain was drawn, and he had to stop for a second in front of Mikey's bed. Mikey was a little Asian kid, adopted, who had something wrong with his bone marrow. His parents were sitting together on one side of the bed, and Brennan lifted his hand, smiled, and wiggled his fingers.

"How are you, Mikey?" he asked. "Feeling better?"

"Okay, Mr. McCalmont," the boy said.

"Hi, Mikey," Kate said.

"Evening," Brennan said to the parents, then stepped around the curtain.

Louey had tubes down his nose. That was a first. Brennan felt his smile shift just a little, but he covered it, then said, "The Loueyville slugger." He stepped forward, conscious of Linda on the other side of the bed, and kissed Louey's forhead. He couldn't lift his lips from the boy's forehead, and he let them rest there, getting control of himself the entire time. "Louey," he whispered.

Then it was time to play his part, and he moved back, circled the bed, and kissed Linda hello, still not letting his eyes really fix on hers, then held his hands out with the bag dangling between them.

"Wait until you see this one," Kate said, her voice sarcastic, but it was a game, they all were playing a game..

Louey shook his head, the tubes catching light. An IV was hooked up to his right arm, set on a slow drip.

"Come on, guess," Brennan said.

"A water pistol," Linda said, smiling first at Louey, then at Brennan. "Two puppies."

"I don't know," Louey said, his words slow and a little drugged.

"No guesses at all?" asked Brennan. "You want hints, or you just want the surprises?"

"No hints," Louey said.

Brennan made a small drum roll in his throat, then pulled out a foam rubber basketball with a backboard and a plastic rim. He watched to see if Louey smiled, but Louey just stared.

"For the world championship horse match," Brennan said, stepping closer and sitting on the edge of the bed.

"Oh, my gosh," Linda said.

"Here, let me stick it up here," Kate said.

She climbed up on one of the chairs and stuck the backboard against the window. It had a round rubber suction end that spread out on the glass.

"They give you two balls," Brennan said, digging back in the bag for the spare. "Go ahead, take a shot."

He handed Louey a ball. Louey lobbed it with his left hand up at the ring. It bounced off the window a few inches away.

"Try again," Linda said.

Louey shot again. This time it came pretty close. The ball bounced off the rim, and Brennan watched Louey getting just a little excited.

"Okay, here's the other thing," Kate said, stepping down from the chair. She grabbed the bag Brennan had brought and pulled the book out. "Sports, right? Let's see who knows the most, the Silver Bullet or Louey. Here we go. What's the longest distance anyone ever walked backwards?"

"That's not a sport," Louey said, shaking his head.

"It says here it is."

"How are we supposed to know?"

187

"Come on, you sportaholics are supposed to know everything."

"Three thousand," Brennan said.

"Five thousand," Louey guessed.

"Mom? Any guesses?"

"Why would anyone want to walk backwards?"

"I don't know. Take a guess," Kate said, obviously enjoying this.

"Two thousand miles."

"Eight thousand miles," Kate said. "He walked from Santa Monica to Istanbul. It took him over a year."

"Imagine walking backwards for a year," said Linda.

"The longest dog walk is seven thousand, three hundred, and twenty-seven miles," Kate said, still reading.

"I'll bet it wasn't the dog's idea," Brennan said.

"You couldn't take McGregor on a walk like that," Louey said.

Brennan grabbed one of the balls and took a shot at the basket. It didn't go in. It bounced back on the bed, and Louey shot, missing badly. The ball hit Linda in the head, and she raised her hands, a little overdramatic, and made a phony smile. But Brennan smiled back and listened to Kate, getting ready to read another question. He looked at Louey only out of the corner of his eye. It was quiet, as it sometimes got. Brennan glanced at his watch and saw it was twenty of eight. Twenty of and twenty past, the times when angels go through a room.

FOUR

RUNNING. Brennan followed Standish Avenue up to Mountain View Terrace, then arced down Birch. Good houses all around him, good air, birdbaths and manicured lawns and a few late sprinklers. It was a Saturday, noon, and Brennan ran with an easy grace that lopped off sidewalk blocks at a beautiful rate. He glanced once at his jogging watch, a present from Linda when she had seen he was really serious about this running business, and punched the time: 22:54. He had been running for nearly a half hour, and he didn't feel it. His blood came right; his arms hung loosely to protect against lactic acid build-up; his legs felt strong enough to go for miles. His mind was clear, sharp. The air was right for September, and far away he smelled woodsmoke and the scent of bare earth after raking. He took in glimpses of things as he passed: a new Datsun in the Parkers' driveway; a tractor sprinkler going over the Farbers' lawn; a dead pine in a yard he'd never looked at closely before. This was his reward, he realized, the ability to run with a clear mind, to chase thoughts. He depended on these runs now. All the running magazines had said he would, and he had never believed them, but it was true, it was exactly as they said. He didn't think he would ever become one of those guys who had to have his jogging shoes in his briefcase, always asking the desk clerks for good runs, but it was a calm addiction he felt growing.

He rounded the bend up Birch and went down Dudley a little, then crossed toward Highland. He was in the $60,000 range easily now, with exquisite houses on either side. Make it $150,000, this was 1986. Kate had an expression that said, "Get 1986 with yourself," but Brennan wasn't quite sure what that meant. No, he understood what it meant—get modern, get cool—but he didn't quite see its being said to him. Stay with the times, or the times stay you, was his motto. His sneaker picked up a pebble, tossed it. Brand-new Nikes, Yankees was the name, which seemed fancy enough without the flying stripe down the side. Who was that? Mercedes, or Hermes? Maybe Mercury? There was a company now that had the guy with winged feet delivering flowers, hurtling over desks and jumping water coolers, Happy birthday from Olympus. That was okay. That was better than the new gimmick everyone had of renting belly dancers or strippers or clowns to come and dance all over your desk when your birthday rolled around. How could anyone like that stuff? Brennan wondered. How could you want to sit there and watch them dance around, all the people in your office hooting, the guys getting excited, the women disgusted, and for what? He would hide his birthday when it came in December. He had already made Linda swear she would never send anyone to his office or anywhere else. No surprises. No balloons in the car, no ridiculous assortment of people playing "This Is Your Life, Brennan McCalmont."

He punched his watch again and saw it was 33:12. He could head back now. It was always easier once you headed for home. He glided down past the Cunnicks', then took the easy incline toward the Herbrichs'. He passed the giant beech tree on Appian Way and reached up to touch the leaves of four or five birches, his hand whooshing through the leaves and turning them back. Tree fur, he thought, then let his legs carry him, able to stand back and admire his own coordination. Smooth. Six feet, 179 and dropping. Now, when he sat, he could feel muscles in his legs he had never had before. There were small ripples and shakes of muscle, pockets of tendon, dimples in his ass. The Silver Bullet was riding again. He was in the kind of shape that had people wondering if he had cancer, his cheeks were starting to be so gaunt, but the people asking were fat, blubbery, Pop-Tarts. He was four pounds over his high school playing weight. Four pounds. Now, when he looked at the films Harvey sent, the last two arriving just the other day, he could see himself again. Close his eyes, and there he was, Bulleto man, the king of the court. But you had to be careful. He had read articles lately about men who ran too much, who ate too little, and who ended up with middle-aged anorexia. They couldn't even see themselves becoming beanpoles. For a few strides this took Brennan's thoughts, but then he let it go. He liked to eat too much. It wasn't a threat. Even tonight he knew the menu: baked chicken, baked potatoes, a vegetable of some sort, and a Duncan Hines cake. He didn't know about the Duncan Hines, but maybe a small piece, a sliver. He would have to eat a slice since it was a small celebration for Michael, a homecoming, and everyone would expect it. The only thing was, Brennan now thought of food in terms of miles. A potato chip was a quarter mile or so, something like that. Better to burn hardwood. You didn't want the creosote to build up in yellow chicken fat around your hips.

He was heading back up toward Hillside, then looping around, before he let himself think of Louey. Louey was on his mind too much, and he had to try to blank him out now and then. They had brought him home from the hospital like a newborn, wrapped in a blanket, his head bald—no longer spotted with hair, but bald, all bald. His immune system was shot. A cold can be as deadly as cancer, the doctor had said. You had to protect him against everything. Brennan thought of the chemo as a tide these days, carrying everything with it, washing away kelp and shells and dead fish. An undertow. What was the use, he wanted to ask the doctor, of giving him medication that would let a cold take him? It seemed like burning down a house to get rid of ants. But the fucking medical profession had you. Breisky had his graphs and blood smears and slides of tissue to back him up. He was safe in his bunker, sandbagged deep, his procedure against cases of malpractice probably established years ago. He was a pro, and Brennan felt outclassed, a lightweight going up. Breisky had whys, that was the thing. He wasn't looking for reasons. He could point to cells and blood tests, and the answer was right there for him, clear and steady, all science. But Brennan couldn't accept it. It was a fucking spinning world that had to turn an eleven-year-old boy back into a baby. Had to take his hair, and his weight, and carve him into a cheap rubber doll. Sometimes, when Breisky was going on with his charts and forms, Brennan wanted to grab him and press him against the wall. He wanted to grab the damn smug lab coat, the little fucking peck of rubber showing from the stethoscope, and shake the bastard until he admitted he didn't know a goddamned thing. Not a thing. It would be like fights when he was a kid, getting another kid down and making him eat grass, or say his father was a whack-off, his mother swam after troopships. He wanted to see Breisky like that, reduced and shaken and a snotty red glaze to his face.

Down Sinclair and up Prospect, Brennan kicked up the pace, hoping it would stop that line of thinking. It wasn't helpful, didn't lead anywhere. He had been over it and over it. Linda was doing it, too. She had put off reading her real estate course work until she had enough time to concentrate on it. He had found her reading a book of philosophy the other day, a collection of philosophical proofs she had used in college. She said she hadn't understood them then, but now they were making sense. They were slow going, and her lips moved when she read them, sometimes reminding him of prayers. Still, she kept them by her bed and underlined passages from St. Anselm and Thomas Aquinas. The Ontological Argument, Five Proofs of the Existence of God, the *Meditations* of Marcus Aurelius. Brennan thought he should read some of them with her, maybe it would help to discuss them, but she had said no, it was okay, she liked doing it herself. She still read *Glamour* and *Redbook* most of the time, but the philosophy was sneaking in like a chaser after beer. She had said the other day after dinner, "If God exists outside the natural world, you can't prove Him by natural rules, so the argument is pointless," which was the first time Brennan had ever heard anyone give a reason why religious arguments were so stupid. It wasn't dorm conversation, though; it was something deeper she was going for, and sometimes, when she turned the pages and scratched a new underline, he suspected her of traveling away from him.

For the length of half a block, cutting through Highland and Colonial Avenue, he trotted directly beneath a gray squirrel that ran on the power line above him. Storing up for winter. Brennan kept his pace exactly in time with the squirrel's. The squirrel stopped once, then sprinted ahead, and ended up crossing a very thin line that hung perpendicular to the road. It reminded Brennan of the rope he and Harvey had strung across the Deerfield in one of the few places it was good to swim. They got the rope from Harvey's dad, a construction guy, and they had made it into a swing. Then, when they were bored with that, they strung it out into a tightrope. Day after day they walked it, getting four or five strides away from the oak tree on the east bank. The tree had a round burn around the trunk by the end of the summer, a circular tattoo or the mark of a man who had escaped hanging, which had climbed out of sight when Brennan looked for it in a summer not too long ago. But of that summer when he was ten, maybe Louey's age, Brennan could only remember hot days and hazy nights and beautiful open meadows just down the river. Brennan had learned to fork the rope with his toes. The rope scraped until he had blisters, but it was a good feeling to take a step forward, arms out, the rope bowing and swinging, the water moving softly beneath. Two steps, three steps, four steps. Each step was a brand-new experience, a completely new balance, and there was no experimenting; everything was immediate and quick and sudden. He had never made it across. The farthest anyone had gone was halfway, and that was Harvey, who was surprisingly good at it. Harvey always hummed that tightrope music, the organ music they play in the big top, so that each time he started across he sang, "Da, dah, dah, da, dah . . . da, dah, dah, dah, dah, dah . . . ," his breath and balance causing the song to disappear for seconds at a time.

What he wouldn't give to see Harvey walk the river once more, he thought as he rounded onto New Providence, cut through Standish again, looped through the Mountainside shopping center, then headed down Woodland. Water under the bridge. Water under the rope. Time seemed to him to be speeding up. He had a few more gray hairs, patches of black fur on his back, the first showing of veins in his legs. His balls, he had noticed, had become pendulous and full, castanets he had to scoop into a jock before each run. Maybe it was a testament to full maturity and virility, he didn't know, but it made him feel a little like a specimen in its prime. His was the kind of head a big-game hunter would have wanted if he were allowed to hunt humans. Brennan McCalmont, bagged west of the New Jersey Meadowlands, a specimen just edging out of his prime. But a rare buck, a fine head, a sable-flecked *Homo sapiens*. Brennan pictured his head above a fireplace somewhere, a British gentleman below raising a

195

brandy snifter at him. Come after me, is what Brennan would have said, even though he knew that in the real predatory world the hyenas would go after Louey first.

He punched his watch once more and saw it was almost exactly an hour, 59:41, just as he cruised into his front yard. Six hundred calories dropped, he thought. A bunch more capillaries formed, making death from a heart attack that much more improbable. He imagined his chest a giant web of veins and arteries, a stump throwing out shoots left and right. Even as he thought this, he heard Kate yelling something at Michael, and Brennan began to yell himself, shouting, "We see him now, the winner of the Boston Marathon, Bill Rodgers, is coming into view." Then he was around the house, his legs still pumping. McGregor began barking. Kate and Michael stood on either side of a huge pile of leaves. He ran at them, and Kate screamed, jumping to one side and shouting that he was as sweaty as a pig. Michael, much smarter, held his rake up to protect himself. But Brennan didn't want them. He ran the last few steps, staggering, making a crowd noise in his nose and throat, raising his hands in victory. "A world-record time . . ." he called, then fell into the leaves, the blood still firing around his body, his legs great, the scent of leaves and combed grass as old as anything he knew.

Behind the wheel of the station wagon, driving to the Rialto on Broad Street, Brennan felt full and satisfied. The dinner was wonderful. He had eaten too much, but what the hell. He had had two slices of Duncan Hines, wedges of sponge with chocolate icing, but he had gone easy on the butter and salad dressing, so it was a compromise. You had to know where to save. Chip away at the weight, that was the lesson he had learned. You didn't just zip it off. That's what women always wanted to buy. He couldn't believe the magazines Linda and Kate sometimes brought into the house. Ten days to slimmer thighs, two weeks to graceful buttocks. Jocks knew better. Muscle was just sweat made hard.

Driving now reminded him of days when they'd gone up to see Linda's mother, the kids all small and needing the rest room every ten minutes. He looked in the rear-view mirror and saw Michael sitting still, Kate beside him, Louey leaning against the door. Louey looked like a ghost. His skin was white and so soft it made Brennan think of light. Brennan looked at him for a second or two in the mirror, then reached over and took Linda's hand. 'Good dinner," he said quietly, and she squeezed his hand back. Kate leaned forward and put her head between them, her eyes suddenly large in the rear-view mirror.

"It won seven Oscars," she said.

She talked with her hand on her chin, her teeth clicking a little.

"It was nominated for seven, for Pete's sake," Michael said, his voice unchanged by college. "How many times do I have to tell you?"

"Won seven," Kate said again.

"Name them," Michael challenged.

"Best-looking, best music, best African dancing." Kate giggled, knowing this was the way to get to Michael. "What were the other four?"

"Name them."

"Dopey, Sneezy, Doc, and Grumpy," Linda said.

"Can you really name all seven dwarfs?" Brennan asked her.

But Kate wouldn't let Linda answer.

"Best spear chucking, best character with syphilis in a leading role, best flamingos."

"That's more than seven," Louey said, his voice weak.

"Good clue, Sherlock," said Kate.

"How did you know she has syphilis?" Linda asked. "I thought no one had seen this."

"Someone told me," Kate said. "Our English teacher said the book's much better. She said it was Hemingway's favorite book on Africa."

"Nominated. I'll bet you five dollars," Michael said, leaning up a little, too. "Dad, you hold the money. It has to be a real bet."

"You want to bet him, Kate?" Brennan asked, glimpsing her in the mirror quickly before finally pulling around Baron's Drugstore to park. He took a ticket from the little ticket machine that had started a big controversy in the local paper, forcing taxpayers to pay again for using a municipal lot. He had to drive over by the Playfair for an open shot.

"Is Mr. Brown University submitting a formal challenge?" Kate asked. Brennan knew she was covering now. She didn't want to plunk down five against Michael.

"Yes, Ms. C Minus at Westfield High," Michael said.

"Do you two realize you're paying for him to become this obnoxious?" Kate asked them. "College has done nothing for his ego."

"Do you want to bet or not?" Michael asked.

"It's not worth it. Why should I give you the satisfaction?"

"See? She knows I'm right. Give me five, Louey," Michael said, reaching across behind Kate's back, but she lurched backward and trapped his arm against the seat.

"Let's just watch the movie," Linda said, getting out.

The Rialto was divided into three sections. *Rambo* and *The Color Purple* were playing in the other two theaters. Brennan followed the little red felt ropes toward the white neon sign that said *Out of Africa*. The place wasn't that crowded for a Saturday night. When he mentioned it as they came in, Michael had said, "Videos," and Kate had stung him with that phrase, "Get 1986 with yourself." Now he stood for a moment looking down at the money in his hands, his feet shuffling forward over a nubbly plastic mat, wondering if he had been short-changed. Five people at four-fifty a head was what? Twenty-two something. Twenty-two fifty. He had given her thirty dollars and got back—no, it was right, it was simply the puniness that had surprised him. A family night out at the movies was going to cost him a cool thirty, maybe forty dollars. It was no wonder people were watching videos.

Michael stopped at the refreshment stand, and Brennan handed him another ten without thinking. Louey wandered over to the far side of the lobby to play a video game. Kate tried her best to act as if she weren't with her parents on a Saturday night. He started to ask where Jason had been lately but then decided against it. He took Linda's hand and held it. It felt good to have her hand in public. She leaned into him and kissed his cheek, the back of her hand just lightly brushing his cock. "Ho-ho," he said, and she smiled.

"I want some popcorn," Linda said.

"Michael, popcorn," Brennan said. Michael was ordering Pom Poms and red licorice and Milk Duds.

"You want the big mama?"

"Sure, why not?" said Brennan.

"With butter or without?"

"Is this a multiple-choice test?"

"I'm only asking."

"With," Linda said.

"Get 1986 with yourself," said Brennan, knowing it didn't quite fit.

Suddenly Kate squeezed up next to Michael.

"See?" she said, pointing to one of the large posters next to the entrance. "Seven Oscars. I told you."

"Nominations," Michael said without turning.

"Oh, wrong-o, Mr. Mind."

"Oh, *contraire*-o, Ms. Mindless."

"Five bucks."

"We didn't even bet."

Brennan let go of Linda's hand and went over to see what Louey was doing. He noticed a few people, not many but enough, glance quickly at Louey as they passed. They looked at him the way people look at retarded kids, quickly and fleetingly, but sharply enough to consider the difference between themselves and the retarded guy. The hat, really, didn't help. If anything, it made the baldness underneath that much more conspicuous, like a man wearing a bad toupee. Brennan could remember kids up by the Deerfield getting ringworm. They had shaved off all their hair and worn the tops of their mothers' stockings over their heads, but that was nothing compared to this. Louey's eyebrows were gone, and his teeth were starting to loosen. He looked bad. Louey knew it, too, and that didn't help matters.

"How's the battle going?" Brennan asked, coming up to stand at Louey's side. Missiles shot back and forth. Louey leaned close to the screen, his fingers stuttering on the fire button.

"Okay."

"You feel all right?"

"I feel fine."

Louey hit the button about five times, but the aliens were on him, and he was blown up. Another fighter appeared on the screen. It wasn't a game Brennan had seen before, but the strategy was familiar. He nailed something that looked as if it might carry Darth Vader, the warlord. It was a big, menacing ship.

Michael came over then and said Linda and Kate had gone to the ladies' room. Michael handed Louey the package of Milk Duds. "Hit the center of those flying saucers, and you score triples," Michael said. Brennan took a few kernels of popcorn off the top of the barrel. A door to the second theater opened, and Brennan heard Rambo gunning down fifteen helicopters.

After the movie Brennan took them all out for ice cream. He knew it would cost him another twelve or fifteen bucks, but he didn't care. He walked next to Linda down Broad toward the Baskin-Robbins. It was a cool September night, the stars high and distant, the trees almost finished turning. The streets smelled of dust and the peat moss that had been scattered around the trees in small circles. The ground around the trees looked like coins of countryside.

"So the whole thing was a big coffee ad," Michael said to no one, but deliberately provoking a reaction. He walked next to Louey. Kate walked in the middle of them all, the center dot on the five of clubs.

"You're so stupid," Kate said. Brennan had heard her crying through most of the show.

"Well, listen, as soon as Robert Redford showed up with that plane, you knew it was over. I mean, how Hollywood can you get? You knew he was going to crash and you'd get a fade-out to a creaky old Meryl Streep writing her memoirs in Norway or wherever it was."

"Why do you want to spoil everything?" Kate asked him. "Why do you always have to be so cynical?"

"It's my great gift to the world."

"You know that flamingo scene could have been dangerous," Louey said. "Flamingos can clog up propellers."

"So can sea gulls," Brennan added.

"They can even mess up jets, but that's beside the point," Michael said. "The point is that they put a bunch of African scenery up on the screen, put Meryl Streep there as Mrs. Lonelyhearts, then brought Robert Redford in as the macho hunter. What I don't get it why he wouldn't stay with her. Was it the syphilis or what? Or were we supposed to believe he was just too independent and macho?"

"Oh, shut up," Kate said.

"Did you like her clothes?" Linda asked Kate. "Laura Ashley must have a boutique in Nairobi."

"Or a mail-order catalog."

"She's a pretty woman," Brennan said.

"Did you like the movie, Dad?" asked Louey.

"It was okay. I thought it was pretty contrived."

"What isn't contrived?" Kate asked, getting a little warm now, Brennan saw. "You people have no imagination. Why do you always have to analyze everything to death?"

"It's all the hoopla, that's why. This was supposed to be the big film of the year, and it wasn't. It was really a Hollywood film, the kind they do best. It put two big stars in a beautiful setting, then had them slowly fall in love. But really, Kate, what happened in the film? What happened between them? Robert Redford was outacted by the African chief who came by and grunted into the camera," Michael ended.

Baskin-Robbins was between the old music store and the Broad Street barbershop. Brennan held the door for everyone, then followed them inside. A few cardboard cutouts of banana splits and chocolate sundaes floated above the counter.

"What's the limit?" Louey asked.

"The sky's the limit," Brennan said.

Michael and Louey ordered banana splits. Kate ordered a small cup of rocky road. Linda ordered a cone of fudge chocolate, and Brennan ordered French vanilla. When the orders came, Kate and Linda went over and sat at a small white table against the wall. Brennan ate his cone standing. Louey and Michael came over a few minutes later and sat at a second table, huge dishes of ice cream before them.

"I'd like to stay with you, Meryl," Michael said to Louey, blinking his eyes with love, "but I have to go shoot another wildebeest."

"Oh, make it a rhino," Louey said in a high falsetto.

"A rhino? Of course, my dear. A rhino it is. Is there anything else you'd like me to slaughter? Maybe I could hack my way through a herd of gazelles? If you'd like, I could bazooka an elephant or two."

"No, just stay and have tea with me forever and ever. Play the phonograph again, would you, Sahib?"

Brennan was enjoying the act, mainly because it was good to see Louey in such high spirits, but when he looked at Kate, she was staring down at the table. Brennan made a cut sign across his throat just as Linda said, "That's enough, you two."

After the ice cream they walked back to the car. Brennan couldn't keep himself from tallying up the night. A rough guess was around forty dollars. Forty dollars to take his family out to a movie, it seemed impossible, but there it was. Pretty soon, he thought, movie theaters were going to start taking charge cards.

"Thanks, Mom and Dad," Kate said as they were easing out of the parking lot. "I enjoyed it even if no one else did."

"Thanks, Mom and Dad," Louey said.

"Thanks, Mater and Pater," Michael said.

"You're welcome," Linda told them, turning in her seat to touch one.

Brennan couldn't see whom she touched. It was dark in the back seat, impossible to see his children clearly. Searching for them in the rear-view mirror, he saw only shapes.

Standing on the sideline, a light sweat already greasing his chest and temples, his helmet fitting his forehead nicely for once, Brennan watched the cheerleaders yelling at the bleachers behind him. They were Red Oaks cheerleaders, wives and girl friends of the men around him. There were three or four good-looking younger women, probably girl friends, but most of the cheerleaders were forty, leathery-looking women who carried black purses and plastic bags full of deli sandwiches. Between cheers they sat on red plastic coolers and pulled on their cigarettes. One, a tall, magnificent black woman in her middle thirties, shook a red and white pompon repeatedly at the crowd of only two or three hundred, her free hand holding a can of Pabst, shouting in between swallows, "Kill, kill, kill."

It was a day for surprises. Since morning he had kept a small knot of nerves in the center of his stomach. Butterflies were something he thought he had done away with long ago, but they were there, full and concentrated and throbbing. Get a lick, he remembered, was the remedy, but the game was still a few minutes from starting. Bonow was out in the center of the field, flipping the coin against the Merchants, his helmet off, his goat shoulders narrowed and hard and brilliant red. Brennan moved his feet back and forth on the grass, pawing lightly with his cleats, the game rising in him so solidly he could hardly breathe. His bowels felt weak, his bladder full, but he couldn't tell if it was simple nervousness or a real need to go back beneath the bleachers. "Baby, call it," one the cheerleaders yelled, and Brennan turned to see a woman his own age jumping up in the air, a pompon stretched out, her landing a delicate little jump, spring, kick, straight out of the early sixties. Gidget or Judy Garland or the sweater girl—what was her name? He wondered if he looked as ludicrous to her as she did to him. Two more cheerleaders moved next to her, and together they began to clap and chant and kept it going long enough so that the big black cheerleader put down her beer and came over. She joined in the cheer, then called some of the other women over, and soon they all were locked in a Rockettes line, kicking back at the grandstands, their blue jeans whistling. "Hey, hey, hey," they called, losing their balance as a line in soft collisions, once or twice coming close to crumpling.

A few players around him began to clap, and at first Brennan thought it was to go along with the cheerleaders. Then he saw Bonow running off the field at a slow trot, his helmet tapping his right thigh pad, his head nodding. "We're on D, on D, first D," he called. Brennan saw the defense slap on their helmets and felt relief, even though he knew he wouldn't start, at knowing the offense would stay off the field a few minutes longer. "Ho, baby, get at them," someone yelled, and Brennan felt someone pound his shoulder pads. Someone slapped the side of his helmet hard, an ear ringer, and Brennan took it and slapped back, not quite right for a quarterback, but he wanted the hit to loosen him. It was Mussman, the big center, and Brennan found himself saying, "Take it to them, baby, rock them," at the same time aware that he was drifting backward. His blood was rich now, and he closed with the other players, careful of his toes and feet with all the cleats. Bonow stood in the center of the closing circle, his weary smile gone now, his face dead and serious. He held up a cigar, a thick brown White Owl, and spun it deftly in his hands. Then, with a quick move, he lowered the cigar and bit it in half, tucking the loose shreds into his cheek neatly and well. A lizard, Brennan thought, and watched the big wad take shape in Bonow's cheek, while Bonow nodded again and again, chewing and pumping himself, saying in a voice that was no longer a coach's, "We get them now, we get them."

Brennan felt himself losing control. He was aware of letting go, which was sweet and mellow since it meant he was old, but it pleased him tremendously to be able to do it. "Stick 'em, stick 'em," he shouted, and someone hit his shoulder. He hit back and leaned into the swell, deep in the pack, 1964 again. He heard Bonow's voice, tense and sharp, his words not clear. It no longer mattered. Brennan heard, ". . . take this game to them . . . you got to be the ones. . . ." Then there was a tremendous swing of ferocity around the pack, a sense of going feral and wild, and Brennan was squeezed between two bigger men, his chest huffing, his hands closed into fists. "You going to get them?" Bonow shouted, and Brennan amazed, heard himself shout back, "Yessss," as the circle broke and the kickoff team sprinted onto the field.

"Stick, stick, stick," someone next to him screamed.

Brennan closed his eyes, afraid for an instant he would faint. He felt suddenly that he was crying, his eyes blinking. It was a flood returning, time moving too fast. He thought of his parents, of Louey and the red plaid blanket he wore high up in the stands. He felt ridiculous for letting it all get to him, but there was no stopping it. It was like dreaming of buffalo, this dream of men running across playing fields, their cleats throwing up flecks of dirt, their breath wild and hard and free. It was a second season, his own afternoon. He closed his eyes and wanted to thank someone for letting him play this long, for letting him get the feel of it all again, but he was afraid to push his mind in any particular direction for fear the feeling would leave him. Then, above the trees, he saw the ball going up, and he squinted to watch it fall, dropping through the scattered crowd on the other side, a blue-shirted Merchant advancing to catch it. A horn went off, someone played a roll on a snare drum, then he heard the deep grunt of men running at one another. He could not see, but he knew when the ball-carrier was about to be hit, heard the quickened feet, the short intake of breath, the ayyyyyy of the shoulder dip and the final tuck. Then a whistle went off, shrill and changing pitch, as the referee ran toward the tackle, and Brennan sank back, away from the sideline.

"Okay, D, be on them," Bonow yelled.

Between the players' shoulders Brennan watched the two teams line up. It looked confusing from ground level. It had been too long. He had watched too many games from a TV perspective, high in the press boxes, Howard Cosell pointing out details. It wasn't like that on the field, but he had forgotten how fast it all was, how difficult it was to keep your wits. He was relieved this kid Haynes had shown up. Haynes was a big, dumb kid, but he had a bullet arm, quick feet, the ability to go for a big play. He seemed to Brennan like a country boy, a Bob Feller stepping off the cornfields to hurl thunder. Once, in practice, Haynes had missed the receiver, but the ball had struck the goalpost dead on and started it wobbling. The whole team had watched while the pole gradually quieted. It was something mythical, like Robert Redford knocking out the clock in *The Natural*, Brennan had thought at the time. Now he sensed it was a strange sort of dumb luck, something brutish and thick without enough intelligence behind it to take on any meaning.

The first play was a simple off tackle that almost broke for a touchdown. Brennan saw it coming, but it happened too fast to shout anything. Rose, one of the linebackers, just tripped the Merchants' back as he was making his break to the outside. The Merchants' linemen started yelling and hitting each other on the shoulders, while Bonow shouted, "Shit, come on, you guys. Close it down." The middle linebacker, Dunham, a young kid who hadn't gone to college, trotted five steps to the sideline and closed his fist against his chest.

"You want a fist defense? You want a fist against these guys?" he yelled to Bonow.

"Go fist. Rotate them in back."

Dunham hustled back, called the defense, then broke his huddle out. The Merchants were already coming out, the flanker and split end twins right. "Watch the pass, passsss, passsss," Bonow shouted as the Merchants' quarterback took the snap, faded, then began to roll right. Brennan saw the pattern clearing, the same linebacker, Rose, frozen between two curling receivers, while the tight end ran a flare to the sideline. The quarterback read it nicely and drilled the ball into the flanker, a ten-yard curl pattern, first and ten.

"Come on, Rose," Bonow shouted. "They're eating you up, boy."

Brennan looked up in the stands. Louey was there. So was Linda. Michael had taken the early train back to Providence. Kate had had some sort of reconciliation with Jason and was out with him all day. Brennan started to wave, stopped, then figured it didn't matter. He waved from his chest, just a short wave, but neither of them saw him. When he looked back at the field, he saw the Oaks jumping up and down. Someone had fumbled.

"Offense! Get the O out there," Bonow yelled.

Brennan stepped up to watch. Haynes trotted onto the field last, cool, collected, used to this. The offense circled around Mussman. Haynes ducked into the huddle and called the play. Brennan knew it was an off tackle, nothing fancy. It would get everyone loosened up, and that was important. First licks. The snap came, and Haynes spun, giving Glass the quick hand-off, and Glass took it for three yards before getting pushed back. "Here we go, here we go," someone close yelled. "Come on now, big O," one of the defensive linemen called. The lineman sweated freely and sucked from the hook of a water bottle. He looked exhausted already.

Haynes passed next. It was a beautiful play, one Brennan doubted he could have thrown himself. Haynes dropped two steps, straightened, then threw a tight little square out to Sales, the flanker. The ball never hung. It was thirty yards, flat, zipped with perfect control. Sales was well covered, but it didn't matter. He took it, shook the

206

defensive back just enough, and ended up in one of those ridiculous tackles where the defensive man hangs on to one leg while the back tries to pull away. A second defensive back was right on it, and Sales had to duck before he was slaughtered. Still, it was a gain of five. Haynes pushed his shoulder pads back like Joe Namath and spit as he walked forward. Brennan watched, knowing it would be a while before he got in. The kid was better than Brennan. Maybe he wasn't better, maybe Brennan had been his equal once, but who knew? It was like comparing baseball players of different generations, DiMaggio and Mays, Pie Taynor and Wade Boggs. You had to give in to age. Playing right was only a question of synapses, nerve relays, reactions. The kid was close to twenty years younger than Brennan, his circuits fresh, his confidence bordering on arrogance. It was possible, Brennan realized, perhaps for the first time, that he wouldn't get in at all. No, that wasn't right. One way or the other he would hold for extra points. He had been to more practices than Haynes and knew how Knoblock, the kicker, liked the laces. It all was worked out. Brennan would get in almost every quarter. He could almost count on getting a letter.

Deep in the blanket, deep in Linda, Brennan moved with the garden around him. "Shhh," Linda said, though they were quiet, he was sure of that. Her legs came up, loosened now that he had pushed the blanket a little off them. He felt himself glide deeper, deeper, and all around was the smell of the garden, the rough-clodded earth under his knees, the night cold and bright on his back. "Nice, so nice," Linda whispered in his ear, and he reached one hand under her jacket, a thick, heavy letter jacket he had from high school, and touched her breasts. She arched into him, adjusting to some position she alone understood, and he lifted slightly to let her move under him. He closed his eyes, then opened them, listening to the cornstalks rustling above him. Beneath them, matted in the soft soil, he saw remnants of the garden: stalks of cucumbers, vines from beans, green caps from the tomato plants. He moved the blanket a little farther off his shoulders, and then it slipped away entirely so that they were exposed, their hips naked. He kissed Linda as completely as he could, falling into her, asking open, open, and she let him enter deeper and deeper, their skin connected, the grind of their hips just one more sensation. He moved more slowly, concentrating on the kiss, realizing the kiss was it, that was the trick, the secret they had held for so many years. They could kiss, had kissed, and now, his penis glossy and smooth in her, it was the kiss he felt sustaining them.

"Are you cold?" he asked quietly, whispering because Louey was asleep upstairs, the house was asleep.

"No, I'm fine. It feels lovely."

"You're lovely."

He kissed her, and it was there once again, the wonderful warmth of their flesh and hearts and breath. His back felt chilled, but not too much, and his hips felt fierce against her. He slowed even more and took her hands and spread them out, straight out, until their hands were together on the dirt. Then it was just four points, their mouths, their groins, their hands, and he felt the soil under them, the pumpkin draining the last of the garden slowly away.

"Finish," she said, and he closed his eyes, riding on her hips, shuddering deeply even before. She lifted her legs higher, and he felt wonderfully solid, together wtih his wife, a chance at renewal. He kissed her again, sad because he knew this would be the last kiss like this for a time, then let himself go. "Ah, ahh," he whispered, thinking he would like to fill her.

A few minutes later he rolled off and held her against his side, just lifting the blanket around them. Air still came in, but he knew she would be warm enough against him. Through the trees he saw the stars and the moon bright orange and yellow. A harvest moon, a coin, a hole in heaven.

"Are you okay?" he asked her.

"Fine."

"I was worried I was too heavy."

"No, not at all. You're skinny now," she said.

"We fit better."

"We always fit perfectly."

"But now it's better. I was too fat."

"Don't get too skinny, though. I hate skinny men. I hate men who are all bones."

"All right."

"We should get up. Kate should be coming home."

"Maybe she's out in the yard someplace with Jason," he said, pulling the blanket tighter around them.

"Oh, you're terrible."

"Do you think she's a virgin?"

"I don't know."

"I don't think she is," he said.

"Why?"

"I don't know, I just don't think so."

"Would you be mad if she wasn't?"

"No."

"Not at all?"

"No, I don't think so. Are you going to tell me now that she confessed to you or something?"

"No, I don't know if she is or not," she said, moving closer to him. The air was getting colder. "Do you think Michael is?"

"Yes, unless he's got a computer program for it."

"He had Strip Poker."

"That was a little perverted, wasn't it? Playing strip poker with a computer?"

"Michael's just immature. He'll find someone soon. He told Louey he had a girl friend or some girls he hung around with. Louey told me last night."

"Hangs around with is more likely."

Linda reached down and pulled on her jeans, then moved against him again. Brennan thought about putting on his own pants, but it felt too good to be naked outside. He put his arm under his head and studied the stars.

"Are you mad you didn't get in today?" Linda asked.

"I got in. I held for kicks."

"I mean as a quarterback."

"It was a close game. We won."

"But you didn't get in. Wasn't that the whole point of going out there?"

"It was good to be out there anyway. I felt a lot of old things."

"That's because there were a lot of old things out there. Did you see the cheerleaders?"

"They were a hard bunch, weren't they?"

"I think they were drunk by the end of the game."

"I think so, too. I think seeing them making out with the players was a good indication."

Linda laughed and pressed her face into his neck.

"I think they should have let you in," she said. "It wasn't exactly the Super Bowl."

"No, but people want to win. Haynes was doing okay."

"Louey hates that guy. He says Haynes is cocky."

This is what Brennan had been waiting to ask about for most of the evening, but he was afraid to bring it up. Now that it was out, he wanted to know how Louey had taken the fact that his dad had ridden the pine.

"What did Louey think of the whole thing anyway?"

"He was disappointed. He wanted to see you play. He said Haynes is a thrower and you're a pitcher. Is that right?"

"That's right."

"And he said you had played in the scrimage he saw before he went into the hospital. He said you looked better than Haynes."

"Did he really?"

"Yes."

He put his arms around Linda. A clod of dirt bit into his back, but he didn't care. He felt cold now, the wind coming in under the blanket. He turned and looked at the pumpkin growing like a heart. Again he imagined the whole garden draining into the warm center of the pumpkin, the season's growth a single missile of sap.

Brennan climbed out of his car, grabbed his briefcase, and started to the door. It was Friday evening, the tenth of October, forty-two degrees. In the kitchen he found Kate and her friend Janey making

Tollhouse cookies. Janey was a knockout but didn't know it. Or maybe she knew it enough since she wore tight pants and little wiggle skirts that always made Brennan want to hoist her over his lap and give her a spank. Spankable fashions, that's what he thought of them. She reminded him of that cartoon character in the back of *Playboy*, the one with the big butt and the huge mujumbos, who was perpetually surprised at everything. Little Annie Fannie.

"The king has returned," he said, putting his briefcase down, the first heat of the kitchen hitting his blood. "You may continue what you're doing."

"Oh, God, he's on one of his queer kicks. Ignore him," Kate said to Janey.

But Janey giggled and turned. A streak of dough went up from her lip.

"Hello, Mr. McCalmont," said Janey.

"And hello to you, Janey. What's this? A bake sale for the chess club?"

"Dad, you always do this."

"What? Come home? I live here."

"You know."

Brennan went over and took a fingerful of cookie dough. "God, that's good," he said, and tried for another, but Kate boxed him away with a wooden spoon.

"Dad, wait until they're cooked."

"They're better now."

"I think so, too," Janey said.

"See? You're outnumbered," Brennan told her, and dabbed between them to take another fingerful.

"I'll tell Mom," Kate warned.

"Oh, please don't. She'll ground me."

Brennan gave Kate a kiss on the neck and made her smile. Then he backed off and ran a glass of water.

"You-all staying with Louey tonight?"

"Yes," Janey said.

"All right. Did Mom say what time we're supposed to be going? Where is she anyway?"

"She's at the beauty parlor. She said to tell you to be ready at seven."

"I haven't been bowling in twenty years, I'll bet."

"You're going bowling?" Janey asked, taking a sheet of cookies from Kate and popping them in the oven.

"That's what they tell me."

"Whose idea was it anyway?" Kate asked, stirring the batter some more, then flecking out little pods of cookie dough on a second sheet. "I mean, aren't we a little old, gang?"

"No, we are not a little old."

"My mother always says that whenever you're bored, and you think bowling might be fun, forget it immediately," Janey said. "She hates to bowl. She says it's her definition of nothing to do."

"Thanks," Brennan said, drinking the water.

"No, I mean, other people might like it," Janey said, blushing. She was even prettier when she blushed. She turned to Kate, but Kate just shook her head.

Brennan leaned against the sink and tried to see out. The window was foggy, but he could just make out the pumpkin.

"You think we should bring the pumpkin in? It's what? We're already in the middle of October. Do you think they keep growing?"

"It won't hurt to leave it outside," Kate said.

"I just don't want anything to get at it. Maybe the raccoon will get it."

"The raccoon would have gotten it by now if it had any interest in pumpkin."

"I guess you're right," Brennan said.

"Thank you, Sahib."

"Where's Louey?"

"Watching TV. It's time for 'Star Trek,' remember? He's circling the planet Telethon."

Brennan grabbed one more fingerful, then went looking for Louey. He took out his wallet, flipped it open, then talked into it in a tight, nasal voice.

"Spock to *Enterprise*, Spock to *Enterprise*, beam me down a six-pack of Bud. Spock to *Enterprise*, throw in a couple of packages of Cheez Doodles, over and out."

Louey raised a hand from his place on the couch. McGregor sat with him. "Hi, Dad," Louey said, but didn't turn to look. Spock was telling Kirk something serious beside the captain's chair. Kirk had a faraway look in his eyes, a man of vision.

"It's great to see you, Louey."

"Shhh, wait until the commercial."

"I've worked my life away so you could watch 'Star Trek,' do you know that?"

"Shhh."

"Does anyone care?"

"Shhhhhh."

"Okay, that's it. If you want to help me in a few minutes, I'm going to bring in the pumpkin. I don't want anything to get it."

"Okay."

"Maybe we'll just beam it into the kitchen."

"Okay."

Brennan patted his knee for McGregor to come closer, but McGregor didn't move either. He didn't care. He headed up to his room, climbing the steps with a good feeling falling on him from nowhere. The weekend was here. Things were just starting.

Ten minutes later he was down in a pair of jeans and a flannel shirt. He grabbed his hooded sweat shirt from the closet and yanked it over everything. The sweat shirt said RED OAKS across the chest.

"You guys are helping," he told Kate and Janey. "This is an annual pagan rite."

"Dad, it's fine where it is," Kate said, sliding a sheet of cookies out. The smell filled the room, and Brennan stood for a moment enjoying it.

"It will take only a minute," he told them when the cookies were safely on top of the stove. "I think the whole garden drained into the pumpkin."

"Oh, Dad."

"Seriously. The whole garden just slowly poured into the pumpkin. It did."

Janey looked at him strangely. Brennan smiled at her, aware that he would have to control himself not to flirt with her. He wondered if other fathers flirted with Kate.

"Come on," he said. "I just want you to hold the doors. I'll wrestle it in."

"Are you really going to do it right now?" Kate asked, shucking the large oven mitten she'd worn to handle the cookies. "Why do you get on such kicks?"

"Oh, I'm just wild, that's why."

Janey laughed and said she would help. Louey came out then, limping badly, his body even thinner than before. He was due for chemo again in two weeks. He was just getting over the last dose.

"Louey will help, won't you, Lou?" Kate asked.

"I just need two volunteers to open the doors. Here we go now. Kate, why don't you go get those markers you have? We'll draw faces on the pumpkin and see who makes the best one."

Kate shrugged, then went upstairs. Brennan stepped out on the porch, slapping his chest and breathing deeply. It was fall, his season, and he felt ridiculously full of health. A hundred and seventy-five pounds, his high school weight. His legs were rocks, coils, and his belly as rippled as a golf ball.

He jumped down the back stoop and went out into the garden. The pumpkin was larger than he had realized. It came up to his knee, maybe above it, and the vine went all through the grass. He picked up the vine and shook it. Small tremors answered in every part of the garden. With his pocketknife he cut the vine away from the top of the gourd.

"You all ready?" he called.

Louey held the inside door open. Janey was out on the back steps, her arms across her chest. Brennan squatted in front of the pumpkin and hooked his arms around it. It was like hugging a barrel except the pumpkin smelled soft and tired when his nose came close to it. "Easy, old fellow," Brennan whispered, then lifted, the strain spreading nicely in his back and legs. It was heavy, but not too much to carry. He waddled across the lawn and climbed the steps. At the door he had to back past Janey, and he smelled her perfume above the heavy scent of the pumpkin. "Got it?" he asked her, already knowing she did, but wanting to establish her position so he wouldn't bump into her.

"Got it," she answered.

He shuffled past Louey and put the pumpkin down on the kitchen table. As soon as it was down, he grabbed some newspapers and tucked them underneath. Finally he went into the bathroom and came out with the scale.

"Put this under when I lift it," he told Louey.

"Okay."

Brennan lifted the pumpkin once more, set it on the scale, then let the pumpkin go.

"How much?" he asked Louey.

"Thirty-four pounds."

"A record."

"We've never weighed one before."

"So that makes this one a record. Here," Brennan said, and grabbed a pencil from the pad near the phone. He wrote "PUMPKIN 1986— 34 lbs." on the kitchen doorjamb next to the horizontal lines marking the kids' heights.

"We bought one once that was fifty pounds," said Janey, closing the doors.

"Ah, bought. Anyone can buy anything," Brennan said, coming back to the table. "This one was grown. This one has a whole garden inside it."

"You're nuts," Louey said.

Brennan lifted the pumpkin again, and Louey took away the scale. Kate came back with the markers. "I'm not working on the pumpkin," she said, but Brennan, surprised, as always, at how much easier it was to get other people's kids to go along with things, knew Janey was all for it.

"Listen," Brennan said, "I'm going to draw lines on this thing so that there are four equal spaces."

"Quarters, I'd guess you'd call them," Louey said.

"Maybe you would at that." Brennan laughed. "We're each going to draw a face on the pumpkin, and the best one will become the dominant motif, the *je ne sais quoi*, of the whole pumpkin. It will become the face for the season."

"Dad, this is ridiculous," Kate said.

"I like it," Louey said.

"So do I," Janey said.

"Listen, Kate, quit being a wet blanket. Get us some cookies. Artists need nourishment."

Kate huffed a little, but Brennan knew it was okay. Everything was okay. It was Friday, and the weekend was here. Tomorrow morning he would wake to the smell of eggs and bacon, to toast clicking in the toaster, to butter smoothing over the grainy texture of whole wheat bread.

He drew the lines on the pumpkin, then sat down behind his quarter. Kate came over with cookies. Louey sat next to him, and Janey on the other side. Kate sat opposite.

"Sad or happy?" Louey asked.

"Your choice."

"How about scary?" Janey asked, already dabbing at her side of the pumpkin. "Can you have crooked teeth and things?"

"You can have anything you want," Brennan told her. "The trick is to make it lifelike."

"I want to draw one of Michael," Kate said, finally sitting and taking a red marker.

"Try it."

Linda came in before they were done. She carried two bags of groceries. Brennan jumped up and grabbed the bags and carried them to the counter. "Well, this looks like fun," Linda said, smiling, happy. She kissed Brennan as he sat back down.

"Nice do, Mom," Kate said.

"Oh, you look cute," Janey said.

"Do you like it?" Linda asked, taking off her coat and turning like a model. "That Sheila kept wanting to cut it, and I kept telling her no. I don't know about the bangs."

"No, they're great," Janey said.

"They're stunning," Louey said, not looking up from his painting.

"You look wonderful, honey," Brennan said.

Linda went into the bathroom, and Brennan listened to the floor creak as she checked herself in the mirror. When she came out, she began putting the groceries away.

"You're the judge," Brennan told her.

"What am I judging?"

"You have to decide what should be the dominant image for the 1986 pumpkin season."

"Are you going to carve it tonight?"

"I doubt it."

"We have to be ready by seven. We're eating there," Linda said.
"Okay."

"You're supposed to dress fifties style."

"Dad always dresses fifties style," Kate said.

Linda came over and looked at the pumpkin. She squeezed around the table. "Oh, Janey, that's great," she said. At Kate's quarter she asked, "Is that supposed to be Michael?"

"Can't you tell?"

"Actually, it's a pretty good likeness."

"Michael should be the pumpkin," Louey said. "It should be in honor of his absence."

On his side Brennan was drawing a pine tree. When Linda came by, he leaned forward to cover it. He held the pumpkin close to his chest and wouldn't let her see.

"You're ridiculous," Linda said.

Brennan grabbed a paper napkin and hung it from the sharp stem. "All great paintings have cloths over them," he said, and let the napkin drop. It covered just his quarter.

"We've got to get going," Linda said. "You have to get dressed."

"I know. We'll make the decision when we get home."

Brennan sat for a moment longer, reluctant to leave. He dotted some more grass around his pine tree. Far in the distance he squiggled an impression of the Deerfield River. He smelled the pumpkin once more, wondering why it always reminded him of damp screened porches and muddy welcome mats.

A hoop skirt. Walking into Echo Lanes, the electric door hissing open in front of him, Brennan had the sensation of entering a time warp. Pam Samuels stood in front of a new Volkswagen Golf, given to anyone with a three hundred score in league play, her wide gray skirt flouncing away from her like a giant rocket cone. A pink poodle rested down near the hem, a little silver leash snaking up the side of the skirt. The poodle had sparkles for eyes and a few more sequins around its throat for a collar. Underneath, Brennan saw, Pam wore two or three starched petticoats, with anklets and saddle shoes. Her blouse was white and plain, but her hair was pulled back in a ponytail. She looked like something out of "American Bandstand," or *Grease*, or "Happy Days."

"What do you think?" she asked as Brennan held the door open for Linda and Phil and Margaret Dedich. "Is it too much?"

"Oh, my God." Margaret laughed. "I haven't seen one of those in years!"

Margaret came forward and touched the hem of the skirt.

"Oh, how I remember the feeling of those petticoats. My sisters all wore skirts like that. How dreamy."

"Did you make it?" Linda asked, coming forward now. Brennan knew she probably didn't like the skirt. She wouldn't be caught dead in anything like it, but she was Pam's friend and had to fuss over it. Brennan looked at Phil Dedich, who was smiling and shaking his head.

Then Freddy came over, carrying a tray of beers, and Brennan saw he was dressed in a white T-shirt, black motorcycle pants, and pointy roach killers. He had slicked back his hair with Vaseline or something, and as he walked past a video game, the lights made little moving pictures over his temples.

"Hey, Daddy-o," Freddy said.

"Christ, it's Fast Freddy," Phil said. "Where'd you park your bike, Fonz?"

218

"Hey, cats, you've got to get into the swing. You guys are squares-ville."

"If he talks like that all night, I'm leaving," Margaret said, letting go of Pam's skirt. "Where did you two get all this?"

"At the sock hop," Freddy said. Then he motioned with his head down the bowling alley. "We've got lane fifty-two."

Brennan followed the group, a little stunned to be back in a bowling alley. A quick glance told him nothing much had changed. Maybe the lanes looked in better shape, and maybe the overhead score-keeping devices were computerized, but everything else looked the same. There were still racks of balls behind the lanes; there were still little shuffleboard games over by the bar and an electric bowling machine where the pins jumped up if you slammed the disk at them.

The first forty lanes were taken up by leagues, their bowling shirts reading like the Yellow Pages: Gus's Auto Body, Phil's Sunoco, Boyle-Midway. Brennan watched a few of the guys nudge each other as Pam walked by, her skirt hitting everything on either side of her, her petticoats flashing little loops of white at anyone who looked. The skirt looked like a bell, and Brennan couldn't help wondering if this was some sort of sexual game with the Samuelses. First there was the sauna, and now maybe it was dress-up time. The thing was, Brennan could appreciate it. He imagined tipping Pam over, grabbing under the skirt, and doing the breaststroke through all the lace and undies. Maybe she got excited thinking Fast Freddy was a greaser, a Lucky Strike guy, who smelled of oil and lube jobs. Part of Brennan envied them; part of him never knew if the Samuelses were crazy or not. Sometimes they struck him as the kind of couple for whom everything was fun and games until they came flying apart in some sweaty divorce. They tried too hard, that was it. Even this bowling date, which was the first event in a new thing the women had cooked up—each one of them was responsible for something fun one weekend night a month, twelve events in all, with an emphasis, Linda said, on doing something, not just drinking—was a sort of stage set to show off their new costumes. He had never known a couple so actively trying to be madcap.

"Here we go," Fast Freddy said, putting the tray of beer down on the scoring table, "here we go, cool cats."

"He really is going to talk like that all night, isn't he?" Margaret said.

"Twenty-three skiddoo," Phil said. "How's that? Is that jive enough, Freddy?"

"No way, Daddy-o. Think of Wolfman Jack. Think of Cousin Brucie. Remember him?"

"Cousin Brucie? I haven't thought of him in years," Linda said, scooting around on one of the wooden benches to make room for the rest of them.

"Palisades Park is easy to reach," Freddy sang in a little jingle, "boating, swimming, something, something . . . beach."

"Cousin Brucie, Cousin Brucie, Cousin Brucieeeee," Linda called back, and made them both laugh.

"WABC is all talk now," said Freddy. "They let everyone go. Now they have Dr. Susan Forward, the pop psychologist who can cure your problems between commercials."

Brennan squeezed past Pam, crushing into her skirt a little, and grabbed a beer. Want to get gone with me, he almost said to her. But Phil Dedich had already beaten him to it. He took Pam's hand and spun her, pretending to be dancing to bebop but really, Brennan suspected, just doing it to see her dress fly up. The trouble was that in the first turn Pam slammed a beer glass off with her skirt and the beer spattered all over the floor next to the lane. The skirt was a buzz saw.

"That skirt's like the hat that guy Odd Job wore in the James Bond movies," Margaret laughed. "How did we ever wear them?"

"The world was wider," Linda said.

"You think so?"

"Sure," Phil said, taking a drink. Freddy had a towel that he threw over the puddle of beer. "That's a wonderful theory. Think of cars. Even cars were wider. I bet you had trouble getting in the car to come over here, didn't you?"

"Not really," Pam giggled.

"Well, so much for that theory," Linda said.

"Are we going to bowl?" Freddy asked, mushing his foot around the puddle. "You have to pick out your own balls."

"What do the different colors mean again?" Pam asked, sipping a beer. "Blues are the lightest?"

"Something like that," Freddy said, picking up the towel. "I guess you're supposed to pick one that goes with your outfit."

"But wait," Margaret said, rising anyway, "aren't the Atwaters coming?"

"No, they're going up to that place they have in New Hampshire to close it up. The Bloomers are going with them," Pam said.

"Does that put them out of the once-a-month-do-something-exciting club?" Phil asked.

"No, indeed," Pam said. "They've already got something planned for next month, but they've been very secretive about it. I think they're going to take us to the circus."

"Oh, Christ, I can't stand the excitement," Phil said, his quick grin stretching his neck veins so hard Brennan thought they would snap.

"The circus, or a football game. You know how Jim likes sports," Pam said.

"I thought sports were out," Linda said.

"Not if they have a certain panache," Margaret said. "For example, you can get us out to a Princeton game, but you can't drive us to Yonkers for the races."

"Why not? I love the races," Phil said.

"So do I," Freddy agreed.

"Bloomer said he wanted to take us all iceboating," Margaret said. "He's been going on and on about it ever since he went with a friend of his from the office. He says you can go a hundred miles an hour."

"Didn't the Hardy Boys have an iceboat?" Brennan asked.

"No, they just had a roadster," Phil asked.

"I think we'd better get out bowling balls," Margaret said.

Pawing over the balls, hoisting them up against his chest, Brennan thought of the Hardy Boys. He had read most of them over when Louey was on the kick, and he had been surprised at how taken he was with them. It was all nostalgia, probably, but he liked reading about cabins and lakes and roadsters. The world was wider, Linda was right about that. Every book had some new gimmick, a boat bought from the reward for solving the Mystery of Cabin Island, or motorcycles purchased with loot from the Mystery of the Chinese Junk, but it wasn't that so much as remembering what it was like to be beside a lake in the summer, with long days of vacation in front of you.

He was still thinking about this when Phil came up to him and said, "You ever hear about guys getting their fingers caught in a ball and pulling their arm sockets out?"

"No, but I heard about guys throwing the ball and their fingers got stuck and they went flying down the lane after them."

"Wouldn't your fingers break off first?" Phil asked.

"I don't know."

"I had a friend who put these fake rubber fingers in bowling balls whenever he came to the lanes. People used to die."

"You any good?" Brennan asked, still going through the balls.

"At bowling? How could anyone over eighteen be good at bowling?"

"I don't know. I thought maybe you used to bowl."

"Do I look like some bowling guy? Listen," Phil said, stepping closer, "what are those two dressed up for? It isn't Halloween yet, is it?"

"They're just playing or something."

"I think they're nuts. Pammy Baby looks like the top of a mustard pot. You know, the kind with a little brush inside."

"I think it's a sex thing with them."

"Oh, really?" Phil asked, a little exaggeratedly. "You think they dress up in costumes and stuff?"

"I don't know. It's probably more subtle."

"They look pretty fucking subtle to me. Everyone in the place is having a case of déjà vu, and you're talking about subtle."

"I mean, it might be a sexual game, but mybe they're not conscious of it, you see? Something like that."

Brennan finally found a ball that fit his fingers. It seemed tremendously heavy. Phil reached over and asked to try it, and Brennan let him. It was probably too big for Phil, but he moved his fingers in and out, then said, "At least I won't go skidding down the lane. Do you mind if I use it? I'm going to go get the next round."

"I don't care."

Linda came by and offered to pick up shoes for them both. Brennan told her an eleven and a half.

Back at the scoring table, Pam was drinking a beer and smoking a cigarette. Brennan sat down, the heavy ball in his lap, a bit disconcerted to be alone with her.

"Where is everyone?" he asked her.

"Oh?" she said, looking around. "I don't know. Probably looking for balls."

"That's quite an outfit," Brennan said, not sure what else to say.

"Is it stupid? I'm not sure people really like it."

"No, it's fine. It's a gas," he told her.

"A gas? You sound like Freddy."

"I just mean you look great. Not everyone could carry it off. The dress looks great on you."

"Skirt."

"Okay, skirt."

Brennan felt suddenly that he would like to ask her how many petticoats she had on under it. Just saying "skirt" excited him. He knew it was ridiculous, but there it was. What's under there? That was the question men always wanted to ask; that was the question they never stopped asking. Women knew it, too, at least women like Pam.

"Freddy gets these wild ideas, and I just go along. He's always afraid life's going to be boring. Is your life boring, Brennan?"

"No, not really."

"What's not really mean?"

"It means I know pretty much what to expect, but I sort of like that. It frees my mind to think of other things, you know? Does that make sense?"

"Certainly. It's the way I feel."

Then everyone was coming back, Freddy with a polka-dotted ball, Phil with a tray of drinks. Linda and Margaret came from the ladies' room, carrying their purses and shoes.

223

"Don't we need shoes, too?" Pam asked Freddy.

"Sure. Up by the desk. I'll get them in a second," Freddy said.

"Oh, God, this is a production," said Margaret. "I never knew bowling was such work."

"Oh, get off it," Phil said. "If this is work, well . . ."

"Well, what?" his wife asked.

"You ought to try tennis," Phil told her, laughing.

Brennan laughed. He felt good. He wanted another beer. The next round was his; then it was back to Freddy.

"How about a practice round?" Phil asked, the first finished with his shoes. "I'm going to fire at will."

"Go ahead," Pam told him.

Phil grabbed Brennan's heavy black ball and moved to the top of the lane. He held it steady against his chest, then turned to look at them watching him.

"What do I say? Yabadabado?"

"Then you go up on your toes and throw the thing through the wall," Brennan told him.

"Just try bowling it. Be careful of your back," said Margaret, still lacing her shoes.

"My back is as strong as iron."

"But your disks aren't. Be careful."

"Christ, now I'm going to be thinking about my back going out. I'm going to worry about falling down on the lane here and not being able to move."

"It will add excitement to the once-a-month-do-something-exciting club," Linda said.

Phil rocked forward, then ran at the line and threw a gutter ball. He came back rubbing his shoulder.

"That thing must weigh thirty pounds."

Fast Freddy returned with shoes for Pam and himself. He sat down and started putting them on.

"You jack your car up in back just for tonight, too?" Phil asked him, still wiggling his shoulder around.

"No, I rented a cycle."

"Did you really?" Margaret asked.

"Yes, why not? We go whole hog or we don't go at all."

"In other words, if you can't be a pig, you don't want to be anything?"

"Did he really rent one?" Linda asked Pam.

"It's outside," Pam answered. "It was sort of scary at first, but you get used to it."

"You really have a motorcycle parked outside?" Phil asked, coming over and drinking some beer. "You're not putting us on?"

"No, why should we? It's fun!" Fast Freddy said, stamping one foot to check the laces. "You guys can take it for a spin if you want."

Brennan felt as if they were ganging up on Freddy a little, so he interrupted. "I'm going to take my practices."

"Go ahead," Phil said. "Watch your fucking shoulder."

"If I go skidding down the lane, turn the pin collector off, will you?"

"Sure."

Brennan hit four pins on his first throw, then made the spare. He felt awkward doing it, but it didn't matter. He went back and sat at the scoring table. Freddy was writing in their names on the overhead projector. Linda Lou, he wrote. He wrote Margaret Mitchell, Frederico, Amscray Pamscray, and Philo-dendron. For Brennan he wrote Rocko.

"What are these, superlatives?" Pam asked.

"You really have a bike out there?" Phil asked Freddy once more.

"Sure, I told you. I'll take you for a ride later on. It's fun after about thirty beers."

"Let's get this started," Margaret said.

Brennan sat in the scorer's chair and took a long drink of beer. Pam was up, and he watched her bowl, the flip of her petticoats touching and innocent. After her came Linda, then Margaret. Fast Freddy went last and surprised them all by knocking a strike in the first frame. He kept his leg hiked up in back, his arm lifted in a corny follow-through. He didn't move even after the pins had stopped rattling.

"Dazzling," he said, the light careening off his greased hair. "I'm a dazzler."

The lights in the living room were on when Brennan pulled into the driveway. When he climbed out of the car, he saw that the pumpkin had been cut into a jack-o'-lantern. They had picked his side after all. The candle inside it made the pine trees and grass throb like a forest fire.

"How beautiful," Linda said. "They picked yours."

"But they did a better job with it."

"But it was your design. Everyone thinks of faces, but you thought of trees. How did you think of that?" Linda asked, taking his arm.

"I'm just an artist."

"Do you miss the Deerfield house, honey?"

"A little."

"More than a little, isn't it?"

"I miss it."

She kissed him, then Brennan held the door open for her. McGregor was there, his eyes bright, his claws skimming on the linoleum. Brennan let him out and closed the door.

"Who's awake?" Linda called softly.

No one answered. Brennan smelled smoke and hickory.

"Do they have a fire going?" he asked.

"I don't know. It smells like it."

Brennan followed Linda into the living room. Kate was there, lying on an old sleeping bag, asleep by firelight. Louey was cooking a marshmallow. Both of them were dressed for bed.

"What's going on?" Brennan asked. "It's a little late, isn't it?"

Then a sound came from behind two large armchairs. Louey pinched his nose and began making an Indian fife whine, the music that's played when a cobra rises from a wicker basket. Kate jumped up and began making magician motions at the chair.

"From the Orient, the land of mystery and intrigue," Kate said, "from the lands of Zanzibar and Milky Way bars and Good and Plenty, comes Foulah the Great."

It was Michael. He rose up from behind the chair, his hands clasped in front of him like a Buddha.

"What are you doing here?" Linda laughed, going to kiss him.

"It's Columbus Day on Monday. I got a ride with a Jewish kid going home for Yom Kippur."

"You can't get rid of old Mikey," Louey said, taking off his marshmallow.

"I can't believe he's spending a weekend away from his computer," Kate said.

Brennan went over and kissed him. Michael's appearance was maybe a little too well timed. He had just been back a couple of weeks ago, and now here he was again. You pay a couple of thousand for room and board, and all your kid wants to do is come home. Brennan wondered if Michael was homesick.

He couldn't help asking, "Everything okay up there?"

"Fine. I'm racking in the A's."

"This is a treat," Linda said, kissing Michael again. She went to the hall closet and hung up her coat.

"Dad, did you see the pumpkin?" Kate asked.

"Yeah, it was great. Who voted?"

"Janey said yours was the most original."

"I wanted the Mikey Model," Louey said, putting on another marshmallow. "I wanted Mikey to be pumpkin of the year."

"Mikey or no Mikey, I know some people who should be getting to bed," Linda said, coming back in the living room. She moved close to the fire. "That feels wonderful."

"We have to have ghost stories first," Kate said, sprawling out on the sleeping bag again.

"You two can have ghost stories, but Louey has to go to bed."

"Aw, Mom, what's the dif? We have Monday off, too."

"The dif is you'll get too tired."

"How about one ghost story, then everyone to bed?" asked Brennan. "How would that be?"

"All right, but you deal with this monster when he's cranky tomorrow. I'm going to go to bed."

"I'm not a five-year-old," Louey said.

"No, you're at least six," said Michael, flopping down beside Kate.

Brennan went to hang up his coat. Linda kissed the kids good night and started upstairs. Brennan looked at her, and she leaned close. "He came home to see Louey," she whispered, then kissed him good night. He kissed her, then went back in the living room.

"Hey, Dad," Louey said, "Michael looked it up. What's the biggest pumpkin ever recorded?"

"Four hundred pounds," Brennan said, lying down next to Louey. He grabbed a marshmallow and took Louey's fork. "Let me toast one, okay?"

"Okay. How much was it, Michael?" asked Louey.

"Six hundred and twelve, grown in Washington," Michael said.

"And how big was the biggest tomato?" Kate asked.

"Six pounds, eight ounces," Louey said.

"Imagine eating that," Brennan said.

"The biggest potato was eighteen pounds something," Kate said, jumping up to turn off the lights. The light from the fire was warm and peaceful. "And the biggest cucumber was around seventeen."

"What have you all been doing all night? Have you been going through the vegetable records?" Brennan asked.

"It's that book," Louey said. "Kate was grossed out by the good ones like the guy with fingernails a hundred and forty-three inches. He keeps them covered when he sleeps."

"The fattest guy in the world is eight hundred and ninety pounds," Michael said. "He's in a freak shows. He gets wheeled around on the overweight baggage trolleys in airports."

"Oh, God, you should see his picture," Kate said. "He's grotesque."

"They have this decent picture of these fat twins on these motorcycles, and it says they weigh one thousand, five hundred pounds combined," Louey said, more excited than Brennan had seen him in a while.

"Forget all that. Tell us a ghost story," Kate said.

"No ghost stories," Brennan said, taking his marshmallow off and eating it. He handed the fork back to Louey. "I'm all out of ghost stories."

"But you promised. Tell us one from hicksville, where you used to live," Kate said. "They had enough woods there to have good stories."

"Oh, is that so?" Brennan asked, reaching over her shoulders and squeezing her to him a little. "I'll tell you a quick one, then we get off to bed, okay?"

"Okay."

Michael didn't say anything. Louey had another marshmallow going.

"Once there was a man who lived up in the north woods. His name was Emile. He lived there trying to grow the world's largest pumpkin."

Louey shook his head. Michael snorted. Kate squeezed over closer.

"He did. Then one day he noticed his wife was getting taller. She wasn't a great deal taller. At first she was just a fraction of an inch taller. He thought it might be a mistake on his part. He was taller than she was, but she seemed taller. Her clothes looked short, and her head came up to his chin, when before, it had just touched his breastbone."

"Is this supposed to be real?" Michael asked.

"Shhh," Kate told him.

"So he wondered what to do. One day, when he saw her looking at herself in the mirror, he pretended to lean across her and take a piece of lint from the surface of the glass. He deliberately smudged it just where the top of her hair had been. He checked to make sure she was wearing no shoes; he checked all the details. Then, very lightly in pencil, he put a little line next to the medicine cabinet so that he would be able to compare it the next time. He waited a week; then he pulled the same trick. When he compared the new smudge mark with the old one, he saw that she had grown nearly three inches. Three inches! It was impossible she hadn't noticed, but she hadn't said anything. Slowly he began to realize that she didn't want to mention it; she knew she was getting taller, but she didn't say a word."

"You know, I thought Mom was taller this time home," Michael said.

"Would you be quiet?" Kate said.

Brennan could feel her next to him. She had the best imagination of the three. He found himself speaking more directly toward her.

"He began to suspect he was living with a woman who had been kissed by a vampire. She painted her nails red and let them grow especially long. She began to wear only black. At parties he waited for someone else to notice that she was taller or that her face was dark and frightening, but no one seemed to find anything unusual about her. It didn't seem possible that he was the only one to see it. He decided to confront her.

"One night he put a crucifix around his neck and waited for her to come upstairs. He had a wooden stake under the bed, carved from a baseball bat—"

"From a baseball bat!" Michael laughed. "Killed with a Louisville Slugger."

"Oh, shut up," Louey said. "Just listen."

"From a baseball bat," Brennan went on. "He decided he would hold her in the bedroom throughout the night and not let her out. He had a plan to take her outside into the full sunlight because he knew sunlight would kill a vampire.

"He counted on the crucifix to protect him. He had tied it around his neck with a dog leash, making it impossible for her to tear it off. People think crucifixes are automatic protection, but the truth is a vampire can sometimes rip them off his victims. Vampires can smell crucifixes as well, since they can smell blood from any distance, and the blood of Christ is the only blood they cannot tolerate.

"His wife took a long time coming into the bedroom. She arranged her hair carefully; she dressed in a black negligee; then she turned the lights out.

"At once Emile heard wings. He touched his crucifix and pushed up in the bed. She had smelled the blood of Christ, and she was trying to get out of the room. But he had her trapped. He had nailed down the windows earlier, and he had locked the bedroom door after her."

"Why didn't she smell the blood of Christ when she first came in?" Louey asked.

"Shhhh," Kate said.

"He had wrapped cellophane over it."

"Don't wrap it, bag it!" Michael cracked, then lay on his side, laughing into the crook of his elbow.

Kate said, "Would you all be quiet? Who cares why she didn't smell it before?"

"Anyway," Brennan said, "Emile was petrified. The sound of the wings grew louder. He heard her hitting against the windows, trying to get out. Then, suddenly, the bed dipped, and he felt a huge weight step onto the mattress. Through the darkness he saw she had changed herself into a wolf. Slowly the wolf came closer, and Emile smelled the rank odor of its fur, the blood on its lips, the slaver dripping from its muzzle. It began to snarl and breathe on top of him. He reached under the bed for the wooden stick and said—"

"Fetch!" Michael howled.

"That's it, story's over," Brennan said.

"Oh, Jesus, you big jerk, Michael. Come on, Dad. If he says anything else, I'll kill him," Kate said.

Brennan took a marshmallow and ate it raw. Then he asked Louey to cook him one. He thought about going on but wasn't sure where the story would end up. He was too tired, and the fire felt too good to worry about making something up. He ate two more marshmallows.

"You're weird, Dad," Kate said after a while. "Come on, finish it, please?"

"I'm too tired."

"I'd hate to be out in the woods right now," Kate said.

"You're not, sweetie," Brennan said, kissing her. He had one more marshmallow, then stood. "Time for bed."

"I'm not going up there unless you make both of these two swear they won't hide under my bed or do anything strange the whole night. Make them swear," Kate said.

"Kate, are you taller? Didn't that nightgown drag on the floor before?" Michael asked.

"See?" Kate said, jumping up and standing next to Brennan. "I won't go to sleep. I won't let you go to sleep either, Dad."

"Kate, I'd be careful about hanging your feet over the bed," Louey said.

"Do you have your old baseball bats upstairs?" Michael asked Louey.

"Stop, you guys," Brennan said. "Come on, let's go to bed."

Brennan banked the fire and closed the screen, then carried Louey's marshmallows and fork out to the kitchen. Kate stayed right behind him. "The escort ends when we're upstairs," he told her. She nodded but kept following him.

He cleaned up the sink, rinsed off Louey's marshmallow fork, then turned off the kitchen lights. He heard Louey and Michael laughing quietly upstairs and knew they were planning some sort of ambush. He hoped they didn't wake Linda.

"Come on, honey, I'll walk you up. Once you're in your room, lock the door on those guys."

"I can't sleep behind a locked door."

"Lock it for a little while until they go to sleep. I'm sorry I told you the story."

"No, I liked the story. Tomorrow I'll like it."

He walked upstairs with Kate, holding her hand.

"Okay, you guys," he said, but they weren't around. "Want me to check your room?"

"Please."

He went into her room and turned on all the lights. He looked under the bed and in the closet. Nothing. "Okay, you guys," he said again, and this time he heard them laughing down the hall. Kate jumped across the room and up onto the bed and hid behind him. Brennan put up his fingers like a crucifix.

"We're safe, I think," he said. "Spock to *Enterprise*, aliens approaching. Phasers on stun."

Louey and Michael came in with their bedspreads wrapped around them like capes. The costumes were lousy, but they both crept forward, waving their hands in front of their faces like Bela Lugosi. "Come to me," Louey said.

Michael had fake fangs from somewhere and began mesmerizing Kate by waving his hands at her, saying to Louey, "Get the woman."

"On three, phasers full stun," Brennan said.

"Aye, Captain," Kate said.

"One, two, three," Brennan said, then made a phaser sound.

Kate began shooting a six-gun, and Michael fell on the bed and began writhing. "Finish him off with a baseball stake," Kate said.

Louey was not sure enough of his balance to fall. He found the floor in sections, carefully lowering himself until he could resume the game. Brennan held the sound of his ray gun until Louey was ready, and only when Louey lay on the floor and hexed them did Brennan get him with his phaser.

On Sunday, dressed in his football pants and his Red Oaks sweat shirt, Brennan stepped into Louey's room. The air was hot and close and smelled of Vick's VapoRub. A pile of comics had slid from the foot of the bed onto the floor, fanning evenly across the carpet. In the dim light from the bedside lamp, Brennan made out copies of *The Hulk* and a few of *Sergeant Rock*. Silky, Louey's hamster, spun his wheel.

"You asleep?" Brennan asked quietly.

"You going?"

"Yeah, I've got to get going."

"Is the game still on? It's raining like crazy."

"I called Bonow. He says it's on."

"You like playing in the rain?"

"I don't even know if I'll get in. Besides," Brennan said, sitting on the edge of the bed, "I don't care about that right now. How do you feel?"

"Okay."

"Where's the cold? In your lungs?"

"I don't know. I guess so."

Brennan tossed the comics back on the bed and bent to kiss Louey. The VapoRub was like a shell around his body. Brennan kissed him on the forehead, thinking at the same time how pale Louey looked on the pillows.

"You want me to feed Silky?" Brennan asked.

"Mom gave him some food this morning. You could give him a little more."

Brennan stood and threw a few pellets into the hamster's feed bin. Silky jumped off the wheel and went to the trough.

"So, this cold has you pretty good," Brennan said, coming back to bed. "We might have to run you up to the hospital."

"I don't want to go to the hospital. It's just a cold."

"I know, but you're a little weak right now."

Brennan moved to get more comfortable on the bed. He was conscious of his size and strength beside Louey.

"What's the Hulk been doing?" Brennan asked to change the subject.

"Nothing. Clobbering people. Anybody in their right mind could figure out he's Dr. Bruce Banner."

"Don't some guys know it?"

"They suspect it. And there was a detective following him around in the TV show. In the comics he normally just beats people up all day."

"What's he? Radioactive?"

"No, gamma rays."

"Is that why he's green?"

"I guess so. I don't really know. Maybe I'll turn into the Hulk with all this treatment."

"Maybe. But then you'll have to go into hiding."

Michael came in then, carrying a few more comics. He threw them on top of the bed and grabbed some of the others.

"You done with these?" he asked Louey.

"Most of them."

"Sergeant Rock is the greatest. Every time he hits a kraut, he says, 'Nighty-night, Heinie.' "

"I like the Hulk," Brennan said. "The one I liked best was the Phantom. Nobody runs him anymore."

"Was that the guy with the skull cave and the skull ring?" Michael asked.

"And the jungle Olympics," Brennan said, getting up. "I've got to go, Louey. Don't fight your mother if she has to take you up to Overlook."

"Will you come up afterwards?"

234

"Sure."

"You mean, you're not going to drive through town honking your horn?" asked Michael. "Don't they normally have toga parties after a victory?"

"I'll be up," Brennan said, tapping the hamster cage on the way out, then hustling downstairs. The game started at two, and it was already one twenty-three.

When he stepped into the kitchen, he saw Linda had set out cold cuts. She was making sandwiches on the cutting board. He crossed to the counter and rolled two or three pieces of bologna and cheese together. He dotted the cheese in a little pot of fancy mustard Linda insisted on using, even though he preferred French's.

"How does he look to you?" Linda asked.

"Not good."

"He should go in."

"What did Breisky say?"

"I told you. You weren't listening," Linda said, smearing mustard on a piece of whole wheat bread. She didn't look up.

"I was listening. I just want to make sure I understand it."

"Breisky thinks he should go in the hospital. He says even there he can't predict how the cold will respond to treatment, but he should be watched and his temperature should be monitored. I think I should take him in."

Brennan took a few more bites.

"I'm going to keep Michael home here if Louey goes in," Linda said, adding it as if it were an afterthought.

"Michael can't do anything, honey."

"Louey loves Michael. He looks up to him. It will make him feel better."

"Why don't we just hold on a little? I'll take him in when I get back."

Linda turned with the knife. A small drip of grainy mustard fell on the wooden cutting board. She shook her head, and the knife went back and forth.

"Brennan, it could be penumonia. He doesn't have anything left."

Her voice went up as she ended the sentence, and Brennan held his arms out. She let the knife fall and stepped to him, her body shaking, her face turned against his shoulder. She cried silently, her hands around his back, her breathing fluttered and uneven. Brennan held her, staring up at the ceiling, not sure if he would begin crying himself. He tried not to think of Louey or the damn hamster running on the steel circle. He tried to think of the Deerfield and his own boyhood, the smell of mountain laurel and staghorn sumac, but all he could recover from those years was the image of his mother and father sitting on the front porch, their rockers pressing age into the old boards. They were gone, and the house was gone, and soon, very soon, Brennan knew, Louey would be gone.

He pulled Linda closer and put his head against her hair.

"Honey, he's just got a cold right now. I'll take him up as soon as I get home. I'll be gone only two hours."

"Okay. All right. Dr. Breisky said he wouldn't be up there until five or so anyway," Linda said.

She nodded again, then splashed some water on her face while Brennan tried to eat the last of his cheese and bologna. He didn't feel hungry, but he ate anyway, thinking of it now as pure calories. Feed the fires. Nothing stopped, that was the startling thing. Even now, hurrying to get in a little protein, he had to glance at his watch.

"I've got to run," he said.

"Hurry back, okay? I'm sorry no one's going to watch you."

"It doesn't matter."

Then he was out, running quickly, trying to dodge the rain. It was absurd to be playing anyway. The field would be chewed and people would be pulling groins and hamstrings like crazy. But he still wanted to get in, that was the strangest thing, and even as he climbed into the car, he felt the butterflies appear.

Brennan felt the ball come into his hands, and he spun to pitch to Glass. Just as he got rid of the ball, Brennan felt someone hit him, a solid shot, nothing cheap, and he went down. The body landed on top of him, grunting as it came, and Brennan felt his ribs spring slightly, too old to be taking such abuse.

"Good hit," he said to the Scotch Plains Pirates' lineman.

It was wet and cold under the lineman, and Brennan wondered when the game would be over. The Red Oaks were losing by twenty points or more, the game was a joke, and Brennan felt ridiculous running out the clock for Bonow. He had almost told Bonow to stick it when Bonow said to go in, but he had wanted to play all day and he'd had to watch Haynes stink up the joint.

Now it was like a pickup game, only tackle, and as Brennan climbed to his knees, then to his feet, he couldn't figure what he was doing there. Instinctively he kept his hands out of the mud and water, holding them up like a surgeon, a little surprised that this habit had returned after all those years. The Silver Bullet, he thought suddenly, and he felt calm and a sweet grace moving through him.

Glass had a first down, probably the first one of the fourth quarter, and some of the Red Oaks' linemen were hooting, while the Pirates' defense shouted shit like "It's about time."

"Fuck you," Mussman, the center, yelled at them. He was red in the face and scarred. His helmet had cracked down on the bridge of his nose all day and blood trickled in a wedge under his eyes. Brennan walked with him back to the huddle, using the towel Mussman wore in his belt, then slapped him on the rear.

"We'll get them," Brennan said, and he couldn't tell himself if it was phony or not.

In the huddle he called a pass, the quick slant-in to Sales, the split end, that had worked so well in scrimmage. Webb said, "Don't forget me, baby," and then they broke huddle, Brennan feeling just the slightest swell of confidence. The middle linebacker for the Pirates started yelling something, but Brennan didn't listen. He watched his line spread, saw the men take their spacing, heard them begin their calls.

"Get these assholes," one of the defensive linemen said, and Mussman grunted, "Fuck you, fuck you," over and over.

Brennan took the snap, stepped back, and saw Sales fall, sliding in the mud in a comical way that made Brennan almost throw the ball at him anyway. But then he rolled, back, scrambling, the pattern completely broken. A Pirate lineman came at him, and he faked a throw, pumped, and took the lineman off his feet, sliding around him easily, and suddenly Brennan was out in the clear, drifting, his left eye and ear sensing the pressure. Twenty yards down he saw Webb coming back at him, just what he was supposed to do on a broken play, and Brennan threw it on the run, gunned it, and felt the ball fly on a dead fucking string right to Webb. Webb's shoulder pads cracked, the ball was thrown so true, and Brennan pumped his hand, charged, as Webb was hit by two men.

"Here we go, here we go," Brennan yelled, running downfield.

Just to one side he saw Mussman throw a late forearm at the defensive man who was mouthing off, and two Pirates jumped at him. Brennan veered over, pulled Mussman off, then spit on the ground in front of the two bastards.

"Fuck you," one of the guys said, and Brennan, not sure where it came from, yelled, "You're a fucking pimp."

"Fuckers," Mussman screamed as he came back to the huddle and put up his hands.

"Here we go, baby, here we go," Webb yelled as he came back, and suddenly the huddle was humming, they were moving, and Brennan felt in charge, on top of it all.

He called another pass play, not caring which one it was, because he knew the momentum was with him. He took the snap and dropped back, the ball high, his form good. He watched Sales clear a linebacker, and then Fleming dropped in on a little curl, almost a center screen, and Brennan popped him the ball just in time to catch the linebacker with his legs crossed going the other way.

"Yeah, yeah, yeah," Brennan yelled, and ran upfield. Fleming slipped a tackle, gave a dead leg to another, and he was going until he was clipped down by a quick chop at the forty-five.

Nothing would stop them, nothing, Brennan felt, and he got them back into the huddle. He could feel it all, that fine feral feeling, mad dogs. He wanted to hit someone, so he called a sweep with Glass running, and Brennan led the blockers, not what a quarterback does, but he didn't care. He turned the corner and hit someone low, a chop block, and felt the guy go over him. Then it was all legs, calves with earrings of clotted mud dangling on them, knees and thigh pads, square jocks and dirt everywhere.

First and ten on the fifty.

Bonow yelled something and Brennan turned to him and flipped him the finger; he didn't care anymore, and he called another pass, hoping to scramble this time, hoping to run upfield and collide with someone. But when he dropped back, he felt the right side of the line give, and two defensive men were on him too fast to do anything about it. He tucked the ball and belted into them, bucking, churning forward, but he was pushed back and slammed. He jumped up. "You don't get to me, you assholes," he yelled, and he pointed at them, fired, a madness filling him with feelings older than he remembered.

"That's right," Mussman shouted, and then Webb was back, saying he could run a drag on them if Fleming and Sales cleared, so Brennan called it, dropped, and spotted Webb clearing fifteen yards down, going against the flow. Brennan threw from his toes this time, the laces ticking his fingers, the spiral without a goddamn wobble, splitting the defense. Then Webb took it and knocked one guy over, creamed him, his big ox shoulders coming down and jolting the bastard, and Brennan saw the guy wasn't going to get up easily. But Webb was on a rampage, the kind of kill run tightends sometimes had, kicking and butting and guys shying away from him. Then someone hit him a good lick, another chopped him, and Brennan worried Webb's knee would go. But Webb jumped up and tossed the ball in the defenders' faces, and you knew no one was going to fuck with him.

"Way to run, way to run," Bonow was yelling from the sideline. "Watch your time."

Brennan ran, checking the clock. There was less than a minute, and it didn't matter. Nothing mattered, and Brennan threw the finger at Bonow once more. Even though he didn't hate him, he deserved a finger for keeping him out of the game so long, and Brennan gave it to him. He gave Haynes the finger, too, because he was twenty-one and didn't know shit. Forty-three, I'm going to be forty-three, Brennan thought, and called the slant-in again, hoping Sales would be open. The Pirates' middle linebacker said over Mussman, "I'm coming for your ass, QB," and Brennan winked at him, because he couldn't get to him, or maybe he could, but Brennan knew he'd stick him in the fucking ribs if the guy got close.

He took the snap and hit Sales perfectly, even though the ball was a duck, and then he sprinted out, trying to throw a block, but Sales was down to the twenty.

"Call time out," Bonow yelled.

But that would have been bush. It would have been stupid to kill the momentum, stupid when you're twenty points down to make a big deal about six, so Brennan waved him off, neglecting to give him the finger. He felt the smallest sag in the linemen now, and he reached over and slapped one on the helmet, hard, and said, "We're going to ram this fucker in," and this keyed up some of the other linemen, Mussman saying, "Forty seconds of decent ball."

Suddenly Brennan realized they all were old men, some of them young but old already, too old for football, and he felt as if he were about to cry. "Come on, come on," he said, the venom gone, and in its place the sense that he could experience what he was doing without being part of it. This was the second season, the dream of men running on fields, and he called the play quietly, even and calm, then took the snap.

It was a touchdown, Brennan saw that. The defensive safety covering Sales went down, slipping in the mud, and Sales was open on a goalpost pattern, three steps ahead of anyone, the pattern bringing him to an easy angle for Brennan to hit. Brennan set up, controlled his drop, felt the ball, then let it go, his last pass, he knew, and it was there, a spiral, Sales running under it beautifully. It wasn't caught, Sales dropped it, but it was there, it had been thrown, and Brennan listened to the crowd groan, mostly Red Oaks fans, and he felt such warmth enter him that he began to cry. "You okay? Jesus, you okay?" Mussman asked, setting up for the final huddle, and Brennan nodded, called the last play, time was running, and threw a bomb at Webb that didn't have a prayer. He wished he hadn't been forced to throw that last pass, but he didn't really care. He wasn't hit, wasn't touched, but simply stood in the center of the field thinking how he had missed this, how he had missed it so.

Back at home, Brennan stood in the shower, working the hot spray over his body. He felt bruises everywhere. A red welt was growing on his left shin, and he felt something deep, maybe a bone bruise, on his hip. It was all right. The pain wasn't welcome exactly, but there was something familiar about feeling the abrasions and the way the water made him burn. He was half tempted to call up Freddy and ask if he could go over and take a sauna. The heat would penetrate his bones and chase some of the stiffness.

He climbed out of the shower and dried himself carefully, patting himself with the towel, afraid to rub too hard. He inspected the welt on his shin and saw that it was a three-inch gash, probably made by a cleat shearing down his leg. A scab was already forming. He thought about putting a bandage on it but decided against it. Air healed things, he remembered.

He was in his underwear when Linda came in, pushing through the door too fast. He looked at her quickly and knew at once what was happening.

"Louey's having trouble breathing," she said.

She was trying to remain calm, but she couldn't quite fake it. It was not so much what she said as her look that made his heart beat. It was a look of fear and confusion, surprise that this was finally happening, and he found himself fumbling for a response.

"What do you mean?" he asked, grabbing his pants and pulling them on. "What are you talking about?"

"His breathing," she said, her voice rising. "He can't breathe. He's all congested."

"Okay, all right, I'll take him right now."

"Should I call the ambulance?"

"No, I'm ready. Get a blanket around him."

Linda left. He heard her running through the hallway, that hurried run you heard in hospitals and emergencies. Louey's door slammed back as she pushed into his room, and he heard that, too, knew exactly how she moved. He grabbed a coat and started after her, not bothering with a shirt. He slipped into a pair of loafers, and then he was there, standing in Louey's doorway, watching Linda straining to get a blanket around him.

"Hey, champ, come on now," Brennan said.

Louey lay on the bed, too weak to help his mother. The room was warm, and for an instant Brennan thought he might be breathing too fast himself. He could not seem to make himself move properly, and as he came to the bed, he felt light-headed and a little dazed.

"I'll get him," he said to Linda. "Call Dr. Breisky and tell him we're on our way up."

"Okay."

"Tell him I'll meet him at the hospital."

"Okay."

Brennan bent close and felt the warmth of Louey's bedclothes. His skin was very warm, and his breathing sounded shallow. Louey did not seem to recognize him. Brennan tucked the blanket around him as well as he could, then lifted him. Louey was remarkably light, too light, but Brennan held him against his chest and started across the room. He heard the hamster spinning the wheel. It made little squeaking sounds, and Brennan tried to think of something to say to Louey. "There's your hamster. There's Silky," he said, but Louey only closed his eyes tighter and seemed to grow softer in his arms.

He turned sideways to go down the stairs. Once Louey's foot hit a picture on the wall and tilted it. Brennan turned even more and kept going down, twisting his feet to make sure he stepped on the center of each stair. Louey coughed, and Brennan hugged him closer. A bubble appeared on Louey's lips as they reached the ground floor.

"He's not there," Linda said, hurrying in front of him to hold open the door. "They don't know where he is."

"Keep calling."

"I want to come."

"I think it's better if you call. Call Freddy and get him to bring you up. We'll be okay."

They were at the door, and Linda went through first. She held the door wide, making the hinges bray as he passed through. It was cold and damp outside, evening. He had forgotten how cold and damp it was, and he tucked Louey closer.

"You okay, Lou? You'll be all right in just a few minutes," he said.

Linda held the passenger door open, standing beside the sharp window cranks and handles to protect Louey. He put Louey in and tucked the blanket around him. The car was too cold, the upholstery shiny and hard, but there was nothing to be done about it now. He tucked the blanket even tighter. Linda reached past him and tucked the blanket once more, then she kissed Louey on the forehead again and finally pulled back.

"He's okay," Brennan said as he went around the back of the car. He did not believe it himself, but he had to say it. "I'll be up there in ten minutes."

"Brennan . . ." Linda said.

She was crying. Her voice was very high and tight, and he couldn't look at her too closely or he knew he wouldn't be able to keep thinking straight.

"Call him and come right up," he said.

He kissed her and got in the car. He backed down the driveway as fast as he dared and then gunned the engine, making the tires squeal, but he didn't care. He turned the heat up as high as it would go. Louey didn't say anything. He looked very sick, more sick than a cold, more sick than Brennan had ever seen him.

"You okay, sport?" he asked Louey softly.

Louey nodded.

"You sure?"

Louey nodded once more, but his eyes were rheumy, and his chest heaved in short, stuttered bursts that made Brennan hold his own breath each time Louey took one. He looked over and half imagined seeing the cold settling deeper into his son's lungs.

Driving to Overlook, Brennan wanted to tell Louey about playing, tell him something about how it felt. He didn't want Louey to go to sleep because he worried that people didn't wake up from sleep. Maybe that was a concussion, he couldn't think, but it seemed important to keep Louey conscious.

He drove too fast and skidded once on some wet leaves going up through the Watchung Reservation. He wondered if they should have contacted the ambulance, but that would have taken more time. This was better. This was faster. As he drove toward the hospital, he saw the New York skyline appear over the hills and clouds, and he said, "Look, Louey," but Louey didn't turn his head. "You okay?" he asked again, and Louey couldn't speak very well.

He left his car at the emergency door and bundled Louey inside. A nurse came forward, and Brennan explained as fast as he could: leukemia, a cold, difficulty breathing. He put Louey down on a trundle table, and an intern began to take Louey's vital signs.

Suddenly it occurred to Brennan that Louey could die. He had known it for a long time, but suddenly it was here, right now, his son could be dying. He stayed next to the doctor and held Louey's hand. "Okay, champ, okay," he said, and Louey looked at him. Then Brennan bent and kissed Louey's forehead, his lips staying on the boy's head. When he lifted his face he saw Louey's eyes becoming more glassy. "Louey, Louey," Brennan whispered. The intern asked if Louey was allergic to any drugs, and Brennan said no, said Dr. Breisky was the attending physician. The doctor gave Louey a hypodermic of antibodies, and something else Brennan didn't catch, and Brennan leaned over Louey and said, "You'll feel better in a second."

It was impossible that it had become this serious so quickly, so unexpectedly after all the months and days of chemo and hospital visits. Then Louey was coughing, too weak even to clear his throat, and Brennan squeezed the hand in his and felt Louey's arms coming up. The boy was frightened, and Brennan lay down across the table, careful to keep his weight off Louey's chest. "Okay, champ, okay," and he couldn't keep from crying. Louey's arms were weak, they pulled apart with each cough, but Brennan held on until the intern said they should take him upstairs.

Brennan went with him into the elevator and upstairs, then they were walking down a long hallway. Louey was wheeled into a room and transferred onto a bed and an IV was placed in his arm. Brennan stepped back while two nurses worked, one fixing a tube down his nose, the other checking the IV again, and Brennan had to look away for a second. He was crying freely now, and he couldn't think anything except that his son was dying. Louey, Louey, he said, and looked out at the forest, the rusty treetops, and he wondered what he would do if he didn't have Louey. The leukemia couldn't take him. Nothing could take him. Louey was the one, he was all of it, and he couldn't let Louey go. He pictured Louey playing miniature golf, or playing with McGregor, or running across a football field on a clear October Sunday. He was just a boy, just eleven, and he knew there was no way to forget that look in Louey's eyes, that joy at feeling his feet touch green grass. This was the child he loved, the boy he understood as he understood himself. He wouldn't know what to do without Louey. Not Louey, not his own, not his heart.

JOSEPH MONNINGER is the recipient of a grant from the National Endowment for the Arts. He grew up in Westfield, New Jersey, and now lives in New York City.